SEASON OF THE WOLF

Visit us at www.boldstrokesbooks.com

By the Author

After the Fall

Season of the Wolf

SEASON OF
THE WOLF

by
Robin Summers

2014

SEASON OF THE WOLF

© 2014 BY ROBIN SUMMERS. ALL RIGHTS RESERVED.

ISBN 13: 978-1-62639-043-0

THIS TRADE PAPERBACK ORIGINAL IS PUBLISHED BY
BOLD STROKES BOOKS, INC.
P.O. BOX 249
VALLEY FALLS, NY 12185

FIRST EDITION: MARCH 2014

THIS IS A WORK OF FICTION. NAMES, CHARACTERS, PLACES, AND INCIDENTS ARE THE PRODUCT OF THE AUTHOR'S IMAGINATION OR ARE USED FICTITIOUSLY. ANY RESEMBLANCE TO ACTUAL PERSONS, LIVING OR DEAD, BUSINESS ESTABLISHMENTS, EVENTS, OR LOCALES IS ENTIRELY COINCIDENTAL.

THIS BOOK, OR PARTS THEREOF, MAY NOT BE REPRODUCED IN ANY FORM WITHOUT PERMISSION.

CREDITS
EDITOR: RUTH STERNGLANTZ
PRODUCTION DESIGN: SUSAN RAMUNDO
COVER DESIGN BY SHERI (GRAPHICARTIST2020@HOTMAIL.COM)

Acknowledgments

When I began writing this book, I thought it would be a relatively easy journey. I already had one book under my belt, after all, so this second one would naturally be a piece of cake. But, as is often the case in life, my journey took an unexpected turn.

A few months into writing *Season of the Wolf*, my dad—my rock, my inspiration, and my hero—was diagnosed with leukemia. He fought bravely, with more spirit and humor than anyone had any right to expect. His motto became our family's: whatever it takes. He, and we, would do whatever it took to get him better and home.

Unfortunately, cancer cares little for intention or resolve, and after a courageous six-month battle, my dad passed away in May 2012. He was much too young, and he deserved far better.

Many things, as you might imagine, took a backseat during his illness. I was blessed in a way many are not, with an understanding boss, board of directors, and co-workers, who provided me with invaluable, precious time to spend at my dad's side and with my family.

I was equally blessed to have a tremendous publisher, who gave me the time and the space to finish this book on my own terms. It took a long time after my dad's death for me to begin writing again, far longer than I might have anticipated. But once I did begin to write, I found it was—as writing always has been for me—a balm for my wounded soul.

To my family and friends, thank you for your unending support, encouragement, and love, throughout the writing of this book and, more importantly, throughout my life.

To K, my love, for staying by my side through it all, and for being your wonderful, funny, intelligent, beautiful, loving self. You are still the best thing that ever happened to me.

To my editor, Ruth Sternglantz, for always answering my questions—no matter how inane—at all hours of the day and night.

It is said that we write what we know, which is certainly true. But it is also true that we write the truth of our characters, and sometimes that truth is not the same as our own.

I love wolves, and—despite a recurring adage within this book—do not advocate them being killed. It is a metaphor befitting the character's past, and that is all. Anyone interested in the conservation and protection of wolves and their habitats should check out Wolf Haven International at http://www.wolfhaven.org.

I am also a big, big fan of the American Civil Liberties Union (ACLU), and am deeply appreciative of their commitment to defending the individual rights and liberties guaranteed under the US Constitution. Everyone has rights…even serial killers. You can learn more about the ACLU's work at www.aclu.org.

Dedication

For my dad, whom I love and miss every day.

CHAPTER ONE

B illy lifted the fork to his mouth, savoring the way the delicate crust melted on his tongue. He hadn't had a piece of apple pie in years. He preferred to eat healthy—chicken breasts and brown rice, fresh fruits and vegetables, no butter, little fat. He wasn't one of those "my body is a temple" nut bags. No, Billy's discipline was born of dedication, his body a tool as essential to his trade as a knife to a chef or a badge to a cop.

He chuckled at that.

But smelling the pie that morning, fresh out of the oven with just a hint of cinnamon and brown sugar like his momma used to make, it clawed at his stomach. He'd just had to have a piece of that pie.

"I have to tell you, this might be the best pie I ever ate." He lowered his voice to a conspiratorial whisper, talking to the waitress with the golden hair. "Don't tell my momma I said that."

He hummed to himself between bites, a melody of his own creation, inspired by the morning and, of course, by the pie. He found that music had a way of coming upon him that way, stirring up from his bowels, vibrating up and through his vocal cords in ways he had never contemplated and, he thought, no one else ever had, either. Sometimes he thought he might be a bit of a musical savant, a modern-day Beethoven who, if he ever sat down at a piano, would compose the most fantastic symphony ever heard. Of course, he never did sit down at a piano. It wasn't that he didn't know how to play—although he didn't—but more that somehow it seemed like an utter waste of time.

"This really is good pie," he said as he chewed, looking down at his dining companion. "You sure you don't want some?"

A pair of lifeless eyes stared accusingly up at him from the floor.

"Oh, come on now. Don't be like that." He laid his fork beside his plate and delicately wiped his mouth with the napkin from his lap. The woman—Sally, according to her name tag—lay on the dingy tile, her glossy curls a pristine halo around her head. The angelic aura was an illusion, however, undone by her corneas, which had begun to whiten, and the blood-soaked uniform covering the twelve ragged wounds.

Twelve was an important number to Billy. Twelve apostles. Twelve days of Christmas. Twelve years.

Billy swiveled away from the counter so he could face her directly. His momma had always told him it was rude not to give a person his full attention when he was speaking to them. Billy was nothing if not polite.

"It's not your fault, honey. You just had the misfortune of working this morning. Couldn't be helped. It wasn't anything personal against you or that cook." Billy glanced back toward the kitchen, where the cook was slumped down against the freezer with his throat slashed open. "Nope, nothing personal against either of you."

The gray of early morning was beginning to filter through the slats of the closed window blinds, and Billy knew it was nearly time. *In fact*—he looked down at his watch—*it's a little past time.* He cocked his head like a mutt puzzling over a scratching within the walls, listening for the telltale sound of keys scraping against the lock of the diner's back door. Instead of the sound he was waiting for, Billy could detect the incessant hum of the city waking around him, growing louder with each tick of the clock. Even though it was past time, he knew there was still time, though it was growing shorter.

A furious rapping at the door evaporated the time that was left. Billy sighed.

Of course.

Billy thought sometimes that God had a very interesting sense of humor.

He looked down again at Sally, the accusation at last fading from her blind stare. "But they that wait upon the LORD shall renew their strength," he said. "They shall mount up with wings as eagles; they shall run, and not be weary; and they shall walk, and not faint."

Isaiah 40:31. One of Pa's favorites. Patience—and faith—would be rewarded.

Billy stood and fished around his front pocket, pulling out a fistful of change. He sorted through the assortment of quarters, dimes, nickels, and pennies with his index finger. "I know it was in here this morning. I really need to…ah, there you are."

He lifted up a single penny and inspected it in the faint morning light. Mr. Lincoln's profile seemed to have a harder edge, as if he were expressing his disapproval over Billy's most recent activities. Billy turned the coin over and smiled fondly at the two stalks of wheat lining the sides. He walked over to the cash register, which hung open and empty save for a few loose bills and rolls of change, and carefully set the penny down on the counter next to it, wheat side up.

Billy came back around the counter and squatted next to Sally the waitress, being careful not to step in the blood congealing around her. He reached out his hand, brushing an errant curl from her forehead. He wished he could feel its softness on his skin, but the best he could do was imagine what it would feel like without the leather glove.

The rapping at the door began again, this time accompanied by, "Come on, Sally, open up. I'm starvin'!"

Knowing time was no longer on his side and God seemed to have plans different than Billy's, he picked up his plate, fork, and napkin and took them into the kitchen. He washed the plate and fork and set them in the drainer to dry. The napkin he pocketed to throw away later. Then he exited the diner through the back door, shutting it with a soft click. He stood for a moment in the darkened alley, thinking maybe, just maybe, this was where it would happen. But as the morning's rays began to dissolve the lingering shadows of night, Billy knew it was not meant to be. Not yet.

Twelve years and a day longer.

CHAPTER TWO

Devon James ran down Grant Street, weaving between cranky pedestrians and dodging projectile paper cups and discarded morning newspapers propelled by the fierce November wind. She was late for work—again—though it was hardly her fault. The eighty-seven bus was supposed to run from East Liberty to downtown every ten minutes, at least according to the schedule. If that bus showed up once an hour, it was practically a miracle, complete with burning bushes and choirs of angels. The best Devon could figure, the folks at the Pittsburgh Port Authority managed their bus service like an ROTC cadet put in charge of the Normandy Invasion. They were simply in way over their heads.

Devon had learned quickly upon arriving in Pittsburgh that when planning her day, it was wise to think of the buses as operating in dog years—with the occasional leap year thrown in for fun—where ten minutes in normal, human, have-to-get-to-work time equaled seventy minutes in Pittsburgh-city-bus time, except when the buses skipped an hour if only because they could. So if she wanted to make it to work in time for her 6:00 a.m. shift, the only sure way to do it was to be at the bus stop by 4:30 a.m., which, on a double-shift day like the one she was facing today, was absolutely unthinkable. So she had convinced herself for what had to be the forty-third time over the last nine months that just this once the Port Authority gods would smile down upon her and allow her to catch the 5:22 a.m. bus and make it to work on time, as advertised.

Which was, of course, how Devon found herself dodging the aforementioned pedestrians and paper cups in a mad dash to make it the last four blocks and arrive at work nearly thirty minutes late. Not that running was going to help matters. Devon was going to catch hell. Again.

Good thing they're all bark and no…

Devon skidded to a stop a block from the diner, brought to a halt by something she had never before seen. The restaurant appeared to be closed, and there was a line of impatient customers waiting out front in the cold. She approached the building cautiously, her instinct for self-preservation going from zero to sixty in the time it took to blink. Questions swirled in her mind as she approached the door.

"Hey, Devon, what gives?" one of the regulars asked as she reached the door.

"Yeah," another regular chimed in. "What's with the locked door? Sally didn't go and get foreclosed on, did she?"

Devon tuned out the growing muttering of the small crowd and tested the door. Locked.

"What, you thought we were standing out here for our health?"

Devon ignored the sarcasm, entirely focused on the locked door and what it could mean.

Maybe Sally and Chuck overslept. Maybe they decided to take an impromptu vacation. Maybe Sally's visit to the bank yesterday didn't go well.

They were all reasonable guesses, except that in all the months Devon had worked at the diner, she had never known Sally to miss a day of work. Or Chuck. And Sally, who both owned the place and served as its main waitress, wouldn't have asked Devon to work a double if she'd had any inkling the diner would be taken away. In fact, Sally had sounded downright upbeat about the future when she'd called Devon the day before.

"Shoot, you think I'm going to let those greedy sons of bitches take away everything I've worked for?" Sally said. "Not as long as there's any breath left in this ol' bag of bones."

"You're far from old, Sally," Devon scoffed. Sally was only about ten years older than Devon. She hadn't even turned forty yet.

"You're damn right. And still hotter than a whore in church on Easter Sunday."

Sally was nothing if not forthright. She was also demanding, hardworking, infuriating, and the closest thing Devon had—or would let herself have—to a friend.

"You gonna let us in or what?"

Devon shook herself out of the haze of memory and reflection and pulled the keys out of her bag. She unlocked the door and pulled it open, the bell above it chiming its cheery welcome. She stepped over the threshold. It took her a minute to adjust to the faint morning light pushing into the gloom.

"Holy Jesus."

Devon barely registered the voice behind her. She was too focused on the body of her boss lying on the worn tile, the crimson gashes screaming at her in warning.

Dear Lord, please no.

All the convenient explanations she had come up with moments earlier vanished in an instant. Not that she had really believed any of them were true. Deep down, she had known what she would find when she stepped through that door.

She moved closer, her vision fixed on Sally. She didn't see Chuck but she knew he, too, was dead. You didn't need to feel the blade at your throat to know it was going to kill you.

The diner's patrons called to her from the doorway, but she paid them no mind. Her gaze lingered on Sally a moment longer, a simple act of respect for one who had deserved better, and then it moved across the floor. Scanning. Seeking.

The voices behind her whispered urgently. She could hear their fear that whoever had done this terrible thing might still be within. But the killer was gone. She could feel it.

Finding nothing on the floor beyond body and blood, Devon edged around all that remained of Sally Pendleton. She moved instinctively toward the counter, noting the open and empty cash register. But Devon wasn't interested in what had been taken, or even what remained. She was interested in what she knew had been left.

The penny shone like a lighthouse against a starless night, luring her in with its siren song. She knew before looking any closer, but she looked closer anyway. Two stalks of wheat lined the edges, mirror images bordering the words *one cent* in the upper center. Devon had seen many such pennies in her life. To some people, they were collector's items. To Devon, they were the tangible proof of her eternal damnation.

Adrenaline surged in Devon's veins, screaming at her to move. She began to backpedal, her limbs knowing what to do before her brain sent the signals. The adrenaline worked its will, lifting the fog from her mind until she could finally hear the voice screaming inside her head.

Run!

Devon turned, surging for the door, bursting through the crowded doorway and straight into the eye of a hurricane.

The cops had arrived. There was no escape.

CHAPTER THREE

Despite the heavy clouds and cold wind that had overrun the city early that morning, it was turning into a surprisingly mild day. Jordan Salinger was grateful for the deviation from Pittsburgh's normal November chill, for it enabled her to shed her coat while she carried the last box from the house to her black Jeep Cherokee.

Max, her faithful nearly one-and-a-half-year-old German shepherd, sat watching her in the yard. He had no tether, and he didn't need one. Jordan had trained him too well to worry about him running off. The only time she even used a leash on Max was to comply with the city's leash law when they walked down at Point State Park.

Max had been a gift a year earlier from her partner—well, former partner, really, though she had to force herself to think of him that way—Henry.

"Maybe taking care of him will help you take care of yourself," he'd said. She'd bitched him out for interfering in her life and continued to grumble about it for months afterward, but he'd been right. Of course he'd been right. He usually was.

She'd expected her mother to have a problem with having a dog in the house, but to Jordan's surprise, she'd been delighted. Jordan was convinced that Henry and her mother had conspired against her, but they never admitted a thing. Sometimes, when Jordan was feeling less suspicious, she thought that maybe her mother just enjoyed having another guest in the house—even the four-legged variety— and that maybe it made her feel less lonely. Her mother hadn't shared a house with anyone besides Jordan since her father had died. Jordan had been a teenager then.

Last week, Jordan's mother had left for Florida to spend the winter with Jordan's aunt in West Palm Beach. She'd been making the trip every year since retiring from teaching seven years earlier. It helped her fight the loneliness. She hadn't gone the year before. Jordan wasn't going to let that happen again.

"I don't have to go."

"I'll be fine, Mom."

Abigail Salinger looked disapprovingly over her reading glasses as Jordan pulled the suitcase from the high shelf in the closet.

"Jordan, be careful. Your shoulder—"

"Is fine. All healed up. See?" Jordan dropped the suitcase on the bed and started swinging her arm up, down, and sideways. "Good as new."

"You might fool your doctors, Jordan Denise Salinger, but you can never fool your mother." Jordan cringed at the use of her middle name, both because she hated it and because, as with most mothers, it meant her mom was actually upset. "I see you grimacing when you've overdone it and you think I'm not looking."

Jordan swallowed the sarcastic comment that popped into her head. Her mother was worried about her and Jordan was grateful for her concern, even if it drove her a little crazy sometimes. She sat on the bed and took her mother's hand.

"Seriously, I'm okay."

"I really don't have to go."

"Yes, you do." Jordan patted her mother's hand and then let it go. She went to the dresser and began pulling out clothes. "You go every year. And you've been looking forward to seeing Aunt Martha for weeks." She glanced back at her mother. "You're not the only one with keen observational powers, Mom."

Abigail smiled but still looked uncertain. "Are you sure you'll be all right? This is the first time you'll have been alone for any length of time since you…got out of the hospital."

"You missed last year because of me. There's no need for you to miss this trip. *I'll be fine, Mom. Promise.*"

She hadn't missed how her mother's voice had faded at the end, an echo of just how close she had come to losing her daughter.

Jordan had moved in with her mother four months after she'd been shot. Her rehab had been lengthy and difficult. The hollow-point bullet had hit her between the left shoulder and breast and had shattered bone, shredded muscle, and sliced a major artery. The initial surgery to fix the artery and save her life had been followed by three more over three months, to repair what the bullet had destroyed.

When she was released from the hospital, she'd returned to the apartment she shared with Caroline, her partner of six years. But within a month, Caroline was gone. She couldn't take Jordan pushing her away anymore, she'd said. Jordan didn't deny the accusation and didn't blame her for leaving. The truth was, they had been growing apart long before she'd been shot.

But with her arm needing to be in a sling and the weakness and fatigue that made simple things—like brushing her teeth and cooking meals—infinitely difficult, Abigail and Henry and Ella, Henry's wife, had insisted Jordan move in with her mother.

Jordan had only been at her mother's for a few weeks when Henry brought her Max.

It took months of arduous physical therapy to rebuild her muscles. Her shoulder still ached from time to time, whenever she pushed too hard and especially when it rained, but for the most part, Jordan was healed. At least physically.

Jordan secured the box in the back of the SUV and closed the tailgate. Max recognized the action for what it was and stood, his tail swishing back and forth as Jordan approached.

"You're ready to go to the cabin, aren't you, boy?"

Max chuffed and ran ahead of Jordan into the house, as if he were about to grab her keys and coat so they could get on the road.

Chapter Four

L ieutenant Henry Wayne exited his car, annoyed but un-surprised by the chaos before him. The beat cops were doing their best to secure the scene, but the large crowd of gawkers pressed against the crime-scene tape, unconcerned with whatever evidence they might be about to trample.

"Sergeant! Move that crowd back!"

The woman nodded at Henry, grabbing the closest two officers and ordering them to push the onlookers back and reset the crime-scene tape ten feet farther away from the diner.

Henry spotted Detective Martin Lawson and strode toward him.

"Hey, Lieutenant," Lawson said as Henry reached him. "Come to check up on me?"

Lawson had only been with homicide for six months and had shadowed Henry when he first arrived. Normally a new detective would stay with a mentor for at least four months, but not Lawson. Within weeks, Henry had known Lawson had the makings of an outstanding investigator. The rookie had sharp instincts and a nose for bullshit but was also affable and empathetic—essential tools for getting witnesses to open up. Lawson reminded Henry of another fine detective, one whose ability to find the truth was outshone only by her compassion.

The thought of his partner made Henry sad. He missed her, but more than that, he worried about her. One of these days, he was going to get her to see reason.

He shook off his melancholy, turning his attention back to the rookie detective. "I don't know, Lawson. You need checking up on?"

"Always."

"So what have we got?"

Lawson talked as he led Henry into the diner. "Two Caucasians, one female, one male. The woman has multiple stab wounds. The man had his throat cut."

Henry crouched next to the female, his experienced eyes traveling over the body as Lawson continued.

"Sally Pendleton. Thirty-nine. Owner of the diner along with her husband, Chuck. He's the one dead in the back."

Henry scanned the scene. No footprints. No drag marks. No blood other than that on her clothes and around her. She had died where she'd fallen.

"According to the regulars, Sally and Chuck usually arrived around four thirty to open the diner at six. There's nothing to indicate today was any different."

"Who found them?" Henry stood, carefully stepping around the body to approach the counter. He noted the mostly empty cash register. He didn't think they'd find the killer's prints, but they'd dust it anyway. They'd dust everything, for whatever good it would do. The busy diner was bound to have hundreds of prints, no matter how good they cleaned the place at night.

"A waitress, Devon James. She was supposed to be here by the time they opened, but she was running late."

"Might have saved her life. Why was she late?"

"Bus."

Of course.

"Forced entry?"

"No signs of it, front or back. Front door was locked when Ms. James arrived. Only way to lock it is with a key, and there was a set in Sally's purse and in Chuck's coat pocket."

"Killer might have used them and put them back, gone out the other door." Henry thought the possibility was unlikely, but a good detective had to explore every alternative, even if only to knock them down. In his more than twenty years as a detective, first with narcotics and then homicide, Henry had learned that even the unlikeliest of possibilities was sometimes true.

"For a robbery? What thief do you know that locks up and returns the keys before he leaves? Especially after he's murdered two people?"

"Hmm." Henry inspected the cash register. The drawer had been mostly cleaned out. He dug inside his jacket pocket for a pen and used it to sort through what was left in the register. Three one-dollar bills and a five sitting neatly in their slots, and two rolls of coins, one pennies and one dimes.

"What about the back door?"

"Also locked. But that one is a fire door. Locks automatically when it closes. Killer probably went out that way."

A small object on the counter caught Henry's attention. He peered closer. He hadn't seen a wheat penny in years. Between the Treasury and the collectors, they had mostly fallen out of circulation.

"Make sure you bag this," Henry said, not waiting for a response. He headed for the kitchen. Lawson followed.

"Chuck Pendleton. Thirty-seven. He and Sally were married for eight years. Have owned this diner for the last five."

Chuck was propped up against the freezer, his throat a gaping wound. Blood soaked the front of his otherwise pristine white T-shirt and apron. The floor between and in front of Chuck's legs was sprayed with red, like a macabre, monochromic Jackson Pollock painting. Unlike Sally's twelve stab wounds, the cook had none. Not that any had been necessary.

"Theories?" Henry asked.

"Killer came in through the back door. Locks don't look tampered with, but there's a lot of wear. The techs are checking. Maybe he had a spare key, maybe he knew them. Killed Chuck first, likely from behind. Looks like the carotid is cut, so he probably bled out fast. No signs of a struggle either here or in the dining room, so Sally probably wasn't in here when it happened and didn't hear anything. Then the killer went for her. No splatter, no smears. He killed her quickly and efficiently. My guess is the ME will find the first thrust killed her, and the rest were done while she was on the ground."

Henry thought about it. "Maybe." He looked over the rest of the kitchen. He noticed a single plate and fork in the drainer and a pie resting on the counter with one slice missing. "We don't know it was a him," Henry said, eyeing the plate.

Lawson chuffed. "What woman you know can take a big guy like Chuck?"

Henry said nothing. He knew that despite Lawson's response, his point had been understood. Leaps of logic were fine, even necessary, but assumptions could make you miss things, like a horse wearing blinders. They needed to follow the evidence.

Henry held his hand out about an inch above the pie. It was still minutely warm, like it had been baked that morning. He supposed either Chuck or Sally could have had a piece for breakfast, but somehow he doubted it. Thirty-two years of his wife's baking had taught him a thing or two about pies. Assuming Chuck or Sally had started making it as soon as they'd arrived, that pie couldn't have been done much before five thirty. That would be awfully close to opening time for either of them to sit down and eat a slice.

He sure did miss Ella's pies.

"Bag this plate and fork, too," Henry said. "So where's the waitress? Ms. James?"

"Uniforms have her out front." They stepped outside beneath a bright blue sky. Pittsburgh weather was often like that. Blustering and overcast one minute, crisp and clear the next. Henry reached for his sunglasses, but then thought better of it. He generally saved the shades for when he wanted to come off like a hard-ass.

Devon watched Detective Lawson walk toward her, followed by another man. She assumed he was another detective and mentally braced herself for more questions. It wasn't the first time she had been questioned by the police about a murder. Devon knew the routine. Right now, they were trying to piece together the basic facts and an approximate timeline. The real questions—the hard ones—would come later. She didn't plan to be around when that time came.

Devon eyed the new man, sizing him up as he approached. She had gotten pretty good at that over the years, though she knew that first impressions weren't always the right ones. He was African American, stocky without being fat, like maybe he had been a football player once upon a time. He appeared to be in his midfifties, a touch of gray at his temples. His eyes seemed kind, brown pools devoid of malice or duplicity. You could tell a lot from someone's eyes, though, like first impressions, they could also be misleading.

Detective Lawson made the introduction. "Ms. James, this is Lieutenant Henry Wayne. He'd like to ask you a few questions."

"Ms. James," Lieutenant Wayne said, nodding his head slightly in greeting.

"I don't know what else I can tell you, Lieutenant, that I haven't already told Detective Lawson," Devon said, careful to keep the urgency from her voice. The sooner they'd finished with her, the sooner she could disappear. But she wouldn't be going anywhere if they suspected she was anything more than a waitress who'd had the misfortune of discovering two bodies. "But I'm happy to tell you anything I can."

"This should only take a few minutes," the lieutenant said, his voice a rich baritone. "I know it's been a rough morning."

Lieutenant Wayne placed his hand on Devon's elbow and guided her away from the diner and the crowd, toward a small alcove made by two police cars and what had turned out to be an unnecessary ambulance. Detective Lawson followed silently. Devon thought she detected a deference in Detective Lawson's actions, not out of duty but out of respect. Clearly this was Lieutenant Wayne's show now.

"Can you tell me what happened?"

"I was running late this morning. My shift started at six but I didn't get here until about six thirty. When I arrived, there was a group of customers waiting outside. They said the door was locked."

"And you unlocked it?"

Devon nodded. "The main lights were off. For a minute I thought maybe Sally and Chuck had overslept."

"Were they often late?"

"No. Never," Devon said. An image of Sally's smiling face filled her mind, and a wave of sadness rose up within her. She pushed it back down.

"Did you go inside?"

"Yes. I know I shouldn't have, but I had to—" Devon caught herself before she slipped completely. *I had to see if they were dead. I had to know if it was him.* "I didn't think it might be dangerous." She couldn't tell if he had caught her self-censorship.

"Then what happened?"

"I saw Sally."

"But you didn't try to help her?"

The question caught Devon off guard. Of course she hadn't tried to help. There had been no help to be had, no mistaking the pool of blood or Sally's lifeless baby-blues glazed over in death. She had known Sally was dead before she opened the door, despite all the plausible explanations that had rolled through her head. But did Lieutenant Wayne know that? How could he? Her mind raced for an explanation, and she searched the investigator's face for some sign there was more than curiosity behind his question. Her instinct for self-preservation on overdrive, Devon told a half-truth.

"I was in shock, I guess. She was staring up at the ceiling, and there was so much blood."

The lieutenant's expression never wavered, and he nodded like he believed her. Devon suspected, though, that he didn't. Her heart started to race, and she tried to quiet it.

"What else did you see?"

"I noticed the cash register was open, but that was about it. Then the police arrived."

"You didn't call them?"

"No. One of the customers must have."

Henry nodded again, though Devon didn't think he was confirming her statement. In fact, Devon thought he probably would have known who called the police before he asked the question. Devon didn't think he was trying to manipulate her, but she couldn't be sure. Past experience taught her to assume the worst.

"Did you go into the kitchen?"

"No. Once I realized what was happening, I got out of there. I didn't want to destroy any evidence or anything."

Devon regretted the words as soon as she said them. Lieutenant Wayne's eyebrows rose ever so slightly, in a gesture few would notice if they weren't really looking. But Devon saw it clear as day.

The lieutenant closed his notepad and tucked his pen into his breast pocket. Detective Lawson stepped forward, awaiting instructions.

"Is there anything else, Lieutenant? I'd like to go home. It's been a...horrible morning." Devon tried to keep her voice neutral.

"I think we should continue this down at the station," Lieutenant Wayne said. He smiled, nodding his head toward the crowd on the other side of the police tape. "I'm having a hard time thinking with all this racket."

Devon fought the panic welling up inside. "I don't know what else I can tell you. I wasn't here when it happened."

"I know," he said reassuringly. "And I'm sorry to delay this any further. I know it's hard and you want to go home. But I've got a few more questions I need to ask. Just to make sure I've got everything I need to catch whoever did this."

Over the lieutenant's shoulder, Devon noticed a look of surprise flash across Detective Lawson's face. As quickly as it appeared it was gone.

"Detective Lawson will take you to the station. I'll be right behind you."

Knowing objecting any further would only raise Lieutenant Wayne's suspicions, Devon agreed. She told herself it was simply a matter of routine, that it meant nothing and in a few hours she'd walk out of the police station and leave Pittsburgh far behind. She told herself these things as Detective Lawson led her to his car, but she didn't believe them. She could feel the walls closing in around her.

❖

Billy stood at the back of the crowd, watching the police flittering about, throwing their weight around. He knew police, knew their routines and their predilection to act like they had everything under control amidst a sea of chaos. He wondered what they thought of his work, whether they had any idea this was anything but a standard robbery-homicide.

They don't have a clue.

He took it all in from behind the indistinct and faded ball cap pulled low across his forehead. Despite the sun's glare, he did not wear sunglasses. The combination of the hat and glasses might draw unnecessary attention, whereas the hat by itself was like a dozen others in the crowd.

Although it was amusing to watch the police run around like ants that'd just had their anthill kicked over, Billy was not some run-of-the-mill killer who hung around at the crime scene to marvel at his own handiwork, and he had no real interest in this particular police investigation. He was there for one reason and one reason alone.

He had watched some uniform bring her a bottle of water, watched as she was questioned by first one detective and then another. But his eyes narrowed as the first detective led her over to his car and helped her inside. Billy had not expected that, and it changed things.

He was not close enough to his own car to follow them, so he would have to improvise. He was good at improvising. He was even better at tracking prey that had escaped his sight.

Devon sat in a small conference room and watched the flurry of activity on the other side of the window. At least they hadn't put her in an interrogation room. The small, windowless rooms were good at accomplishing their intended purpose: intimidation. Fifteen minutes in one of those rooms, with the cops hunched over you, flinging questions like accusations, and you were ready to climb the walls. An hour, and you were ready to confess to the assassination of Abraham Lincoln if it would get you out of that room any faster.

She'd been sitting alone in the conference room for more than twenty minutes, watching the unit's detectives work their cases, make phone calls and take statements, search through computer records, and write up reports. But most of her attention had been focused on Lieutenant Wayne, who had arrived shortly after she was shown into the conference room by Detective Lawson. The lieutenant had spent some time at his computer—doing what, Devon didn't know—and now was talking to Detective Lawson on the far side of the squad room. She couldn't hear what they were saying, obviously, but given their surreptitious glances in her direction, it wasn't too difficult to determine that they were talking about her.

Devon rubbed her hands against her arms, trying to ward off the chill that had nothing to do with the temperature in the conference room. She couldn't believe it was happening again. What had she done wrong? How, after all this time, had he found her? Over the past ten years, she had moved nearly a dozen times. She'd changed her name so often she could barely remember the one she was born with. She'd had so many hairstyles and colors that sometimes when she looked in a mirror it took her a few minutes to recognize her own reflection. She'd had more social security numbers than one human being could possibly be expected to remember, only used cash, didn't have a bank account, and kept everyone at a distance. She carried everything that mattered to her, everything she needed, in her shoulder bag. She rarely went on dates and, if she did, never got past a second date. She had sex on occasion, when the need for some kind of intimacy built to the point that she was crawling out of her skin, but she hadn't held a woman or let herself be held in too many years to count.

Devon lived a terribly lonely life, though she almost never allowed herself to think about it. She had no other choice. She had to keep running, keep hiding, keep people from seeing any part of herself that might somehow lead him to her. It was exhausting, this life. Always looking over her shoulder, always keeping herself apart from anyone who might actually come to care about her and about whom maybe she could care in return.

But despite everything she had done, everything she had gone through and given up, he had found her once more.

She saw Lieutenant Wayne heading toward her, and she quickly slid her wall back into place. She was Devon James, a simple waitress who had been late to work, hadn't witnessed anything, and had no story to tell. She would answer their questions and then she would be gone. And she would not look back.

Chapter Five

Hello, Ms. James." Henry closed the door behind him and sat at the conference table across from Devon. He placed a legal pad on the table in front of him and his pen on top. Beside them, he laid a single manila file folder. Then he moved each item, sliding them carefully around until they were perfectly lined up with the table's edge. It was part of his routine, an old interrogation technique designed to unsettle a witness. Wasting time on such mundane precision tended to annoy whoever was sitting across the table. It also tended to draw the person's attention to the file folder and what might lie within. Witnesses with something to hide almost always became fixated on the folder.

Interrogation was a form of psychological warfare, with every action—from the temperature of the room to the placement of the chairs to the pacing of the questions—designed to get into the witness's mind. But Henry's actions at the moment were not about interrogation techniques, or even about routine. Henry was buying a few moments to organize his thoughts.

He had spent much of the car ride back to the station trying to puzzle out what exactly was bothering him about Devon James. He had no doubt that her recounting of the events that morning was true. She had arrived late, unlocked the front door, found Sally Pendleton's body, seen the open register, and had not been the one to call the police. She did not go into the kitchen or see Chuck Pendleton's body, and she did not try to resuscitate Sally.

Even though he believed her story, he did not believe it was the *whole* story.

It was the little things, mostly. When he'd asked her if she went inside, the answer she gave seemed to be different than the one she had started to give. He wondered what she had been about to say.

When he'd asked her why she didn't try to help Sally after she saw the woman lying on the floor—an innocuous question intended to do nothing more than confirm she hadn't touched the body—she gave a completely logical answer about being in shock and seeing the blood and the woman's lifeless body. But the way she said those things made Henry think she was saying what she thought would be the right response.

Finally, when he'd asked her whether she went into the kitchen, she'd told him she didn't want to destroy any evidence. In Henry's experience, people who just found a dead body, especially of someone they knew, tended to think little about preserving evidence, even in this age of endless forensic shows on television.

On the surface, Devon was a solid witness, calm and collected with fairly good attention to detail. That, too, was part of the problem. She seemed too composed for someone in her situation, and though Henry knew that not everyone reacted the same way to violent death, it bothered him.

Still, none of those things were what had made him decide to bring her in for further questioning. It was what he detected beneath those answers and self-possession that troubled him most. Henry sensed fear, and not in the way most people would be afraid after having two coworkers murdered. He sensed a deeply rooted terror beneath Devon's placid surface, an almost panic beneath her cool demeanor that he would bet came from personal experience.

What he'd found in her records only confirmed his suspicions.

Henry couldn't be sure, and he had little to go on besides intuition honed through years of experience, but he was convinced that somehow, someway, Devon James was the key to everything. And that, if given the chance, she would disappear forever—either under her own power, or someone else's.

"Thanks for talking to me a little more. I know it's been a traumatic day. I just want to follow up on a couple of things."

"Okay."

"Have you noticed anyone hanging around the diner in the last few weeks, anyone who maybe didn't belong?"

Devon appeared to be thinking. "No, I don't think so. We get a lot of people coming through there. We have a number of regulars, but many aren't. I didn't notice anyone suspicious, though."

"No one who stood out?"

"No. I'm sorry."

"It's okay. And had Mr. or Mrs. Pendleton mentioned anything to you?"

"About what?"

"Anything out of the ordinary. Had they noticed anyone unusual hanging around? Anyone threaten them?" Henry asked.

"Not that I know of. I imagine Sally would have said something if they had. She wasn't the type to keep something like that to herself."

"What do you mean?"

"Sally tended to say what was on her mind," Devon said, smiling wistfully. "And she tended to have a lot on her mind."

Henry smiled back. "I know the type. My wife, Ella, was the same way. Full of opinions. Of course, her opinions were usually right."

"Sally's too." Devon's face softened. "You said was. Is your wife…?"

"She passed seven months ago. Cancer." Henry read the sympathy on Devon's face, and he believed it to be genuine.

"I'm sorry," she said.

He nodded, unable to voice words past the lump that formed in his throat. He was rarely overcome by his grief anymore, though he missed Ella terribly every day. Something in Devon's expression struck him in the heart. He shook it off. He had a job to do.

"You've been working at the diner for nine months, is that right?" he asked, turning the conversation toward the thing that truly needed asking.

"Yes."

"What about before that?"

"I only moved to Pittsburgh a month before I started at the diner," Devon replied smoothly.

"Oh yeah? Where did you move here from?"

"A small town in Oregon you've probably never heard of. Stanton."

It had a ring of truth, but then a good lie always did. He couldn't say for sure whether she'd been there or not, but Henry suspected if he looked on a map for Stanton, Oregon, he wouldn't find it. But the answer was well crafted, with the bit about it being a small town planting a subconscious thought that the town wasn't big enough to matter. Most people would forget the name as soon as she said it, and if they did happen to remember and found it didn't exist, they would assume they'd just heard wrong.

"So you moved here ten months ago?"

"Approximately, yes."

Henry opened the manila folder and removed a single sheet of paper. He watched her attention turn to the paper. She showed no outward sign of concern. "That's interesting. Did you know that before ten months ago, you didn't exist?"

Devon stiffened. Her gaze darted away from Henry's face, dancing across the table in the way that happens when someone is caught in a trap and trying to figure if there's any way out. Henry waited for her to tell him a story, to make up some kind of excuse or to feign innocence, but she didn't. She looked again at Henry, her eyes now focused but hollow, like she had reached the inevitable conclusion: there was no way out.

"You have no arrests, no warrants. No run-ins with the police of any kind, not even a parking ticket. Anywhere. Nothing in Pennsylvania or any other state I could find. One good thing came out of 9/11—it's a whole lot easier to get public records from across state lines. It's not perfect, there are still gaps and we still live in a world full of bureaucracy, but..." Henry shrugged.

"I didn't realize it was a bad thing to not have a criminal record," she said, her voice devoid of emotion.

"No, of course not. It's a good thing." Henry lifted the sheet of paper, scanning its contents. "You have no car registered to you, no significant assets. You do have a social security number and a state issued ID, but that's about it. And see, the funny thing is that before ten months ago, you didn't even have those things. There was no Devon James."

"I don't understand."

He leaned closer. "I think you do." Henry watched her process the information. It was something he'd seen a hundred times, the way the brow clenched and released, the way the cheeks flushed and the body shifted. Henry didn't think she had done anything wrong, didn't think she was in any way responsible for the murders. He did think, however, she was hiding something and, more importantly, hiding *from* something. Devon James had been someone else once, and had left that someone behind before coming to Pittsburgh.

Henry had caught her in the lie, and now that he had, he thought she would be ready to tell him everything. Instead, she focused on Henry's face, a steel curtain slamming down between them. Just before it closed completely, Henry glimpsed a flash of something raw and desperate. It appeared to Henry very much like a plea to be saved.

A knock on the conference room door stopped Henry before he could press any further. His boss waved him out of the room.

"Excuse me for a minute," Henry said, covering his frustration at the interruption. He closed the door behind him and walked over to Captain Dwight Buchanan.

Buchanan headed up the homicide division. He was in his early forties, young to have made captain, especially of a high-profile division like homicide. There were a lot of whispers that Buchanan had only made captain because his uncle was the deputy police commissioner, but Henry knew better. Buchanan had been a first-rate detective, and while his family connections might have moved him to the head of the promotion line, the captain had more than earned his rank in the eyes of the cops that served under him. "Captain?"

"What's the story?"

"Two dead. Looks like a robbery-homicide."

Buchanan eyed Henry. "But?"

"But I believe there's more to this case than what we know."

"Based on what?"

"Based on the crime scene and the vics. There's no sign of forced entry. The man had his throat slit, but the woman was stabbed twelve times."

"Maybe she knew the killer."

"It's possible. But I don't think so, Cap. I can't explain it, not yet, but I think there's more to this than a robbery gone bad. For one thing, we found a wheat penny left on the counter."

"I haven't seen one of those in years," Buchanan said.

"Exactly. Wheat pennies are fairly rare these days. Not many are in circulation anymore."

"What else?"

"The waitress, Devon James."

Buchanan looked over Henry's shoulder into the conference room. "Is she a suspect?"

"No, sir. A potential witness."

"But she wasn't there when it happened."

"No, sir. She found the victims." The glimpse of whatever Henry had seen before Devon shut down pulled at him. "But I think she knows more than she's saying."

"Based on what?"

Buchanan waited for an explanation Henry wasn't yet prepared to give.

"Give me some time and some room on this one?" Henry asked. Buchanan studied him for a moment, then acquiesced.

"All right, Lieutenant. Run it down. But I'm going to need something more than your intuition on this soon. I've already gotten a call from downtown. Three other robbery-homicides in the last two months, all with the cash register cleaned out, no signs of forced entry, all with dead bodies on them, and no suspects in sight. The brass is viewing this as number four, and your intuition aside, Henry, I'd have to say I agree. If this is related to the others, we need to find this guy. If this is something else…well, you'll need to convince me why this takes precedence. Okay?"

Henry nodded. He understood the pressure the captain was under, but he would bet his home, his pension, and even the watch his wife had given him for their twenty-fifth anniversary that this case wasn't connected to the others.

"Good. I've got a meeting with the deputy commissioner. Do whatever you need to do, Henry."

Henry watched the elevator doors close in front of Buchanan. He looked back toward the conference room, toward the woman with a made-up past, and wondered again what she was hiding from. *Who* she was hiding from. She had a story to tell, but convincing her to tell it was beyond Henry's considerable talents. There was a desperation there, and though he had only glimpsed it, he was certain it was born of pain and fear. On the outside, Devon was strong and unflappable. On the inside, Henry would bet she was broken beyond measure. It reminded him of someone he cared deeply about.

If Henry was right about Devon, and whatever she was hiding from had found her, then Henry was going to need help. A very special kind of help.

He hit number one on his speed dial.

CHAPTER SIX

Jordan looked down at her faithful friend. Max snorted again, his tail thundering from side to side.

"Patience never was your virtue, young man," Jordan admonished. Max's tail wagged harder.

With her mother gone until March, Jordan had decided to relocate to the cabin her grandfather had built about an hour outside the city. She'd been slowly fixing it up over the summer months, once she had rehabbed her shoulder enough to do that kind of labor. She'd been going out every other weekend, replacing windows and storm shutters, patching leaky roof shingles, stripping the floors and refinishing them. She had accomplished a lot, but she still had much to do.

Once the work was completed, she planned to purchase the cabin from her mother and make it her permanent home. She had not yet told her mother or Henry of her plan. It was not a conversation she was looking forward to since the idea that she would *buy* the cabin from her mother was an ongoing disagreement, the latest installment of which had taken place only two weeks ago.

Okay, it hadn't been much of a disagreement, since Jordan hadn't been able to get a word in edgewise, as usual. And truthfully, she knew she was indeed being stubborn, bullheaded, and possibly even a pain in the ass—she refused to dignify her mother's use of the phrase *pain in the patoot*—but she would pay for the cabin. Her mom did okay with her teaching pension and her dad's benefits, but there wasn't much left over. Beyond that, Jordan knew her mom's finances had been strained by taking her in and helping in her recovery, whether the woman admitted it or not. At the very least, buying the cabin would allow Jordan to feel like she had paid some measure of recompense.

But if she was honest, the battle over whether Jordan would or would not buy the cabin was not the real reason she had not told her mother and Henry of her plans. The truth was, she had avoided telling them because she knew they would both see through all her cleverly crafted rationales to the one that really mattered: she was running away.

The theme music to *Murder, She Wrote* played on Jordan's phone. She smiled at the distinctive ringtone and answered. "You playing hooky again?"

Henry laughed from the other end of the phone line. "As often as I can."

Jordan stood at the living room window, watching the wind rustle through the trees. "Yeah, right. You haven't played hooky in twenty years."

"You haven't known me twenty years."

"No, but I do *know* you."

Henry laughed again. "That you do."

Max came up beside her and nuzzled her hand, like he knew it was Henry on the phone. Of course, since Henry was the only one who ever called her—apart from her mother—it wasn't really much of a guess.

"Uncle Henry's on the phone," she told the dog. He whined softly and gave her hand a swift lick. "Max says hi," she said, to Henry this time.

"Give him a good scratch for me. You change my ringtone yet?"

He'd been demanding she change it for over a year. "Why would I? It's perfect for you."

"Yes, because I am the spitting image of Angela Lansbury."

This time it was Jordan who laughed. "So, what's up? It's not like you to call me during the workday."

Henry didn't answer right away. "I've got a case."

This time it was Jordan who fell silent.

"Jordan? You still there?"

She turned and sat on the ledge of the large bay window. "I'm here."

"On the surface, it's pretty cut-and-dried, but…"

"But your gut is talking."

"Something like that."

"I'm not a cop anymore, Henry." They'd had this conversation before.

His answer was instantaneous. "You'll always be a cop, wherever you are. But you should be here."

Jordan stiffened, angry with him for bringing it up and angry with herself for knowing he was right. "If this is what you called about—"

"No, no. No. Not really," he said quickly. She could practically see him backpedaling. "I need your help."

She started to tell him again that she wasn't a cop anymore, but she knew that would get her nowhere. They'd go round and round like they always did, each repeating their point and neither conceding. She pushed it down, swallowing her pride and the bile that rose with it. Henry rarely asked for her help. He was always too busy trying to help her to let her help him. Even after Ella's death seven months ago, it was all about Jordan.

"She made me promise to take care of you, Jordan."

They stood beside Ella's coffin, the sky blue and crisp above the cemetery. But even the sweet scent of spring couldn't erase the death that hung in the air.

"What about you, Henry? Who's going to take care of you?"

"Don't you worry about me. We had thirty-two wonderful years together. She's with God now."

"But Ella—"

"Ella's finally out of her pain," he said. Ella had fought a long, hard battle against kidney cancer. By the end, the vivacious force of will that was Ella Wayne had been reduced to a mere shell of herself, though even in her weakened state, she was still one formidable woman. "And she'll kick my butt all the way from heaven if I fail to keep my promise."

"Not everything's about me, Henry."

"Maybe it should be."

"Maybe I can't be saved."

"Who said anything about saving you?" Henry turned to her, brown pools twinkling in grief and hope. "If I tried to save you, you'd kick my butt."

"Probably. Definitely."

"So maybe the trick is to help you save yourself."

Henry hadn't had much luck in that regard. But he kept trying, and Jordan kept fighting him, though over the last few months he had been getting through more than she cared to admit. She shoved that thought aside and focused on the here and now. Henry had asked for help, and she wasn't about to ignore such a request.

Jordan sighed. "What kind of help?"

"We've got a double homicide. Husband and wife—waitress and cook who owned a diner."

Henry quickly sketched out the details, including the account of the waitress who'd discovered the bodies, Devon James. It sounded straightforward enough, but Henry wouldn't have called if it were that simple.

"You think there's more to it." It was a statement, not a question.

"Something isn't adding up about Devon's story," he said.

"You think she's involved?"

"No, nothing like that. I mean, yeah. Kind of."

"Okay, now you've got me confused. You think she is or isn't involved?" She heard the phone shuffle in Henry's hand, and the once-distinct voices in the background became muffled. A few seconds later, Henry was back, speaking a little more quietly.

"I don't think she was involved in the murders. But I do think she knows more than she's telling."

"So why not bring her in? Question her further?"

"I did. She's here. But she's still not telling me everything. In fact, she's totally shut down."

"You think she's protecting someone? The killer?"

"Someone, yes. The killer, no," he said. "I think she's scared."

Henry was one of the best investigators Jordan had ever known. He always seemed to know the right play, the right amount of pressure to put on a witness. His gut was rarely wrong, and he could ferret out the truth like a bloodhound in a swamp.

"What haven't you told me?"

She could practically hear him smiling. "You haven't lost a step," he said. "I checked her record."

"And?"

"Spotless. Of course, she didn't actually exist before ten months ago."

That added a whole different dimension to things. Henry had to have checked more deeply into the woman's background than they usually did on a basic witness, which meant he'd had some inkling that her story was off before he'd run the check. And his gut had been right. As usual.

She'd seen this kind of thing before, once or twice, and heard tales of it beyond her own experience. Someone with no history would cross the path of an investigation, no evidence of his or her name or existence prior to some point a few months or years earlier. It was almost always a woman, usually a battered wife who had run away from her abusive husband. Jordan wondered if that was the case here. In her experience, battered women were often the hardest to break.

"If I let her go, the truth goes with her. She's going to run," Henry said.

"If she runs, you'll find her."

"I don't think so."

Jordan sighed again. Odds were Henry was right. If this woman had run before, chances were she knew how to disappear. "What do you want from me, Henry?"

"I need your help."

"You said that already."

"I need you to do what you do best. I need you to help me find the truth."

"You don't need me for that."

"Yeah, I do."

Jordan was growing frustrated. "There are a dozen detectives there who could break her. Why me?"

"Because breaking her isn't what's going to get her to open up. She needs to trust somebody."

"She can trust you."

"Yeah, but she doesn't. At least not enough to talk."

"But you think she'll trust me. Why?"

Henry didn't answer. Silence crawled across the line for endless moments. Finally, he said, "Because I think she's broken. Just like you."

Henry's words sucked the air out of Jordan's chest like she'd just been sucker punched. Tears welled as a little boy's face filled her vision. She tried to block out the image but it remained, burned into her sight as if it had been branded on the insides of her eyelids.

"Jordan? You still there? I didn't mean—"

"I'll be there in thirty minutes."

She hung up without saying good-bye, knowing Henry would forgive her rudeness but not particularly caring at that moment. Max sat up at her feet, where he had been lying throughout the conversation. She smoothed her hand over the soft fur of his scalp.

"Well, boy. Looks like I'm walking back into the fire."

Devon waited in the conference room, biding her time until Lieutenant Wayne came back from wherever he'd disappeared to twenty minutes earlier. She waited for him to return, waited for him to ask her more questions she had no intention of answering, waited for the floor to dissolve into a deep black hole from which there was no escape.

Or maybe it already had.

She stared at the wooden conference table, watched her fingers trace aimless patterns over the scarred surface as she tried to figure out how she'd ended up trapped in a police station, caught within a web of lies of her own making. She glanced at the door, wondering what would happen if she just got up and walked out of that room and out of the police station. She wasn't under arrest. She'd seen enough movies to know they had no reason to hold her, and her own experience backed up that knowledge. The only crime she'd committed was related to how she obtained her social security number, but she didn't think they'd had enough time to track that down, which meant they had nothing. She was free to leave at any time.

And yet she stayed in her chair, imprisoned by choice. Years of hard-won experience cried out for her to run, and yet she was so damn tired of running. Of hiding. Of living only half a life.

Lieutenant Wayne knew she was living a lie, had confronted her with that knowledge, but he knew only a fraction of the truth. There was so much more to tell, and for the first time in too many years to count, something inside urged her to tell it. She thought she could trust the lieutenant. He was clearly good at his job—he'd backed her into a corner she hadn't even known was there—and maybe he was even a good man. He had led her into a trap, but she hadn't sensed any malice in his intent or perverse enjoyment in his actions. He seemed to want the truth, to stop the man responsible for killing Sally and Chuck. Maybe, just maybe, that meant she could tell him…

But she had done that before, and the police had not believed her. The pain of that betrayal stung sharply all these years later. They hadn't believed her, just like Lieutenant Wayne wouldn't believe her. And then what? She'd be lucky if they didn't throw her into a psych ward somewhere with only her pain to keep her company—her pain, and the certainty that if she stayed in one place for too long, even locked away from the world, *he* would find a way to get to her. There was no escaping him. She knew that now.

No, it was better to stay quiet, to keep it to herself, like always. Eventually, Lieutenant Wayne would tire of her silence and would have to let her go. Then she could move on to the next place, the next name, and the next half a life.

❖

Jordan shoved her car keys into her pocket, asking herself for the eleventh time what in the hell she was doing. She leaned her back against her SUV, staring up at the three-story station house. She hadn't been inside its walls in fifteen months. She wondered if it had changed at all but knew instinctively that it hadn't. She imagined that in fifty years it would still be there, a little older, a little more decrepit, but still standing. A last refuge in a world gone mad. The thought both comforted and saddened her.

She stuck her thumbs in the pockets of her jeans, a seemingly casual move that was anything but. Jordan called it her fake-it-till-you-make-it stance. The first time she'd done it was right after her father's funeral. Jordan had been fourteen when he'd died of a heart attack. It had come without warning and without reason. His heart had simply…stopped.

Where Jordan's mother had taught her to be compassionate, her father had taught her to be self-reliant. He had been a kind man, but he had also been a survivor. He'd lost his two older brothers in the Korean War, had fought in Vietnam, and had lost his job and means of earning a living when the steel industry collapsed in the early '80s. He had survived all that and come out stronger, a trait he had been determined to pass on to his daughter.

She hoped he could not see her from heaven, because he would be sorely disappointed in her in that regard.

After his funeral, Jordan had found it hard to focus, and she'd isolated herself from everyone. She had always been a bit of an outsider, a bit of a tomboy, though she'd always managed to find friends. No one messed with Jordan when she had a group of people behind her, but after she'd pushed her friends away, some of the boys sensed weakness. For a while Jordan took their bullying, unable to feel anything other than numb. She had no energy to fight, no strength to stand up for herself.

But things changed the day one of the boys made a comment about her dad. Jordan was filled with a sense of despair so deep it nearly brought her to her knees. She was overwhelmed by it but knew she couldn't allow herself to be a victim. She had to stand up—for her father, and for herself. Even consumed by grief and pain and fear, she forced herself to pretend she wasn't. She stood taller, straightened her shoulders, and widened her stance. She stared the boys down, never looking away, barely even blinking. Then she stuck her thumbs into her front pockets, like she couldn't have cared less what they thought of her. Like she knew she would win—even though she knew no such thing.

The boys had left her alone after that. They wouldn't admit it, probably not even to themselves, but they had a certain amount of respect for her after that, and maybe even a little bit of fear.

Since then, the thumbs-in-pockets ritual of faking confidence made her actually feel confident, banishing the insecurity from her soul and giving her the courage to face things head-on. It always worked. Or at least it had, until a little boy named Jacob had died.

Come on, Jordan. Enough with the introspective bullshit. Stop being a coward and get your ass moving.

She pushed off her SUV at last, forcing herself across the street and into the precinct. The station was its usual hive of activity, with officers and detectives buzzing back and forth in a vain attempt to save the world. She bypassed the elevator in favor of the stairs and tried to ignore the looks of astonishment on many of the faces she passed on her way up to the homicide division. She nodded to a few people she knew and was warmed by several genuine smiles of welcome. Jordan didn't stop to talk to anyone, partly because she knew Henry was waiting, and partly because she just wasn't ready. She wasn't back permanently, after all, and she feared what would happen to her heart if she fully let this place and these people in.

Jordan spotted Henry immediately, his back turned to her, talking to a man she didn't know. The man's gaze drifted over her, initially with no reaction. But five seconds later, his attention jumped back to her, his eyebrows lifting. Henry turned, breaking into a blinding smile.

"Well, well. Looking pretty good there, Jordan." He walked over swiftly and enveloped her in a giant bear hug. "Welcome home."

She shut her eyes against the onslaught of emotions. She would not let this place in. She would not.

"What have you done to my unit?" she demanded in mock accusation.

"Your unit? I do believe I outrank you."

"Since when has rank mattered to me?"

Henry laughed. He turned to include the man standing next to him. "Jordan, this is—"

"Wow. The famous Detective Salinger. I've heard a lot about you," the man said, completely sincere.

"I'm sure it was all bad," she said, praying she wasn't blushing.

"Nah," he said with a laugh. "Everyone knows you're a hero."

The compliment felt more like an accusation to Jordan. As if sensing her discomfort, Henry tried to introduce the man for the second time.

"Detective Jordan Salinger, meet Detective Martin Lawson. He's my rookie."

"Your rookie? What am I, property?"

Henry and Jordan answered at the same time. "Yes."

"So, what brings you back, Detective? I thought you were on indefinite leave?"

Jordan looked to Henry. They hadn't exactly talked about her status.

"The great thing about indefinite leave is that it can end very definitely. Like when she walked through the door," Henry said meaningfully.

"I'm not back, Henry," Jordan corrected.

"Maybe not, but you are here," Henry said. "And for that, I'm grateful."

Though Lawson hadn't asked, Henry offered him an explanation. "I asked her to help out on the diner murders. I think she'll have better luck with Ms. James than I did."

Understanding flashed across Lawson's face. "Got it."

Jordan expected Lawson to object. Young detectives were always eager to prove themselves, and Jordan expected Lawson would jump at the chance to demonstrate his interviewing prowess. But Lawson asked no questions. He simply accepted Henry's judgment. It seemed to Jordan that Lawson's acquiescence stemmed from respect for Henry, not just respect for Henry's authority. Jordan liked him for that.

Henry turned to Jordan. "We'll get the paperwork squared away later. But for now, you're acting under my authority."

"Are you sure? I don't want you getting in trouble because of me."

Henry smiled reassuringly. "I'm sure. Technically, as your lieutenant, I have the authority to take you off leave. We can work it out officially when the captain comes back."

"I'm still going to have to get used to calling you lieutenant. You were just another lowly detective when I left."

"Honestly?" Lawson leaned closer and lowered his voice to a conspiratorial whisper. "Him and the captain are the only things keeping us all from being shipped off to parking enforcement."

Jordan looked up at Henry affectionately. "Some things never change, huh?"

This time it was Henry whose cheeks reddened. Jordan let him off the hook. "Okay, where is this waitress of yours?"

"Good luck, Detective Salinger," Lawson called out as he walked back to his desk.

Henry led her toward the conference room, where a gorgeous woman in a blue waitress's uniform sat waiting. Jordan's chest grew unexpectedly tight, and she felt her heart speed up its rhythmic thumping. Devon James was classically beautiful, with high cheekbones and piercing blue eyes beneath cascading blond hair that reached just past her shoulders. She was slender without seeming fragile, and unlike many waitresses Jordan had seen in her life—even the young ones—Devon seemed unbowed by years of pouring coffee and carrying plates. From what Henry had told her about Devon's official history, or lack thereof, it was entirely possible that the woman had never waitressed before coming to Pittsburgh. Jordan wondered what she had been in her last life. Or lives.

Jordan forced her racing heart to slow and her breathing to regulate. This was neither the time nor the place for romance, even if she had the inclination—which she most certainly did not.

Henry opened the door and closed it behind Jordan after she stepped through.

"Ms. James, this is Detective Jordan Salinger." Jordan didn't correct Henry's overstatement. Technically, she was still a detective with the Pittsburgh Bureau of Police. She had her gun and shield, was drawing full salary, and was on an indefinite leave of absence, which she could end at any time—and just had. So legally, there was no misrepresentation. Emotionally, though, allowing Henry to call her detective—that was an entirely different matter.

Jordan reached out her hand to Devon. "Ms. James. It's nice to meet you."

Devon looked at her quizzically, as if the decision of whether to accept her hand was about significantly more than a handshake.

Slowly, Devon's hand slid against Jordan's, uncertain but firm. Devon's skin was astonishingly soft, like a summer lawn beneath bare feet.

Jordan sat across from Devon. Henry remained standing, moving off to one side just barely within Devon's line of sight. Jordan recognized the move for what it was. This was Jordan's interview now.

CHAPTER SEVEN

Billy sat on a bench in the park across the street and half a block down from the police station, giving him a perfect vantage point from which to keep watch. His old, nondescript grayish Buick was parked on the farthest corner of the street. He had his face turned up toward the sun, like he was doing nothing more than enjoying the surprisingly mild fall day. He was dressed in worn jeans and a plain blue T-shirt. He had ditched the ball cap and donned his sunglasses. Urban camouflage. He was another nameless, faceless man that no one who passed by would remember in detail, if they remembered seeing him at all.

His relaxed, sun-worshipping posture belied the intense focus he maintained on the police station, and his growing irritation. He couldn't understand what in the hell was taking so long. She had been inside the station for more than an hour. She should have been done by now. Unless, of course, she was talking.

Billy clucked his tongue in disappointment. He expected her to know better than that. Hadn't she learned anything?

His initial wave of disappointment, however, soon dissipated. She wasn't telling them anything. Who would believe her? The cops hadn't back in Illinois, and Billy imagined that over the last ten years she had gotten very good at keeping his existence to herself. She'd certainly gotten good at hiding. He'd had a hard time tracking her down after Colorado and had lost her trail completely after Memphis. That was nearly five years ago. Five years without a lead, without a single trace. Billy had almost given up looking and then, out of nowhere, there she was. Walking down the sidewalk, oblivious to his presence across the street, in Pittsburgh of all places. Sure, her hair was shorter and lighter, and she had gotten leaner and nearly a decade older since he'd last gotten a really good look at her, but there was no mistaking her.

Billy still couldn't believe it. What were the odds that out of all the cities in all of the United States they would be in the same one at the same time? It was a whim that had brought him to the Steel City, a seemingly mindless decision when he left Louisiana. There could be no explanation except divine intervention. It was finally time to put the past to right.

He'd kept his distance initially. He'd been so close before, but something had always spooked her or gotten in the way. He did not want to take any chances now. He had tried several times to follow her home from the diner, to learn where she lived. But God had other ideas, it seemed, because He put up roadblock after roadblock, frustrating Billy's efforts. Finally, Billy had understood that the Lord meant for their reunion to take place at the diner.

But then she had not arrived when she was supposed to, and Billy had been left empty-handed. God had had a change of plans.

Commit thy way unto the Lord; trust also in him; and he shall bring it to pass.

The knowledge that the time was so near added to Billy's growing impatience.

They must be some methodical sons of bitches. Idiots.

Billy swallowed his irritation. He needed to have faith. It was not his right to question the Lord's will. Besides, the waiting wasn't without its perks. The sun was warm against his skin, and there were all manner of pretty things to look at. Not five minutes earlier, Billy'd had a particularly nice view of one woman walking into the station. She had short dark hair, athletic curves, and one hell of an ass.

The woman had stood outside for a few minutes leaning against her car, staring up at the building, and giving Billy a good chance to study her. When she finally pushed off and headed inside, she walked with a confident swagger. He was certain she was a dyke—something about her style, the way she carried herself, the way she moved— but that didn't really matter to him. He had never bought in to all that Leviticus crap, the way in which so-called Christians warped the Bible to meet their petty concerns and social agendas. He understood the true meaning of the Lord's word, and the Lord didn't give two hoots about which way the woman who walked into the station liked her bread buttered. The Lord was much more concerned with whether His soldiers followed the path He laid out for them. And Billy was nothing if not a good soldier.

❖

"I would ask you to tell me what happened this morning, but I can imagine that might be somewhat annoying to you, Ms. James."

The new detective smiled, and Devon couldn't help but smile back. She eased back in her chair, letting go of some of the tension that had been building within her all morning. Devon had been surprised when Lieutenant Wayne had led the woman into the conference room. She hadn't been expecting anyone other than the lieutenant or maybe Detective Lawson. She certainly hadn't been expecting a woman.

Detective Salinger was striking. Dark haired and tan, but not like she spent hours lounging beside a pool or in a tanning bed. Devon imagined the detective working outdoors, maybe rock climbing or kayaking. She was certainly fit enough to do those things. Detective Salinger's shirtsleeves were pushed up to her elbows, revealing toned forearms and accentuating strong hands. The memory of her hand in the detective's lingered on Devon's skin.

The detective was stunning for sure, but the most remarkable thing about her was her eyes. They were the color of an Irish meadow, so green and bright they shone like beacons in a storm, calling Devon home.

She shook off the crazy thoughts swirling in her mind. Detective Salinger was not here to woo her. She was here to interrogate her. Devon focused her mind and settled her racing heart.

"I was wondering if you would tell me what brought you to Pittsburgh."

It was a request, not a command, and it caught Devon off guard. She debated what to say. It wasn't the first time she had been asked the question, though she hadn't expected it to be the first thing Detective

Salinger asked. Devon's standard answer popped into her head, the one about a bad breakup and remembering her grandfather speaking fondly of visiting Pittsburgh when he was a younger man, but the words that passed Devon's lips were entirely different.

"I was looking for something better. Maybe the chance to build some kind of life."

Detective Salinger's gaze never left Devon's face. She didn't seem to be studying Devon. She seemed only to be listening. Devon had forgotten what it was like to have someone simply listen. It was like they were making conversation over coffee in some little café.

"And you thought you could find that here?"

"Yes." Devon thought back to her decision to come here. She could have gone anywhere, but she had chosen Pittsburgh. "I remembered seeing a show about Pittsburgh once. I think it was on the History Channel or something—about what had happened to the city when the steel industry collapsed, but that the city had fought back, rebuilding itself from the ashes. I guess I liked the idea of that."

Detective Salinger nodded, like she understood Devon's connection to the city's struggle. Like maybe she, too, had such a connection.

"Do you like it here?"

So far, Detective Salinger's questions were far from what Devon had expected. "Yes. Very much."

"What do you like about it?"

"The people, mostly. They don't put on airs. They work hard, say what's on their minds, and live their lives the best they can," Devon said honestly. "People seem to appreciate what they have here."

"Not like where you lived before?"

The conversation turned, and Devon tensed. She answered warily. "No."

Detective Salinger seemed to pick up on the change. "I'm not trying to trap you, Ms. James. I'm not here to hurt you. I just want to find the truth, and I need your help to do that."

Devon didn't respond. How could she? She believed the detective, but she also recognized the road they were going down. It led to one place, and it was not a place Devon wanted to go. Or maybe she did. Something was rising within her, something that had begun earlier while she was being questioned by Lieutenant Wayne and that was now threatening to overwhelm her. If she wasn't careful, it could destroy her. But maybe it was time to take that risk. "Devon."

The detective's brow furrowed. "I'm sorry?"

"Devon," she said again. "Call me Devon."

She'd been Ms. James all morning, but now, somehow, it felt wrong. Time slowed as Detective Salinger met Devon's gaze. Devon's breath caught in her throat. Would she understand? How could Devon expect her to understand when she barely understood herself? Devon had given her an opening, despite everything she believed, or thought she believed. She watched Detective Salinger's eyes search her own, seeking some kind of truth within their depths. She felt them delving deep within her, so deep she thought the detective might see into her very soul. Devon felt exposed. Raw. Vulnerable. She had to fight with everything she had not to look away.

"Tell me who killed Sally and Chuck."

And there it was. She had opened the door, and Detective Salinger had walked right through it. Now, Devon had to choose.

It had been so long since Devon had trusted anyone beside herself. She wanted to trust this woman, more than she had wanted to trust anyone in years. Maybe even more than she had wanted to trust anyone, ever.

She caught movement out of the corner of her eye. Lieutenant Wayne had shifted, was now leaning against one of the filing cabinets that lined the far wall. It was the first time Devon had noticed him since Detective Salinger had begun talking to her. And that was what all of this had felt like. Talking. Not questioning, not interrogating. Just talking. And Devon was amazed how now that she'd finally started talking, she didn't want to stop.

She wanted to tell them everything. She wanted to stop running. She wanted to beg Detective Salinger to save her.

It was a new concept, and it violated every rule Devon had established for herself over ten long, hard years of keeping herself alive. She wanted to trust Detective Salinger, but her mind railed against it. It went against every instinct, every synapse, every lesson she had learned since this long nightmare began. But she wanted it, felt the need of it coil in her belly, trying to force the words past her throat despite the signals coming from her brain. She felt like she would explode from the force of it, and she would become a casualty of the war within herself.

It was the ultimate battle, trusting someone after all she had been through. All she had seen.

All she had done.

It was the ultimate battle and, Devon somehow knew, her last chance to save herself. Either she took a chance and risked everything, or she condemned herself to a life spent forever running.

And then she looked again at Detective Jordan Salinger, and everything about this woman told Devon that she was safe. That she would not be betrayed. That everything would be all right. She looked into those emerald eyes, and she knew the battle was over.

She barely recognized her own voice as she spoke words she had not uttered since she was seventeen. "His name is Billy Dean Montgomery, and he's my father."

CHAPTER EIGHT

Of all the things Devon James could have said, Jordan had not expected her to say that. An abusive husband, a jealous ex-boyfriend, maybe even some coworker whose crazy switch got flipped after too many times being turned down for coffee. But her father?

The words were a fist to Jordan's stomach, sucking out the air she needed to voice any kind of response. She looked over to Henry, whose raised eyebrows and parted lips told her he was as stunned as she was.

Jordan turned back to Devon. The woman seemed eerily calm, like a great weight had been lifted from her shoulders. When she spoke, her voice was devoid of emotion. Devon spoke the way a witness to a horrific accident would, like she was somehow not affected by the events that had led to the broken, mangled corpses and the twisted, charred wreckage.

"My real name is Madison Montgomery. I was born in Des Plaines, Illinois, but I grew up in a small town to the west called Roscoe. It was just me, my mom, and Billy."

Jordan noted that Devon referred to the man who seemed to be at the center of everything by his first name, rather than by anything that would acknowledge a familial connection. Maybe it was easier for Devon to think of him that way. As a stranger instead of her own flesh and blood.

"When I was young, I adored Billy. He used to go on these fishing trips every year, sometimes twice a year. I always wanted to go, but my mom wouldn't let me. I was too young, or I had school, or Billy needed the time to himself. After every trip, he used to give me a special penny, one with stalks of wheat on one side. He said it was a tradition his father had started with him, and now he was passing it on to me. A bond between us. I didn't understand what it really meant until later."

Jordan noticed Henry's eyebrows lift again, but he said nothing.

"Mom said the fishing trips were Billy's release, his way of coping with the pressures of his job."

Jordan made a mental note to ask about Billy's job, but it proved unnecessary.

"He was a sheriff's deputy."

The air fled Jordan's body once more. The guy was a cop. That would explain the lack of fingerprints, DNA, or any other kind of forensic evidence at the scene. Jordan could see Henry was thinking the same thing. Things had just gotten a lot more complicated.

"As I got older, things changed. Billy could be…scary. Mom never said anything, but I knew. You just did not cross Billy Montgomery. No one did. Certainly not Mom." Devon paused, then added in a voice barely above a whisper. "Certainly not me."

Jordan wondered what Devon was leaving out. There was something, Jordan was sure. In her experience, survivors of domestic abuse often spoke the way Devon was speaking now, glossing over details and only hinting at the fear and pain they'd endured. There was definitely abuse in Devon's past, and it didn't matter if it hadn't been physical. Psychological abuse was just as damaging as a physical beating, sometimes more so, though Jordan was convinced Devon's story was about to turn undeniably violent.

Devon inhaled deeply, like she needed the extra oxygen to push the next part of the story past her lips. Jordan's heart swelled in empathy.

"In November 2000, I came home from school one day to find Mom and Billy sitting at the kitchen table, waiting for me. Billy announced he was taking me fishing. He looked at Mom as he said it, like he was challenging her. At first she said nothing. She got up and went over to the stove and started stirring the stew she had going on the burner. It took me a minute to realize she'd said anything, but the way Billy snapped his head in her direction, I knew she had. Then she said it again. 'No.'"

Devon swallowed thickly. "Such a simple word, but in that moment, it was like TNT. Billy lunged at her and grabbed her by her hair. She screamed, but he didn't care. He swung her around and punched her in the face. Not a slap, a punch. He hit her so hard he knocked her to the floor. Blood was pouring from her nose. I was frozen. My feet wouldn't move. I couldn't even scream at him to stop. I was such a coward."

Devon's gaze fell to the table, clearly awash in the shame of her inaction. Jordan had to clench her teeth to keep from speaking, had to grip the table to keep herself from reaching out. Devon was wrong. She had not been a coward, just a scared girl shocked into submission by the horror of what she was witnessing. Her urge to deny Devon's self-accusation, to pull Devon into her arms and hold her until the pain of memory eased, was strong. Jordan had to fight with everything she had to suppress the need to make Devon's pain go away.

"Then Billy dragged my mom up to her feet. I saw her fear, but she didn't cry out again. She didn't fight, didn't even flinch when he reached over and slid the knife out of the block on the counter. He just turned around so he was behind her and put the knife to her throat. He didn't say a word. He didn't need to. I knew what was going to happen. I heard myself begging him, pleading with him not to do it. Mom stared at me, but there was no more fear. All I saw was sorrow, like she was apologizing to me for what he was about to do. For what would come after. And then Billy slit her throat."

"Jesus." Jordan distantly heard the word slip from Henry's lips. She probably would have said the same if she'd been able to force any sound from her throat. Despite everything she had seen in her years on the force, every terrible tale a witness had ever told her, Devon's story was horrific beyond measure. It wasn't that Devon had witnessed her own mother's murder, or that her father had committed it, or even the gruesomeness of the crime. It was the coldness of it. The murder of Devon's mother had not been a crime of passion or even rage. Though the violence may have started as an explosion of anger, the murder had been full of contemptuous calculation.

Devon continued to speak as if on autopilot, but Jordan saw the tears gathering, tears Devon seemed to be refusing to let fall by force of will alone. Jordan wondered how strong this woman had to be to keep herself together.

"When her body fell to the floor, something inside me snapped. I moved without thinking. I didn't care about the knife in his hand or that he was bigger than me. I ran at him with everything I had. I guess he wasn't expecting it because he stumbled backward and we fell into the stove and then to the floor. I started whaling on him, but it didn't take long for him to push me off. He stood over me, smiling this sick smile, and I knew I was done. That's when I saw the flames behind him."

Devon smiled hollowly and shrugged, almost apologetically. "I guess when we fell into the stove, something caught. A towel maybe, I don't know. In seconds, the curtains were on fire, and there was all this smoke. Billy must have smelled it because he turned his head, just for a second. I scrambled to my feet and kneed him in the crotch. He never saw it coming. Then I reached for the closest thing I could find. I swung as hard as I could with Mom's rolling pin. I nailed him in the side of the head, and I ran out of the house."

Devon let out a breath, like she'd been holding it for years. Jordan found herself doing the same and attempted to quiet the pounding of her heart. Devon looked at Jordan, as if maybe she thought Jordan was going to pull out her handcuffs and arrest her on the spot. Devon had left her father in the house to die. Bastard deserved it, as far as Jordan was concerned. Legally speaking, it was a clear case of self-defense, and Jordan would fight anyone who said otherwise.

"What happened after you left the house?" Jordan asked. She was surprised by how steady her voice sounded given the blood rushing in her ears and her still-racing heart. She thought she caught a fleeting smile of relief, or perhaps gratitude, cross Devon's lips. Jordan hoped it meant Devon understood she was still safe with her. With them.

"I stood out on the front lawn, watching the fire engulf the house. I couldn't seem to look away, I think partly because I expected to see Billy stumbling out the front door. But he never did. I guess the fire department arrived because the next thing I knew I was being dragged away from the house and a fireman was asking if I was all right and if anyone was in the house. I told them yes, but before they could go in, the house exploded. Billy kept a propane generator in the garage, and they said later that's what had caused the explosion.

"It was days before they were able to recover the bodies. The house was completely leveled. I told the sheriff what had happened. He didn't believe it. None of the other deputies did, either. They questioned me for days. I guess they finally believed me when they pulled the remains from the house. The sheriff's official report said everything happened the way I said it did."

If Devon thought Billy was responsible for the murders in the diner, she believed he'd survived the fire. Jordan couldn't keep herself from asking, "Did they do DNA to be sure?"

"It was a small town. They didn't have a lot of need for DNA testing there, so no."

"So they weren't positive it was Billy and your mother," Jordan said. "Or even that it was two bodies."

Devon smiled sadly. "They said they were sure. One of the deputies said there was evidence that my mother's throat had been cut. I guess that was enough to confirm my story. I didn't think about it much until later."

Jordan had run into this kind of thing before. Small-town cops were often ill prepared for big-city crimes, and they sometimes closed cases based on assumptions rather than facts. She knew it was usually a matter of inexperience or no budget to properly investigate, or both, but that knowledge didn't make her want to kick that sheriff's ass any less.

"I went into foster care after that. It wasn't great, but it was okay. One of my mom's friends took me in. I lived with them nearly two years. Her husband never really knew what to say to me. Neither did the kids. But Debra was nice enough."

Jordan could picture Devon in that house, being eyed with suspicion, never fitting in. Never feeling loved. Jordan's heart broke at the thought.

"I worked hard and got good grades, enough to get a scholarship to Northern Illinois University after graduation. I tried not to think much about what had happened. I thought it was all behind me. I was wrong. A few weeks after school started, I came back to the dorm and found my roommate dead on my bed."

So this was the origin of Devon's belief that Billy had survived the fire. "And you thought Billy was responsible." A statement, not a question. The investigator in Jordan, however, was not yet convinced. Devon shifted uncomfortably. Jordan perceived a mixture of frustration and worry in Devon's movements.

"Her wallet and some jewelry were missing. The cops said there were no signs of forced entry or obvious signs of a struggle, though a couple of people reported they thought they had heard what sounded like an argument and a man's voice," Devon said. Then she looked at Jordan meaningfully. "And her throat was cut."

It was far from conclusive, but it was more than coincidence. The likelihood of Devon knowing two people killed by having their throats cut was extremely slim, let alone three if you counted Chuck Pendleton. Unless Devon was the killer. Every instinct told Jordan that was not the case. She just didn't sense a killer inside of Devon.

"Did you tell the police about Billy?"

"I tried. They didn't believe me."

"Why not?" Jordan asked, anger creeping into her voice. The sheriff's incompetence after the fire was bad enough, but the thought that the police had let Devon down a second time was intolerable.

Devon smiled her first genuine smile since they had begun talking, and Jordan felt herself blush.

"Her stuff was missing, so they figured she'd walked in on someone robbing her. But like I said, there was no forced entry and no sign of a struggle. And Billy was supposedly dead."

"But the witnesses—"

"The witnesses were shaky. They weren't sure what they heard exactly. They eventually decided they hadn't heard anything after all."

Jordan was all too familiar with witnesses' forgetfulness. One minute they were sure they had heard or seen something, the next they weren't sure of anything. These memory failures usually happened right around the time they realized that being a witness might mean they had to testify in court someday.

"So the police...what? Sent you home? With your roommate's murderer on the loose?"

"Not exactly," Devon responded. "They questioned me for... well, for a while. When they finally let me go, they told me not to leave town. I got the definite impression I was their only suspect."

Jordan couldn't believe what she was hearing. She had thought the cops were simply incompetent, not downright stupid.

"I'm sure they thought I was crazy," Devon rushed on. "I can't really say I blame them. I probably would have thought I was crazy, too."

"I don't think you're crazy," Jordan said quickly but firmly. Her gut—and years of experience as a cop—told her Devon was telling the truth.

Jordan read the gratitude, and the relief, on Devon's face. She saw Devon's tears well up again, and even though Jordan knew they were likely a positive autonomic response to her belief in Devon, she would have given anything not to have been their cause.

"What happened after they sent you home?"

"I couldn't go back to the dorm. I…I was scared. He was out there, somewhere, waiting for me."

"Forgive me for asking this, but why didn't he try to kill *you*? Why go after your roommate?"

Devon didn't answer immediately. Jordan watched her process her response. "I don't know for sure. I was usually home earlier in the day, but not that day. I have always thought he intended to kill me, but for some reason he killed her instead."

Jordan suspected there was more Devon wasn't saying, but there would be time for that later. "So what did you do when you left the police?"

"I just…I knew he was going to come for me. I knew if I stayed, he would kill me this time. And frankly, I thought if *he* didn't get me, the police would."

"So you ran."

Devon nodded. "I didn't even go back to the dorm for my things. I had thirty-five dollars in my wallet, and I went straight to the bus station and took the first bus out of town. I've been running ever since."

It was just as Henry had suspected.

She's been on the run for ten years. Christ.

"You've moved a few times, I suspect."

"I've lived in different cities, changed my name and my hair. I didn't want to take any chances. For a long time, I thought I was safe. And then this."

After all that time, he had somehow found her again. Either this guy was frighteningly resolved in his twisted desire to kill Devon, or he was one lucky son of a bitch.

"Why do you think Billy committed the murders here, today?" Henry's voice snapped Jordan out of her thoughts. "Did you see him?"

Jordan looked at Henry questioningly, but his face was unreadable. She wasn't sure where he was going with this and had half a mind to pull him out of the room to find out, but Devon answered before Jordan could act. "No. I never saw him."

"Then why are you sure it was him?" Jordan bristled at her partner's implied accusation even though his tone held no trace of challenge. He was asking the question gently, almost like he was trying to help Devon acknowledge the last piece of the puzzle. "Sally's throat wasn't cut."

"No. But I'm sure you found the penny."

Henry nodded, and Jordan understood. Devon had not seen Chuck's slashed throat when she had entered the diner that morning, but she had seen the wheat penny, left behind like a calling card.

CHAPTER NINE

Henry had heard enough, and one look at Jordan told him she had heard enough, too. He had been right to call her in, though the story Devon had told them was far beyond anything he had expected. Henry still had a number of questions, about the ten years Devon spent on the run, about why Billy had waited two years to come after her at the college, and about how Billy had found her so many years later in Pittsburgh. There would be time to learn those answers, with Jordan's help.

Henry moved toward the door, and through the unspoken communication they had built during their partnership, Jordan followed.

"We'll be right back," Jordan told Devon as she exited the room. Henry didn't miss the reassurance in Jordan's voice, nor how Jordan quickly but gently squeezed Devon's shoulder as she walked past. Henry smiled to himself. Yes, he had definitely been right to call Jordan. She left the conference room door open behind her, a signal to Devon that they were not trying to hide anything from her. Henry walked to the center of the bullpen and turned to his partner.

"You found a wheat penny?" Jordan asked.

"Yes. On the counter."

Jordan ran a hand through her cropped hair and began pacing. It was a familiar habit, one she employed anytime she was trying to process her thoughts. Henry's heart swelled. It was good to have her back, even if only temporarily.

"She could have killed them. Planted the coin at the scene," Jordan said.

"Yes."

"But I don't think so."

"Neither do I. The evidence doesn't support it. It's not as easy to slit someone's throat as they make it look on television. It takes some strength, and skill. And she would have had at least some blood on her clothes. The only way she shows up to discover the bodies in a clean uniform is—"

"Is if she stashes the bloody clothes nearby. And the weapon. There wouldn't have been time for anything else. And you didn't find anything, did you?"

"No."

"We also have to acknowledge the possibility that she's making all this up. About her father."

"Yes."

"It's…it's an unbelievable story."

"Yes."

"To watch your father brutally murder your mother, so suddenly and cruelly. She had her whole family taken away, then was taken in by strangers, but clearly…I mean, thank God they took her in, but can you imagine? Feeling so isolated, so alone. And then to have your father, who's not actually dead like you and everyone else think he is, stalk you, murder your roommate. And to have no one to turn to, no choice but to run, to become someone else, over and over again. Never feeling safe, never trusting anyone."

"Yes."

"And on top of everything, the bastard's a cop! A small-town cop, but a cop nonetheless."

"Yes."

Jordan looked at Henry, her certainty bright and unshakeable. "I believe her, Henry."

"So do I."

"She's in danger."

"Agreed."

"You know there's more to this story yet."

"Yes."

Jordan exhaled slowly. "Okay."

"Okay?"

"Okay," Jordan said, nodding. "I'm in. All the way."

Henry smiled broadly. Jordan rolled her eyes, but she couldn't hide the grin tweaking the corners of her mouth. She punched him lightly in the arm.

I'm keeping my promise, Ella. One step at a time.

"What do you want to do?"

Jordan looked back toward the conference room. Henry followed her line of sight. Devon was watching them, a mixture of confusion and hope on her face.

"I want to get her out of here," Jordan said.

"Safe house?"

"No, I don't think so," Jordan said, turning back to Henry. "This guy's smart, Henry. If everything Devon said is true, then he's killed at least twice before this, faked his own death, and somehow managed to find Devon after a decade. And he was a cop. I'll bet you ten to one he's read every police procedure manual out there. He'll know what to expect from us. Better we do things he doesn't expect."

What Jordan was saying made sense. "So we're staying off the grid, then?"

"For now. You know where we should take her?"

Henry knew exactly where Jordan meant. "Yep."

"We need to get a better sense of just who this guy is, Henry. What he's done. What he's capable of."

"Which is exactly why I brought you in, Jordan."

Jordan grew quiet. She frowned slightly. "I thought you just needed my...brokenness."

The wound beneath her words clenched Henry's heart.

"I thought you would connect with her, yes," Henry said, pushing back his guilt. "I won't deny that. But you also happen to be the best profiler I know, and even before Devon told us about her father, I thought we might need those skills of yours. And now I'm sure."

Jordan looked up at him through haunted eyes. "What if I'm not up to this?"

Henry squeezed her shoulder. "You are."

Jordan shrugged off his hand almost defiantly, her fear flashing to anger in an instant. "You say that, but you don't know. What if I let you down? Let her down? I can't have any more blood on my hands!"

Jordan's words echoed off the walls of the squad room. The silence that followed was deafening. Everyone was watching Jordan now. Her face paled.

Henry reached out a hand to steady her. She wasn't really angry with him. They'd had this argument before. She was angry with herself, hated herself, for the two cops and the little boy she could never bring back.

Slowly the ever-present hum of the squad room returned, filling the lingering silence. No one wanted to make Jordan feel any worse than she already did. They all knew she blamed herself, just as they all—or at least most of them—knew what had happened hadn't been her fault.

"I need you on this, Jordan," Henry said softly. "I need your insight. I need your skill. Most of all, I need my partner."

Jordan stared up at him unblinking. Finally, her decision made, she blew out a breath and nodded.

❖

Devon didn't know exactly how she ended up standing in the doorway of the conference room, but there she was, just the same. Blood on her hands, that's what Detective Salinger had said. No, not said. Shouted. Regardless, it was something Devon understood all too well. Blood. There had been so much blood. There still was.

Something else she understood was the pain lacing the detective's words. Detective Salinger had recovered some of her color, but she still seemed unsteady. Devon could stay away no longer and walked cautiously over to the two detectives.

"Ms. James," Lieutenant Wayne said as Devon approached.

Detective Salinger turned to Devon. "Sorry about that," she said quietly.

"I'm the one who should be sorry," Devon said. The statement was directed toward Detective Salinger, but was really meant for both her and the lieutenant. "I'm sorry for the trouble I've caused, for both of you. Maybe I should just—"

"No," Detective Salinger interrupted sharply, then softened her words. "No. That wasn't really about you. Don't worry about it. We're going to help you."

"But—"

"We need to get you out of here," Lieutenant Wayne chimed in. "Take you someplace safe."

"But maybe he'll leave me alone." The words rang hollow in Devon's ears. She did not for one second believe Billy would let her go. Not now that he had found her again.

"I don't believe that, and neither do you," Detective Salinger said, placing her hand on Devon's arm. It was a gesture of support, but the simple touch ripped through her like lightning.

"Come on," the lieutenant said, "let's get you out of here."

Detective Salinger slipped her hand from Devon's arm, and Devon wondered if she'd imagined reluctance in the parting. She told her mind to quit playing tricks on itself, and she followed Lieutenant Wayne out front to his car, with Detective Salinger to her right and slightly behind. Devon felt like a dignitary with her own Secret Service detail. She noticed how both detectives had positioned themselves around her, how their heads were in constant motion, scanning their surroundings. She couldn't imagine that Billy was there, waiting for her, let alone that he would try anything right in front of the police station, but she was comforted by the two detectives' protectiveness nonetheless.

When they reached the car, Lieutenant Wayne walked around to the driver's side while Detective Salinger opened the rear passenger-side door for Devon. As Devon was about to get in, she was overcome with a sudden feeling, one she had felt before. Like someone had walked across her grave, wasn't that the expression? She paused, one foot inside the car, and scanned the horizon. She saw nothing, but she couldn't shake the feeling.

"What's wrong?" Detective Salinger asked, her hand going to the gun at her waist as she looked around with a new urgency.

"Nothing," Devon said distantly, still searching for something she couldn't define. She forced herself to shake off whatever was plaguing her. She felt the tension radiate off Detective Salinger's body and touched her shoulder. "Really. It's okay."

The detective relaxed slightly beneath her hand. Devon gave her a small smile. "But thanks."

As she got in the car, she could have sworn she saw the detective blush.

❖

Billy walked to his car with a leisurely gait, being careful not to draw any undue attention. He had been surprised when Madison had walked out of the building flanked by one of the male detectives from the crime scene and a woman, the same woman he had watched enter the building earlier. He supposed they could be giving his daughter a ride back to her apartment, but by their protective formation as they escorted her to the car, he doubted it.

"Maddie, Maddie, what am I going to do with you?" he said to himself once he had slipped behind the wheel. She went by Devon now, but that was not her name. It could never be her name.

He watched the female he now assumed was a detective open the car door for his daughter.

So very chivalrous.

His heart sped up when Maddie didn't immediately get into the car. He watched her head rotate slowly, as if she was looking for something.

Does she know I'm here? Watching her? Is it possible my darling daughter senses me?

He savored the adrenaline rush as Maddie looked in his direction. But after a moment her head turned, and she appeared to say something to the detective. Then she was gone, safe inside the car but not from Billy's watchful gaze. He almost felt disappointed that she had not spotted him, but he pushed that feeling aside.

"It's not time yet," he said to no one. "But soon. Very soon."

He waited for the detective's car to pull away from the curb and for several other cars to pass before he pulled out onto the street behind them. He wondered where in the world they were taking her and, despite his impatience to finally have her so close at hand, reveled in the knowledge that the game had just gotten far more interesting. God worked in mysterious ways, indeed.

CHAPTER TEN

They drove in silence for the first few minutes, and Jordan was grateful for the time to think. The guilt that plagued her, that had reached a brief but sudden boiling point with Henry in the squad room, had left her feeling drained, and she couldn't afford to feel that way. She had no idea what the next few days or even hours would hold and she needed to be at the top of her game. Little Jacob Dubois falling lifeless to the ground filled her mind's eye. She shook her head, as if that would clear the image she had not been able to escape for fifteen months. There would be plenty of time for it to haunt her later, and she would let it, for that was her penance.

"You okay?" Henry asked quietly, attempting to respect some semblance of Jordan's privacy.

"I'm fine."

"You know no one thinks it was your fault except you, right?"

"Just drop it, Henry. Okay?" She couldn't help her irritation. Henry said nothing, but she knew he understood. He always did.

She needed to get her mind back on-task. Thankfully, Devon provided the distraction she needed.

"Where are you taking me?"

Jordan turned in her seat so she could face Devon. "My house."

Devon seemed concerned. Before she could object, Jordan said, "It's perfectly safe, I assure you."

"No, that's not...I mean, I'm sure it is," Devon said quickly. "But it's *your* house. I don't want you putting it at risk. Not for me."

Devon's concern touched Jordan. "It's fine, really. And actually, it's my mother's house."

That only seemed to trouble Devon more.

"She's not there, don't worry. She's gone down to Florida for a few months. She spends the winter with my aunt down there." Devon seemed only slightly relieved.

"It's the safest place right now," Henry added. "We want to keep you off the grid, at least until we know more."

Jordan watched understanding cross Devon's face. Devon understood more than anyone how capable Billy was of finding her; she'd lived it. The usual places they would take a witness in protective custody weren't really an option. They could take Devon to a motel, but with no prep time, they wouldn't know the layout and couldn't be sure such a location would be secure. No, their only real options at the moment were either her house or Henry's, and given she would be the one with Devon twenty-four seven, her house made the most sense. Plus, she had an added security feature.

"Do you like dogs?" Jordan asked.

"Yeah, very much. I've never been able to have one."

"Why not? A dog would be great protection for you." Jordan wanted to add *and might have helped you feel a little less lonely*, but she held it back. It wasn't her place to say such things. Too personal.

"Yeah, just I was moving so much, sometimes on really short notice. I worried that somehow a dog might get left behind." Devon seemed to be debating saying more. Jordan felt the melancholy behind Devon's words. It had to be one hell of a lonely life, never putting down roots, never allowing yourself to get close to anyone, never having a place to truly call home. Never holding on to anything for fear of losing it.

Jordan couldn't stop herself from speaking this time. "Must have been lonely."

Devon said nothing, smiling pensively before settling back in her seat and turning to stare out the window.

❖

They pulled up to a red brick two-story house on a quiet street fifteen minutes from the police station. Daisies peeked cheerfully at Devon from flower boxes hanging from the front-porch railing. They reminded her of the house she grew up in. Her mother had loved daisies.

Devon brushed off the memory. She hadn't thought about her mother in years, other than in the nightmares that plagued her deep in the night. They were always the same, a nearly perfect reenactment of the day her mother had died, except in Devon's dreams, the last look her mother gave her was one of accusation.

It took her a moment to register the car door being opened for her and Detective Salinger standing beside it. Devon got out of the car and Lieutenant Wayne was at her right side in an instant. Both detectives searched for threats, just as they had back at the police station. Seeming satisfied, the lieutenant closed the car door behind Devon and Detective Salinger led them up to the house.

The detective inserted her key smoothly into the lock, and Devon heard a soft whine as the door opened and suddenly understood the detective's question from the car ride.

"Back up, Max. Wait."

The German shepherd did as he was told, reversing course just enough to let the three of them through the door. He stood attentively, his big brown eyes shifting first from his master, then to Devon, and finally to Lieutenant Wayne. The dog began fidgeting uncontrollably when he saw the lieutenant, his tail wagging thunderously. Max shifted from side to side but came no closer, as if he could not contain his excitement at seeing the lieutenant but knew better than to disobey Detective Salinger's command.

"Max, sit." The dog sat in an instant, although his whine indicated he was not happy about it.

"You're such a mean mom," Lieutenant Wayne said with a chuckle. Detective Salinger rolled her eyes at him but grinned. She turned to Max, who immediately turned his attention to her. They stared at each other for a moment in some unspoken language Devon had only ever witnessed between the best-trained dogs and their owners.

"Okay."

Max was off like a shot, bounding past Devon straight for the lieutenant, knocking her off balance in the process. Strong arms caught her as she stumbled, and she looked up to find herself nose to nose with Detective Salinger.

"Sorry about that," she said. Her voice seemed to have dropped an octave, and it sent a shiver through Devon. "He gets excited when Henry comes to visit."

"It's okay," Devon said shakily. She hoped the detective would chalk it up to the close encounter with the rambunctious pup. In truth, the slight tremor in her words had nothing to do with the dog and everything to do with feeling Detective Salinger's hands pressing into her arms and her breath whispering across her face. Devon stood up, stepping back just out of the detective's reach. She needed to get a little distance in order to wipe the memory of the touch from her skin.

Both women turned to find Max on his back, his tongue lolling out of the side of his mouth as Lieutenant Wayne scratched his belly. Detective Salinger laughed.

"He missed you."

Lieutenant Wayne smiled broadly. "Well, we men have to stick together. Don't we boy?"

Seeming to remember there was a new person in the room, Max brought his tummy rub to an end. He rolled to his feet and approached Devon, cocking his head.

"Devon, this is Max. Max, this is Devon. She's a friend."

Devon moved her hand forward slowly, palm up, so as not to startle the dog. Max seemed extremely good-natured, but Devon knew that German shepherds were an intensely protective breed. The last thing she wanted to do was somehow send Max's instincts into overdrive.

The dog leaned forward, sniffing Devon's hand from fingertip to wrist. After a few seconds, apparently deciding he approved of his new houseguest, he began to wag his tail. He gave her palm a swift lick and stepped closer, forcing his head into Devon's hand. Detective Salinger laughed again. Devon decided she really liked the sound of her laugh.

"Guess you pass," Lieutenant Wayne said with a wink.

Devon knelt so she could give Max's ears a proper scratch. "How long have you had him?"

"About a year."

"He's very well trained," Devon said, standing. Max went to Detective Salinger's side, seeking out his next head rub.

"Thanks. We work at it. Max was a present from Henry." She ran her hand lovingly over Max's head and he leaned in to the touch. "So I wouldn't be alone," she added almost absently.

Lieutenant Wayne appeared slightly startled by Detective Salinger's admission, but said nothing. Devon got the impression that it was a rare occurrence for her to be so forthcoming, and she couldn't help but wonder why that was.

"You have what you need for the night?" he asked, turning the conversation back to what had brought them there. Devon had nearly forgotten. For a few blissful minutes, life had seemed almost normal. She wasn't used to it but missed the feeling immensely when it was gone.

"We should. I'm going to put Devon in my room. I'll take Mom's."

"I don't want to put you out," Devon said, although she couldn't imagine sleeping in Detective Salinger's mother's bed. It seemed so intrusive. Not that the thought of sleeping in *her* bed was any better.

"You're not, I promise," Detective Salinger said.

"Well then, I think it's time for me to get back to work."

"Send me whatever you get," Detective Salinger said. "I want to lay it all out, see if we can't figure out his next move."

Lieutenant Wayne smiled, and Devon detected more than simple acknowledgment in the curl of his lips. The slight reddening of Detective Salinger's cheeks confirmed it, whatever it was. Devon thought the interaction had nothing really to do with her, and yet she couldn't help but feel she was responsible for it—for the disruption to their lives, for the danger she was putting them in, and for so many things she could detect at the edges but not fully understand. "Lieutenant—"

"Please," he interrupted, "call me Henry. *Lieutenant* seems a little silly at this point, don't you think?"

"Okay, Henry. I…" Devon wanted to apologize to him, to both of them, but she swallowed it. They had offered their help, and the least she could do was thank them for it. "Thank you."

"Don't you worry about any of this," he said, as if reading her mind. He headed for the door. "Stop punishing yourself for what he's done. They were his actions, not yours."

Devon swallowed thickly. If he only knew.

Detective Salinger walked him to the door. "I'll have Lawson bring your truck by later," Henry said. "He can take a cab back to the station."

"Be careful," she said, handing him her car keys.

"*You* be careful," he answered. "Both of you. I'm going to go see what I can dig up, see if we can't get a lead on Mr. Montgomery. You two just stay safe."

Detective Salinger nodded, but Henry wasn't finished. "I mean it, Jordan. Watch your back." His voice dropped so Devon had to strain to hear him. "I have a feeling."

She nodded again, and Henry left. Devon couldn't be sure, but she thought she heard the detective say, *So do I*, as she closed the front door.

The first time Billy heard the Lord's voice, he had been eight years old. His pa had been a preacher, and a good one at that. His sermons were full of fire and brimstone, righteous and poetic and utterly hypnotic. He could have the entire congregation screaming hallelujah in near-ecstasy one minute and weeping before the glory of the Lord the next.

Billy used to love hearing Pa preach. Every Sunday, Billy would get up extra early so he could finish his chores and race down to the church before anyone else got there, ensuring that he was in the front row when the service began. All the old ladies in their Sunday finery—which in West Virginia amounted to little more than a clean dress and maybe a knock-off brooch picked up at the five-and-dime— would arrive shortly after Billy, marveling at the boy's devotion to hearing the word of God. In truth, it wasn't the Lord's words that had Billy up before the rooster crowed every Sunday, but the power his pa commanded when speaking them.

Billy knew that preaching was the Lord's plan for his pa; that's where Pa's power came from. In that church, Matthew Montgomery was the hand of God, following the path the Lord had laid out for him and richly rewarded for his faithfulness. Billy could only hope the Lord had such a plan for him, and that one day he would be privy to it.

That day came on a Sunday like any other, while Billy was mucking out the chicken coop before dawn. He was halfway done when pain seized his head, more pain even than when his pa whipped him in the barn with his good leather belt. Billy dropped his shovel and fell to his knees, clutching his head and praying for the Lord to take the pain away. He blacked out but never fell to the ground, as if the Lord was holding him in the palm of His hand.

A voice called out to him from the darkness, telling him that He had great plans for him, and that all would be revealed in time. The voice told him to watch for the sign, that the eagle would guide the way out of the mist. Most of all, the voice said, Billy must have faith. He would be tested, but if he remained faithful, his destiny would be fulfilled. Then a bright white light shone from a great distance, growing closer and more intense until it consumed his mind. Billy opened his eyes and found himself on his knees in the chicken coop, the shovel on the ground in front of him. Billy knew beyond all certainty it had been the Lord's voice he heard that day. He had been given a gift, and he would not waste it. He would look for the sign and when he found it, he would go wherever it led.

True to the Lord's word, Billy found the eagle, and it had led him down a beautiful path. He had been tested many times over the years, but he had retained his faith and now, finally, it had led him here.

"Then shall ye call upon me, and ye shall go," Billy said quietly in the car, *"and pray unto me, and I will hearken unto you."*

Billy watched the male detective exit the house from his vantage point down the street. He watched the man get into his car and pull away, probably back to the police station or some new crime scene. It was the middle of the day, after all, and the man was most likely in the middle of his shift.

Billy waited to see if the other one or his daughter would reappear, but after half an hour, he had seen no sign of them. It appeared this was where they planned to keep his Maddie from him. Like that would stop him.

He wondered about the other one, the female cop. It seemed strange that he had not seen her at the diner. Maybe she had been late to work or had the morning off. But that didn't seem quite right. Maybe she wasn't even a homicide detective, but some other cop they had pulled in because she was female. Like having a female TSA agent screen a female passenger.

No, that didn't seem right, either. He assumed, in this age of women in the military and all, that the Pittsburgh BP had to have at least a couple of female homicide detectives. So why bring in someone from outside? Maybe his first supposition had been right after all.

Billy shook his head. His mind was going in circles. But something about the woman that morning, about the way she had stood out front of the police station leaning against her car and staring up at the building, was sticking in Billy's craw. Like she was hesitant to go inside.

Billy was good at noticing the little things, always had been since Pa had first taken him hunting as a boy. "You have to pay attention, Billy," his pa had said. "You have to look for the signs. The signs are everywhere if you know how to read them and are diligent enough to seek them out." The signs his father had been referring to were far different than the one God had told Billy to watch for, but the lesson applied just the same. And the signs he was considering now were telling him something was a little off about this whole situation.

When he had followed them from the police station, Billy had assumed they would be taking Maddie to a safe house somewhere, or maybe a motel. But the house they had gone into didn't read like a safe house, at least not one that he'd ever heard about. Sure, the best place to hide someone was in plain sight, and there were plenty of police departments that used residential neighborhoods for witness protection, with safe houses looking like any other homes on nondescript blocks. But this place, with its flowers on the porch and manicured hedges and fall wreath on the front door looked too… lived-in.

Another piece to the puzzle forming in his mind. Another piece that didn't quite fit.

A car passed by, the third one in the last half hour. For a quiet neighborhood, it sure was busy. He watched the car parallel park down the street. The driver got out and pushed a button on his remote, presumably locking the doors. Instead of heading up to the house he'd parked in front of, however, the driver glanced back down the street toward Billy's car.

It didn't last more than a few seconds, but it was enough to tell Billy it was time to go. There was a reason police put safe houses in residential neighborhoods, after all. Suburban housewives bored with their soap operas were sure to notice an unknown car with a man sitting behind the wheel for hours on end.

Billy waited for the man to go into the house before he pulled away from the curb and drove away. No need to draw the man's suspicions any further by hightailing it out of there while the guy was still looking.

He would rather have sat on the house the rest of the day to be sure they didn't leave, but he had a strong feeling they wouldn't be going anywhere. He'd return later, well after they had fallen asleep, to finish this thing once and for all. He couldn't wait to see the look on his daughter's face when they were finally reunited.

Chapter Eleven

Jordan gave Devon a tour of the house she had grown up in. She had not had a visitor other than Henry or Ella since moving back into her mother's house, and it felt strange showing Devon where the towels were kept, the way that the hot-water tap in the upstairs bathroom tended to stick, and how to pour the first cup of freshly brewed coffee so the coffeepot didn't leak all over the counter. Yet it also felt strangely normal, almost nice. She felt like she was thirteen again, showing a friend around who had come for a slumber party.

They arrived at Jordan's bedroom last, and she felt a mild sense of trepidation as she reached for the door handle. She hadn't invited a woman anywhere near her bed in nearly a year. Not that she hadn't been with anyone, nor that this was that kind of situation. Jordan told herself it was just awkwardness about having a woman in her room even though somewhere, deep down, she knew there was more to it. She felt exposed. Raw. Like she was opening the door to some part of herself instead of to a simple bedroom.

Jordan opened the door, stepping through the threshold and off to the side. Unlike the rest of the tour, during which she had prattled on—nervously, much to her chagrin—about every nuance and flaw of the old house, here Jordan stood silently, allowing Devon to explore the room on her own terms.

For more than a decade, Jordan's mother had kept the room exactly as it had been when Jordan had left it for college at the age of seventeen. During her college years, she had been grateful for the preservation, for the room was familiar and safe, a space in which she always knew she belonged whenever she came home. After that, Jordan had begun thinking it was silly of her mother to keep the room as it had been, that she could put the space to a better purpose. She had told her mother as much, but her mom had always replied, "I have all the space I need, Jordan. This space will always be for you, whenever you want or need it."

Not long before she was shot, Jordan's mother had finally changed her mind about the decor. It was as if somehow she had known Jordan would be needing it again, and not as some shrine to her childhood. Gone were the Indigo Girls posters and athletic trophies, replaced by Jordan's favorite Ansel Adams print and photos from her life: her college graduation, the white-water rafting trip she and her mother had taken just before she entered the police academy, her academy graduation, the day she got her gold shield. It was her mother's attempt at reminding Jordan of who she still was as opposed to who she had been. Jordan had added to the photos over the last year, including one of her, Henry, and Max working on the front porch of the cabin. Max had the audacity to look disgruntled at the mess the sweaty, grimy humans had made of his prime napping spot.

Devon stopped before the photos atop the dresser. Jordan watched her study each one in turn, watched the myriad emotions flicker across her face. When she came to the newest photo from the cabin, a slow smile turned up the corners of Devon's mouth. She looked over at Jordan.

"These are nice photos."

"Mostly my mother's work," Jordan explained, as if she needed to apologize.

Devon carefully picked up one of the photos. "Is this your mother?"

"Yes." It was taken the day Jordan became a detective. Her mother stood with her arm around Jordan's shoulders, her face lit up with pride, matching Jordan's. Caroline stood beside Jordan, too, but the smile on her face did not quite reach her eyes. Jordan had never noticed it before, but now she could see the distance between them, despite her arm around Caroline's waist.

"She's lovely," Devon said softly, and Jordan understood that she wasn't referring to her mother.

"Her name is Caroline," Jordan said. "We aren't together anymore." She wasn't sure what made her add that last part.

Devon hummed thoughtfully. "It's good to have such moments captured."

Jordan couldn't help but wonder if Devon had any photos of her own. She decided the answer was most likely no, and the reality of that truth pierced her like an arrow through her heart.

"You know, if there's anything back at your apartment that you want, we can send someone over to your apartment later—"

"No, thanks," Devon said, shrugging. "There's nothing there that means anything."

The confirmation cut through Jordan. She wanted to reach out but decided such a move might only make Devon feel worse. "Well, I think my clothes will fit you," Jordan said, changing the subject. She walked over to the closet. "Actually, they might be a little big," she said, sifting through the hangers.

"You can't be serious?" Devon said with a laugh. "You're tiny."

Jordan's head whipped around. "I am not *tiny*."

Devon held her hands up in surrender. "Not what I meant. You are a force to be reckoned with. I just meant you're no bigger than me. More muscular, sure, and toned…"

Devon trailed off, and Jordan grinned at the flush staining the woman's cheeks. A flirty retort almost crossed Jordan's lips before she caught it. The here and now was neither the time nor the place.

"Anyway," Devon said with a nervous laugh, "I think your clothes will fit me just fine, Detective."

"I think we're past formal titles now, don't you?" Jordan asked, echoing Henry's earlier words. She stepped back from the closet. "I mean, you are going to be wearing my clothes and all. You might as well call me Jordan."

Devon tilted her head, seeming to study her, and Jordan wondered what was going through her mind. "Okay," Devon said finally. "Jordan."

Jordan's heart fluttered as her name passed Devon's lips for the first time. There was something in the way Devon said her name, throaty and soft and sweet all at once, like honey lacing a glass of whiskey. It rang in her head, reverberating down her spine until it settled deep in her belly. A slow, steady warmth spread outward from there, reaching into all the cold, empty places inside. It was like nothing Jordan had ever felt before.

Her mind swam and her heart began to race. She could feel the walls she had so carefully constructed over the last year and a half, the ones which had started to fall at the simple act of Devon saying her name, begin to rise high, protecting her heart once more. And for the first time she could remember, she wasn't sure she wanted them to. Still, old habits were hard to break for a reason, and Jordan breathed easier when she felt the last stone in her defenses slide back into place.

She remained unsettled, her thoughts about what had just transpired churning in her mind, until a loud, low growl pierced the air. Jordan tensed, assuming the sound had come from Max, but the dog sat staring up at her, his head cocked to the side as if to say, *What are you looking at lady? It wasn't me.*

That's when she noticed Devon's hand across her stomach and the sheepish look on her face. Jordan chuckled. "Hungry?"

"I guess I am," Devon said with a matching chuckle.

"That's not surprising. You probably haven't eaten since, what? About five?"

"More like eight last night. I skipped breakfast."

Jordan slapped a hand on her thigh. "Well that settles it. A late lunch it is."

Henry sat staring at the notepad in front of him, going over the scraps of information he and Lawson had cobbled together. It wasn't much. All they'd really been able to do was confirm part of what Devon had told them.

They'd been making calls and searching databases since returning to the station. He'd filled in the captain, who—once Henry had laid out Devon's story and the evidence so far—agreed that the diner murders were unrelated to the recent robberies. The captain would go to bat with the brass about using Jordan as a consultant on the case. As much as Henry wanted Jordan back full time and officially, he'd settle for what he could get. And he'd make Jordan's status work for them. Given what they already knew about Billy, the more outside the box they could take things, the better off they were.

Henry scanned the page before him, working the details through in his mind. Devon James, real name Madison Montgomery, was born in April 1985 to Marie and Billy Dean Montgomery in Des Plaines, Illinois, not long after the couple had moved there from West Virginia. They relocated to Roscoe, Illinois, sometime around 1989, whereupon Billy had taken a job as a sheriff's deputy. It wasn't clear whether the job had precipitated the move or vice versa. Beyond the sheriff's office, Billy's job history was thin—a lot of odd jobs here and there, but nothing very solid before Roscoe. On a blind inquiry to the Illinois State Police, Henry had been surprised—and delighted—to learn that Billy had applied to be a state highway patrolman in the mid-1980s but had been turned down. The state police kept records going back decades, and they had already forwarded Billy's application and, even better, fingerprints. No photo, but the fingerprints would be helpful. Marie had taught part-time at the local kindergarten for a couple of years, but tax records indicated she hadn't worked after 1992. In November 2000, when Devon was still fifteen, a fire at the Montgomery home had claimed the lives of Marie and Billy. The house had exploded and burned to the ground.

The local newspaper ran several stories on the fire and ensuing investigation, and listed the obituaries and funeral services for Marie and Billy Dean Montgomery. They were buried in different cemeteries on the same day. Henry suspected that had been Devon's doing, not that he could blame her. None of the news reports mentioned anything about Marie being murdered, save one. A story in a nearby town's paper a few days after the fire had a couple lines about the police investigation and said there was evidence of foul play in reference to Marie's death. But that was the last mention of it anywhere.

He hadn't yet gotten a copy of the autopsy reports, the case file on the fire, or Billy's personnel file from the sheriff's office. He'd put in the requests but knew small towns were often the last to upgrade to electronic records. Everything he was looking for was likely in a box in some dank basement somewhere, if it still existed, and the department wouldn't be in any hurry to dig up the files on a twelve-year-old case, let alone one that involved one of their own. Henry sighed. Short of going out there and finding those files himself, he'd be lucky to get his hands on them by Christmas.

CHAPTER TWELVE

S o what was it like? Growing up in Illinois?"

The question startled Devon. One minute they were making idle conversation as they washed and dried the lunch dishes, the next minute...for a few blissful moments, she'd nearly forgotten Jordan was a cop.

"It was okay, I guess."

"That's not really an answer," Jordan said, handing the final plate to Devon to dry. She shut off the faucet.

"I know," Devon said, trying not to sound defensive.

"Was there any other family besides you, your mom, and Billy?"

"I had a grandmother—my mom's mom. But she was in West Virginia and I never really saw her. She died when I was five. Mom said her daddy had died when she was a girl."

"What about Billy's side?"

"There was no one. He didn't have any siblings, I don't think. He never really talked about his parents, though I heard him once say his father had been a preacher. Mom never talked about them, either. I never knew them."

"What else do you remember?"

She set the now-dry plate on the counter and wiped her hands. Jordan had turned so she was leaning back against the sink. She watched Devon expectantly. Devon sighed. She walked over to the kitchen table and sat down. She knew what Jordan wanted to hear.

"For a long time, it was normal, I guess," Devon said, meeting Jordan's gaze. "At least, I didn't know any different. I was an only child, with a mother and a father who loved me."

Jordan stayed leaning against the sink. Devon appreciated the space.

"My mom worked some when I was younger. She taught at my school, though I wasn't in her class. Then she stopped working. I never really knew why. She always seemed a little sad about it, but she never said anything. I didn't really care, honestly, because it meant I got to spend more time with her. Everyone always thought she was kind of quiet and shy, but when it was just the two of us...I remember she had such an imagination. She was always telling me stories about faraway lands and beautiful but brave princesses who battled dragons and evil kings."

"No princes to rescue the princesses?"

"Never," Devon said, smiling broadly. "Mom always said a lady needed to know how to rescue herself because there wouldn't always be someone around to rescue her."

"Smart woman."

Devon grew pensive. "Yeah. I wish she'd been able to take her own advice."

"When did things change?"

"I know earlier I said things changed, but I'm not sure they changed, so much as I became more aware of what was really going on. The differences in my mother when Billy was around and when he wasn't. The differences in me."

"He was gone a lot?"

Devon hesitated. They were edging toward territory she didn't want to go anywhere near. "He worked a lot. Picked up extra shifts when he could. With mom not working, there wasn't much in the way of extra money."

"So when he was home, how were things?"

"When I was younger, they were great. I really did adore him. Maybe it was because he was working all the time. You always want what you don't have, and what I didn't have was a lot of time with Billy. But when I got older, maybe ten or eleven, I started noticing things. The way my mom got quiet when Billy was home. She hunched her shoulders more, and she never did that when he wasn't around. She always seemed just a little bit sad, but she tried so hard to hide it."

"Did he hit her?"

It had been so long ago, and she rarely thought of her childhood anymore. Anytime she did think back that far, her mind caught on the memory of her mother's murder, and it cast a long, terrible shadow over her memories. "Not that I remember. Not that I saw. Not until that day."

Jordan settled into the chair next to Devon's and rested her forearms on the table. Her voice grew quiet. "The day he killed her."

Devon nodded.

"But before then, your mother was afraid of him."

Devon nodded again, more slowly this time. She knew what her mother had felt, what *she* had felt back then, but had a hard time separating it from the other fear, the one that came later. The one that came after the darkness and desolation and pain and terror. The one that came not from the unknown, but from the knowing.

"It was like a shadow. I don't know when exactly I became aware of it, or why. But once I recognized it, it was always there. I could *feel* it, this cold malevolence surrounding him, radiating from him. I just knew what would happen if we crossed him, if we displeased him. So we didn't. And we weren't the only ones."

"What do you mean?"

Devon hoisted a memory up from the depths, one that could give her nebulous perceptions form and substance. "We never really saw any of the guys Billy worked with—they never came by the house, and we never went to the station—except at the annual Fourth of July picnic. One year—I was probably ten or eleven—I was sick. Billy insisted we go, so we did. I was too sick to play, and I finally got bored listening to Mom and the other wives talking about recipes and gossip, so I went off to find Billy. He and the guys were playing poker. I hung back, just watching them, all laughing and smiling—even Billy was having a grand old time. It was down to Billy and another deputy. The deputy showed his hand, a straight flush. Everybody started patting him on the back, and he leaned forward to pull in his chips. Then Billy cleared his throat. He wasn't smiling anymore. He turned up his cards. He had a royal flush, ace high."

Devon remembered the looks on the other men's faces, the thickness of the silence that descended over the table.

"The one guy remarked that it was Billy's second royal flush of the afternoon. The other men looked at him, like they couldn't believe he'd said that. Then I saw the look on Billy's face. I had never seen it before, but I came to know it well. His eyes narrowed and his lips curled up in this sickening smile, and he asked the other deputy if he was calling him a cheat. The others at the table stepped in so fast. They were practically falling over themselves to apologize, telling Billy that of course no one would accuse Billy of cheating. They told Billy to take the pot."

Devon had never told anyone this story. She had never shared what it was like to realize she and her mother weren't the only ones who were scared of Billy.

"I didn't really understand what had happened, but then Billy turned his head toward me, seemed to notice I was there for the first time. He was staring at me, that same, sickening smile on his face. And in that moment, I understood what it was to be terrified."

Henry leaned back in his chair, his head throbbing, the pain clouding over logical thought. He had been at it for hours, but he felt like all he had to show for it was this damn headache. He squeezed the bridge of his nose, methodically moving his thumb and forefinger in small circles. It was a trick Ella had taught him long ago. Whenever he was frustrated by a case, he got headaches like the one he was having now. Something about squeezing his sinus cavity and the rhythmic motion of his fingers helped him clear both the pain and his mind. It was the only thing that seemed to work. Another of the little miracles his wife had performed for him in her lovely but too-brief life.

The trick worked, like always, and Henry felt the pain lifting, taking the fog with it. He scanned his notes once more, working through the other details he and Lawson had gleaned from their search. The Illinois Department of Children and Family Services showed that Devon had entered the foster system upon her parents' deaths and had lived in a group home for a few weeks before being placed with Debra and Dale McMillan. She lived with them for nearly two years, and then left for Northern Illinois University in DeKalb.

In his experience, colleges could be very difficult about releasing student records without a warrant, but because of the murder of Devon's roommate, campus security had been more than happy to oblige. Along with Devon's student file, they had faxed over everything they had on the murder, including the full report from the local police. That had surprised Henry. Campus cops were usually quick to wash their hands of real crime on school grounds, but NIU's cops had done a surprisingly thorough job of keeping track of the formal investigation.

The report confirmed that, four weeks into the 2002 fall term, Devon's roommate, Jessica Morgan, had been found dead in their room. Devon had discovered the body. Campus security, which had already been called by another student who reported hearing a loud argument, arrived shortly after Devon had entered. Jessica's body had been lying on the bed, her throat cut. The campus cops quickly called the local authorities and did not question Devon themselves, given the seriousness of the crime.

The formal police file outlined the physical details Devon had told Henry and Jordan earlier. Questioning of the floor's other residents had yielded no significant information and no suspects; no one had seen anyone who didn't belong. A couple of students, including the one who had called the campus cops, had thought they heard some kind of argument between a male and female but, upon further questioning by the local authorities, they realized they hadn't heard anything.

Henry shook his head. He could imagine how the cops had helped the students to their supposed realizations. It happened all the time. Some cops got a story in their minds and actively worked to eliminate any evidence that didn't fit what they thought they knew. That had clearly been the case with these cops. The report indicated they had locked on to Devon as a person of interest early on. The room had been dusted for prints, but apart from those belonging to Devon, Jessica, and a couple of other students, none could be found. The report indicated that there was a lot of blood on the bed, but there was no indication of spatter beyond the bed. The bloodstains on Jessica's clothes and Devon's bedspread all belonged to Jessica. The forensic investigation had yielded nothing else of value. They'd done a complete search of the dorm and surrounding grounds, and the murder weapon was not found.

The autopsy indicated bruising to Jessica's wrists and thighs, as if the killer had wrestled her to the bed, kneeled on her legs and held her wrists. She'd also had a light bruise on the first two knuckles of her right hand. There was no bruising to the head and no trace of drugs in her system, which meant she most likely hadn't been unconscious when she was killed. The blade had sliced through both the jugular and carotid, which would have sprayed blood up and out in a wide arc. The lack of significant splatter at the scene told Henry that whoever had killed the woman took the brunt of the splatter—though Henry would have liked to see the crime scene photos to be sure.

Henry tried to imagine Devon overpowering Jessica and holding her down, but he couldn't. Although Devon wasn't tiny, she was neither big enough nor powerful enough to keep Jessica pinned to the bed while slitting her throat in the way the autopsy suggested. In order to make the bruises on Jessica's thighs, Devon's knees would have had to have been pressing into them with all her weight, her feet off to either side for balance. That wasn't an easy position to maintain, and Jessica would have been fighting for her life. The bruising on Jessica's wrists could have been caused by Devon holding them pinned above her head, but how would Devon have held Jessica's hands down while also slicing her throat? Devon would have had to hold both Jessica's wrists with only one hand, and Devon's hands were just not big enough for that. And slitting someone's throat—especially from the front—was no easy task. It took some power to get through all that muscle and sinew. The killer had to have either been a very big girl or, more likely, a man.

None of that, however, had seemed to matter to the local police. Although there had not been enough evidence to arrest Devon or even officially name her a suspect, their conclusion was there in the report, clear as day. *No reasonable suspect beyond Madison Montgomery.*

They had interviewed her three times, the last one about a week after the murder. While the first interview had been simply to take her statement, it was clear that by the second interview two days later, they had already begun to see Devon as a suspect. When they brought her in the last time, the interrogation—there was no other way to describe it—had lasted five hours. No attorney had been present.

During that first interview, Devon had indeed tried to tell the cops that she thought her father was responsible for Jessica's murder. They'd asked her why she thought it was her supposedly dead father, but the only response recorded was the manner of Jessica's death and a "feeling"—the cops had actually put it in quotes—that her father was somehow responsible. She'd asked them if they'd found a wheat penny, but no such evidence had been found.

It was clear the cops had not believed her from the start, though Henry supposed if it had been him, with the evidence they both had and didn't have, he might not have believed her, either. The main difference between him and those cops was that he would have seriously investigated her claims. The cops had called the Roscoe sheriff's office and spoken to one of the deputies, and that was about it. They hadn't even gotten the case file from Roscoe. The sheriff's department considered it case closed, and so the DeKalb cops did, too. In their eyes, that meant Devon was either supremely delusional or hiding something.

During the final interview, they had tried to break her. The transcript read like something out of a bad police movie. They had used every trick in the book, including some that were clearly illegal, to get her to confess. It hadn't worked, Henry assumed, because she hadn't done anything wrong. They'd had to let her go and told her not to leave town. The final note in the file indicated that a few days later they tried to reach her for another interview but had been unable to locate her. A warrant had been issued for her arrest, and the case had remained open, unsolved.

Henry put aside the DeKalb file and scanned the campus police report. It was thin, since they'd handed the case off, but one of the campus cops had taken a few notes of his impressions, from the initial complaint call to the arrival of the local cops. The call had come into the campus police approximately ten minutes prior to their arrival. The caller, a female in the suite next door, had called to complain about noise coming from Devon and Jessica's room. She reported a loud argument, followed by a couple of thumps against her wall and moaning. The caller said she banged on the wall but the moaning continued, and she was tired of Jessica and her boyfriend going at it all day and night when she needed to study.

The campus cop noted that they normally didn't respond to sex complaints, but the argument the caller described had concerned him. He had arrived to find the door open. Devon had been standing in the middle of the room, staring at the body on her bed, seemingly in shock. He'd immediately called the DeKalb police and had guided Devon out into the hall to wait. From the doorway, not wanting to disturb any evidence, he had surveyed the room. There was no obvious sign of a break-in. The campus cop theorized that Jessica had let the killer into her room willingly. He also noted a small reddish smudge on the wall in the hallway outside the room, about five feet past the door.

Son of a bitch. Henry flipped to the notes from the official investigation. He could find no mention of any such smudge, or any other mention of the campus cop's report. Either they'd missed it or they'd excluded it, and either way it bothered Henry. The mark in the hall could have been unrelated, he supposed, but if it wasn't, it indicated the killer had been out in the hallway after murdering Jessica. And the timeline was significant, too. Devon had no blood on her and no discarded bloody clothes were found on scene, according to the report. Only ten minutes passed between the call to the campus police and their arrival, nowhere near enough time for Devon to commit murder, get cleaned up, dispose of the bloody clothes and the murder weapon, and get back to her dorm room. That should have been enough to exclude Devon as a suspect.

Henry shook his head again. The gaps in logic the cops had been willing to overlook in order to make Devon fit the crime were astounding. He wondered what other evidence they had missed. Had they overlooked a wheat penny left at the scene? When this was all over, he was going to drive out to DeKalb, Illinois, and have a word with the excuses-for-cops involved in this travesty.

Henry put aside the files and thought about the diner murders. He hoped the Pittsburgh Mobile Crime Unit detectives would be able to link something at the scene to Billy, some shred of evidence that could not only prove his involvement but that would indicate where and how to find him. Henry had sent Billy's fingerprints to the lab to see if they could find a match in the diner. Henry didn't think they would—Billy seemed too careful for that—but they'd try.

Henry would still need to follow up with the investigating officers in DeKalb, but he wasn't in any hurry. The state cops hadn't asked questions since Billy was nothing more to them than an old application collecting dust, but cops with a cold case and an outstanding warrant would be more inquisitive. Henry wasn't about to let the locals screw this up for Devon again, and he certainly wasn't about to let them arrest her.

Something else was bothering him, beyond all the bad police work. His mind went back to the house fire. Though he didn't have the reports he needed to prove it, the newspaper articles had all said two bodies had been found. Two bodies had been buried. So if they had found two bodies and one of them wasn't Billy Dean Montgomery, who in the hell had died with Marie Montgomery in that explosion?

A dozen possibilities ran through Henry's mind, each one more outrageous than the last. There was simply no way to know, short of having the body exhumed and DNA tested. And that wasn't an option for the time being. As next of kin, Devon was the only one with the legal right to allow them to dig up the grave. But there was no way to have the body dug up without confirming that Devon was Madison Montgomery, and with the warrant out for her, Henry would have no choice but to turn her over.

He was breaking the law by harboring Devon. He had never broken the law before, never even thought about it, had never so much as jaywalked, but he was surprised to find that instead of making him feel guilty, he felt kind of good. Not that he was about to go out and knock over a liquor store anytime soon, but he realized that for the first time in his life, upholding the law was not his first priority. Doing the right thing mattered more, and that meant protecting Devon and bringing Billy Dean Montgomery to justice.

CHAPTER THIRTEEN

Devon lay awake in Jordan's bed, Max's rhythmic breathing serving as a metronome for her thoughts. The shepherd was curled along her side, his head tucked into the nook between her breast and arm. She gently stroked his silky fur, feeling ever safer with each rise and fall of the dog's strong chest. Max's back legs spasmed once, then again. Devon smiled, imagining the rabbit Max was no doubt chasing through the field of his dreams.

She rested her head on her biceps, Max's fur tickling the tip of her nose. She thought back over the strange, terrible, wonderful day, trying to reconcile the horror of how it had begun with how she felt now. Warm. Protected. Perhaps even…content?

Talking about her childhood hadn't killed her. As afraid as she'd been to talk about her past—to put words to things of which she had never, ever spoken—it had felt okay, even good, to share them.

Guilt settled over her at that last thought, pressing down upon her with its weight. She shook it off. Didn't she deserve to feel good, to feel content? Didn't she deserve, even for the most fleeting of moments, to feel something other than guilt? Or fear? Or numbness?

Yesterday, or even that morning, she would have said no. She would not have allowed herself to think such thoughts, to feel such things. There was no escaping her past, or her shame. It was her burden to carry, the stone she deserved to have tied around her neck, dragging her down into the frigid obsidian waters of her everlasting guilt.

But now there was a light shining above her, calling her out of the depths. Maybe this load was not hers alone to carry, not anymore.

Maybe she deserved more than this half life she had been living for so long. Maybe, just maybe, there was a way out of Billy Montgomery's long, decrepit shadow.

It felt foreign to her, this hope welling inside, like a stranger sleeping in her bed. She nearly laughed at the irony as she lay in the bed of Detective Jordan Salinger, a woman who twelve hours earlier had been nothing if not a stranger. But now? She was a stranger no more, though what exactly Jordan was remained elusive. Devon's hope? Her salvation?

It was a lot to put on Jordan, on both her and Henry, but it was all Devon had.

Beside her, Max grunted softly, kicking all four of his legs now. Apparently that rabbit was giving him a devil of a time. Devon stroked his side more firmly and he settled back down into slumber.

After dinner, after all the questions about Billy and her mother and her childhood, Jordan—seeming to sense Devon could take no more—had suggested they play a game. "Your choice," Jordan had said, rummaging through the hall closet and holding out an ancient version of Trivial Pursuit, a Chutes and Ladders that had seen better days, and a deck of cards. Devon had chosen the cards.

Devon had been surprised by the idea, by how oddly ordinary it seemed. In the end, though, she thought it was Jordan who had been surprised—by how good Devon was at rummy. She had skunked the detective four times in a row. As they played, Devon found herself telling Jordan about Mrs. Eleanor Brindle, who had taken her in when she'd fled Illinois and ended up in Colorado and who had taught Devon how to play cards.

"She was a kind, gentle lady, but when she got you across the deck of cards, she was ruthless," Devon had said, laughing with fond remembrance. Jordan's silence made her realize she had divulged something she hadn't intended. She'd waited for Jordan to press her, but instead Jordan had shuffled the deck. As she lay now in Jordan's bed, she felt the familiar panic again as her mind raced. She knew she would have to tell Jordan and Henry the rest eventually, but she wasn't ready. She just wasn't. What would they think of her then? They would arrest her for sure, throw her into some dank, dark pit and turn their backs on her forever.

She still felt Jordan's hand, telling her with a soft squeeze that she understood. She'd looked up into Jordan's face, which reflected the same understanding. She would press no further, at least not this night.

Devon didn't know how long her luck would hold, but she knew the truth was like sand slipping through an hourglass, and eventually the last grain would fall and her time would have run out. She would have to tell them. She owed it to them. All of it. Every last, disgusting, terrible detail. But not yet. That thought followed her into an uneasy sleep, full of shadows.

❖

The night was still and deep, the neighborhood fast asleep and dreaming, Billy assumed, of all manner of pleasant, middle-class aspirations. Camping trips and new-but-responsible cars and Disneyland, with the occasional dirty-schoolgirl or shoot-up-my-office fantasy thrown in. Even the tamest, gentlest of men harbored the capacity for degradation and death.

For all have sinned, and come short of the glory of God.

All men, of course, except Billy Montgomery. Billy was God's right hand, His angel of death, His divine covenant to rid the world of the unworthy. God commanded and Billy obeyed. Billy cleansed man, and woman, of their unrighteousness, and in that cleansing, gave them new life. Purification by pain, by divine design. It was the noblest of callings, for both Billy and for those chosen to receive His blessing.

Billy's actions had a purpose. They were not the lust-fueled perversions of weaker, lesser men. He enjoyed his work, that much was true. But he also knew that was as God intended it, Billy's reward for his continued faithful service and utter dedication to his task.

In all his years working for the Lord, he had lost control only once. It was well past time to rectify that mistake.

The only break in the stillness came from the faint buzzing of the streetlamps. Even the moon was absent, sinking the street into near-darkness, save for the small circles of sulfurous glow cast by the lamps and the occasional porch light. But there was no bulb illuminating the front porch of the house where his sweet daughter lay sleeping. Billy did not think the police guarding her so stupid as to leave it off. No, God had blessed Billy's task with the gift of a burned-out lightbulb. The Lord was good to him in that way, and in so many others.

Billy approached the house cautiously, ever so quietly. He checked the fit of his black calfskin gloves, which weighed next to nothing and molded to his hands like an extra layer of skin. Years ago, he had dabbled with latex but quickly switched back to leather when he discovered that sweaty hands wrapped in latex were altogether unpleasant. His rubber-soled boots made no sound on the sidewalk nor, he was pleased to discover, on the sturdy wooden steps as he climbed up to the front porch. Several hours earlier, once the last house on the block had long gone dark, Billy had crept the length of the house, testing the entry points. The house did not appear to have an alarm system, which was good. The ground-floor windows—like most of the neighborhood's homes—had bars, negating them as points of entry. In the back, Billy found a sliding glass door—easy to jimmy but usually very noisy when opened. Add to that two floodlights at either corner of the house, and the back was far from ideal. That left only the front door.

Billy sank to one knee, examining the two locks—one in the doorknob and a deadbolt. He was pleased to see the deadbolt was a two-sided single cylinder, pickable from the outside. Not that it would have mattered. Since most of the work of a small-town sheriff's deputy was breaking up bar brawls and escorting home the drunkards who had invariably lost their keys, the sheriff had insisted that all recruits spend a day with a trained locksmith. It had proved an invaluable asset to Billy's work.

He slipped his kit out of his back pocket and set to work on the doorknob lock. Thirty seconds later, he felt the tumbler release with a soft click. He paused, listening for any sign that his activities had been discovered, but heard none. He moved on to the deadbolt, and after forty-five seconds was rewarded with another click. He waited again. Still nothing. He smiled as he rose to his feet.

Billy reached for the six-inch tactical knife at his hip. He savored its progression as he slipped it silently up and out of its sheath, reveled in the familiar warm weight of it in his hand, and slowly rotated it. The carbon-steel blade reflected no light, its finish like a black hole casting back absence rather than presence. Freeing it was like releasing a tiger from its cage, the power of it surging up his arm as he tightened his grip around the leather hilt.

Though he knew the detective inside would most likely have her gun within easy reach, Billy was unconcerned. He was the hand of God, and he would slice open the cop's neck long before she ever had the chance to pull her trigger. And then, finally, he would be reunited with his wayward daughter.

That thought put a smile on his lips as he silently pushed open the front door.

❖

Jordan heard the gunshots, felt the bullet tear through her shoulder and knock her backward. She heard herself scream but it wasn't for herself. It was for the boy. The boy whose face turned ghostly pale and whose eyes held hers as they both crashed to the ground. She screamed again, only this time it wasn't the boy's face she saw, but the blank slate of the ceiling overhead.

She blinked, trying to clear the nightmare from her vision. She was in her bedroom, but it seemed foreign. The ceiling fan looked familiar but wrong, and the shadows seemed…off somehow. She blinked again, several times, before it hit her. She was not in fact in her bedroom, but in her mother's room. Devon was in Jordan's bed down the hall. And there was a mass murderer out there, somewhere, hunting for his daughter.

She sat up, kicking at the sheets that entangled her legs like jungle vines. She was covered in sweat, her thin tank top glued to her skin like it was made of paste instead of cotton. She swung her legs, now free of their prison, over the edge of the bed and ran her fingers through her saturated hair.

Damn.

This one was bad. Worse than she'd had in a while. The dreams never really left her, but lately she had been going days, even weeks sometimes, between the really bad ones. The ones that wrung every drop of moisture from her body and threatened to stop her heart. The ones like she'd had tonight.

Her tongue felt swollen and her mouth was an oven, as if she'd just spent a week crawling through the Sahara. She glanced over at the nightstand—3:13 a.m. She stood on shaky legs, waiting a few beats to make sure they would hold her up, then reached for her gun next to the clock. Her weapon had not been more than a foot from her since they had entered the house earlier that day, and she had no intention of changing that pattern. She checked the safety and the clip and slipped out of the room, gun in hand. She paused for a moment outside Devon's door—*her* door—and heard nothing except the muffled sound of Max's familiar snore. She smiled to herself and headed down to the kitchen.

Jordan rounded the bottom of the stairs, casting a glance toward the secure front door, and padded into the kitchen, setting her gun down on the island. She retrieved a glass from the cupboard and the pitcher from the refrigerator and poured herself a glass of water. She set the pitcher down next to her gun, turning toward the sink and the window above it. The night beyond seemed peaceful, almost inviting. This was not the first night she had stood staring out at the darkened world, glass in hand, trying to shake off a nightmare.

She lifted the glass to her mouth and took a long swallow, and then another, welcoming the cool water. She wondered what the police shrink would think of her nightmares. She had refused to tell him, of course, during her bureau-ordered psych evaluation and mandatory counseling after the shooting. Bureau policy and all that. The guy had seemed nice enough, she supposed, and perhaps was even a good doctor. But there had been no force on the planet that could have made her share the nightmares with him, make her tell him how the events of that day kept replaying over and over in her mind every night or how all she could ever remember when she awoke was Jacob Dubois's face and his tiny body falling lifeless to the floor or how she hadn't saved him. She hadn't even told Henry, though she figured he had guessed by now.

She was giving that thought mild consideration when she heard it. A short, low creak of a floorboard settling under foot.

She was moving before her brain could process the sound, flinging her half-full glass in the direction of the sound and reaching for her gun in a single motion. Her fingers just brushed the barrel when she was tackled and hurled backward. Her feet could find no purchase as her assailant crashed her into the kitchen table three feet away. He landed on top of her, forcing the air out of her lungs with the impact. Dazed and gasping for breath, she only vaguely registered the arm lifting above her and the long silhouette extending from it.

Years of training kicked into overdrive in a millisecond. Jordan thrust her knee up with all her might, the sharp whoosh of air against her face telling her she'd hit home. The body sagged against her, enough for her to tug her left arm free and thrust the heel of her hand into the man's nose. He staggered backward, momentarily disoriented, his free hand covering his nose protectively. Jordan's lungs screamed for air but she ignored the demand and pushed forward off the table. Every instinct demanded she move, told her she had no time, that she had to take advantage. Distantly she could hear Max barking and clawing at something, but her mind could only focus on her assailant, who had already recovered. She launched herself at him, registering his surprise as she brought her elbow up and back down in one swift motion. Pain exploded in her arm as it made contact with his right shoulder. The knife didn't clatter to the ground as she had hoped, but she ignored the thought. He was too big and the area too confined for her to have any chance unarmed against him. She had to get to her gun.

She pushed past him, the blow to his shoulder and her unexpected actions knocking him off balance. She dove across the island, her hand connecting with the gun as she tumbled over the other side and crashed to the floor. She rolled as she landed, absorbing as much of the fall as she could with her right side. Her back collided with the refrigerator, arresting her momentum, and she raised her gun.

"Hold it!" Jordan shouted. The man froze in the shadows, his hate blazing bright as he clutched his shoulder now instead of his face. Somewhere, a door crashed against a wall and she heard Max's snarling, thunderous approach. The man must have heard it, too, because in a flash he was moving. Jordan fired three times in rapid succession as the man crashed through the sliding glass door and out into the night, one of the bullets splintering the doorframe where he had been an instant before.

Max barreled into the kitchen and rounded the island, giving chase.

"Max, no!" Jordan yelled with what little force she had left. The adrenaline rush was wearing off as quickly as it had begun, and the injuries she had ignored were making themselves loudly and painfully known.

The dog skidded to a stop at the edge of what remained of the sliding glass door, whipping his head toward Jordan and then quickly back through the door and out into the night. He whined loudly. Jordan imagined the war being waged within the shepherd, torn between running down the intruder and obeying his master. She knew Max was a capable dog, but as well trained as he was, he could not yet take down an armed man. Max would only get killed, and the assailant would still be on the loose.

More thunder from the stairs, then Devon was there, dropping to her knees beside Jordan.

"My God."

Jordan heard the tremor in Devon's voice and wanted to reassure her, but could only force out a soft, "S'okay." Max licked Jordan's face and lay down next to her. She gave the dog a visual once-over to confirm he hadn't been cut by the door's broken glass.

"I'm so sorry, Jordan," Devon said in a rush. "I heard a crash and then Max was barking and I dialed 9-1-1 and—"

"No," Jordan said, gasping as she pushed herself up off the floor. Devon steadied her as she rose gingerly, pain exploding in her side. "No, you did the right thing." She put the pieces together. The hatred in his face. The knife. This wasn't just some random break in. It was him. No other explanation made sense.

"But—"

"He was here to kill you."

That stopped Devon cold.

"It was Billy. And if you'd come down here, you'd be dead."

Devon swallowed hard. "The police are on their way," she said quietly.

"We need to go."

"Go? Go where?" Devon asked, but Jordan ignored her questions.

"I need to grab a few things. Max, stay with Devon." She pressed her gun into Devon's hand, quickly but efficiently showing her how it worked. "Safety's off and it's ready to fire. You see anyone besides me, you pull the trigger." She didn't wait for Devon to respond as she moved past them and up the stairs.

Within minutes she was back downstairs, a duffel bag thrown over her shoulder, her laptop case and Devon's bag in hand. Devon had stopped asking questions, but Jordan could see them lingering on her face. She would explain, but not until they were moving. She took back her gun and herded them to her SUV, starting it up just as the faint sound of sirens floated to her ears. Her cell rang as she pulled away from the curb.

"Jordan, what happened?" Henry asked urgently. "I just got the call. I'm five minutes out. You okay?"

"We won't be there," Jordan said, ignoring the question. She grimaced. She was pretty sure she'd broken a couple of ribs. Cracked them, anyway.

"What are you talking about?"

Jordan quickly filled Henry in. "It was him. We're going somewhere safe."

"Wait for me."

"No. I need you to find this bastard, Henry. Check the hospitals. I'm pretty sure I broke his nose, possibly a dislocated shoulder, and he should be good and cut up from crashing through the glass. And he may have a gunshot wound."

"I want to get you with the sketch artist—"

"It was too dark," Jordan said quickly. She'd been racking her brain trying to call up a clear image of his face, but it was no use. "I didn't get a clear look at his face. It just—"

"I know," Henry said. It had all happened so fast, and the kitchen had been dark. Even still, Jordan hated that she couldn't provide a description. How in the hell would they find Billy if she couldn't even tell them what he looked like? Devon had been a teenager the last time she had seen him, and so her memory couldn't be trusted to provide an accurate description.

"Six feet, one eighty, all muscle, close-cropped hair," she rattled off quickly. She thought harder. "Jeans. T-shirt. No idea what color. He wore gloves. Soft ones."

That was it. That was all she could remember, aside from the hatred she felt directed at her from the darkness just before he fled. Her gut twisted reflexively.

"Okay," Henry said. "Where are you headed?"

"Not over the phone."

Henry paused. "You think he's got an interceptor?"

She traced back the few phone conversations she's had with Henry since he'd first called that morning. She could not recall having said anything that would have given away their location, but her mind was a jumble of pain and memory. "No. I don't know. Maybe? How the hell did he find us so fast?"

Henry didn't answer. She wasn't sure what was worse: that he had found a way to listen in on their calls so quickly, or that he had followed them all that time and they'd never seen him. Jordan was sure Henry was having the same thoughts.

"I'll call you when we're secure."

"Be careful, Jordan. Both of you."

"You, too."

CHAPTER FOURTEEN

Jordan opened the door to the cabin, ushering Devon quickly inside. The ninety-minute drive had been quiet and tense. Devon hadn't needed to look at the speedometer to know that they were flying, mostly on tightly curving two-lane roads. She supposed the speed should have scared her, but whether it was due to shock caused by the previous few hours' events or the confidence with which Jordan handled the SUV, she had been surprisingly unafraid.

Devon had always had a decent sense of direction, and despite not having the slightest clue where they were heading, she felt as though they had been driving in circles before they finally reached the cabin. Once they were safely inside and Jordan and Max had conducted what Devon could only describe as a full sweep of the small but homey cabin, Jordan confirmed her suspicions.

"We're only about an hour out of Pittsburgh. But I had to make sure we weren't followed," Jordan said, moving the duffel bag from where she had dropped it by the front door to the small kitchen table.

The thought made Devon shiver. She hadn't been afraid since they'd left the house, until now. She took a step toward Jordan, who had opened the bag and was riffling through it. "And are you? Sure?"

Jordan looked up at Devon, her eyebrows lifting as if she realized what was going through Devon's mind. "Oh no. I mean, yes, I'm sure," she said, stepping around the table toward Devon. Jordan took Devon's hands in hers. "He didn't follow us. Not this time. The roads around here are labyrinthine if you aren't familiar with them. Some of them don't even appear on maps and are hardly used. If he was following us, I damn sure lost him, and he'll be lucky to find his way back to a main road by Christmas."

Devon trusted that Jordan was right, but it was as if her fear finally topped the levee holding it back. She began shaking uncontrollably.

In an instant, Jordan's arms were around her, and she released a shuddering breath. Her arms hung limply at her sides for a long moment and then, as if of their own accord, slid around Jordan's strong body. Jordan pulled her closer, whispering soothing nothings into her hair. Devon held on a little tighter, until Jordan gasped. Devon sprang back.

"Oh my God, I'm sorry," Devon said in a rush, watching Jordan's hand protectively grasp her side.

"It's not your fault. It happened at the house," Jordan said grimacing. Her face had gone pale.

Devon went to the small refrigerator and opened the icebox, hoping for anything frozen. She found a bag of peas. "Here, let me see."

Jordan appeared as though she might argue, but then seemed to think better of it. She let Devon help her lower herself onto one of the kitchen chairs.

"In case you're thinking of arguing, don't bother," Devon said in a tone that she hoped would brook no argument. "You're hurt, and I'm sure you're not used to accepting help, but you are going to accept it from me." Devon didn't bother to wait for a response. She knelt next to Jordan and carefully raised her shirt. Devon bit back a gasp when she saw the deep blue and purple bruise already forming on Jordan's side.

"You should see the other guy," Jordan joked.

Devon ignored her. As gently as she could, she settled the frozen peas against Jordan's side. Jordan jumped slightly and gritted her teeth, but soon a little of the color returned to her cheeks, the cold seeming to dull at least some of her pain.

"We're going to need another ice pack for your cheek," Devon said as calmly as she could manage. The sight of another bruise forming on Jordan's beautiful skin upset her deeply. She forced herself to keep her tone neutral, even light. "You have any other injuries I should know about?"

Jordan stared at Devon for a moment and started to shake her head, then stopped. Devon watched whatever was going through Jordan's mind play out across her face. "I hit my head earlier," Jordan said, like she'd gotten knocked about in a basketball game instead of having fought off a madman.

"Hold this for a minute, okay?" Devon placed Jordan's hand over the makeshift ice pack at her side, and she went back to the freezer and retrieved two more bags of vegetables. "Let me take a look."

She handed Jordan one of the bags for her cheek. She delicately probed Jordan's scalp, finding a small but noticeable lump on the back of her head. She took the remaining ice pack and held it to Jordan's head.

"You could have a concussion," Devon said quietly. Jordan's pain was almost too much to bear.

"Nah, I have a hard head." Jordan laughed.

But if her intent had been to lighten the mood, it had the exact opposite effect on Devon.

"You need to see a doctor. You might have broken ribs, or internal bleeding. You—"

"I'm fine," Jordan interrupted, standing. "Really. It's no big deal."

"Damn it, Jordan," Devon said sharply, the reality of Jordan's injuries setting in, "he could have killed you." Devon's heart raged. She folded her arms, as if that might somehow keep her heart from exploding right out of her chest. She hated what Billy had done, hated that she had brought him into Jordan's and Henry's lives, a plague that would infect anything and everyone in its path.

"Hey," Jordan said softly, stepping closer, "Let me give you the nickel tour of the place, and then I think we should try to get at least a couple hours of sleep. It's been a long night. Okay?"

The expression Jordan wore—so open and caring and utterly charming—and the gentle reassurance in her voice nearly melted Devon's heart. She nodded her assent and took Jordan's outstretched hand. Max, who had wisely been sitting at the edge of the kitchen watching the scene from a safe distance, followed them. Jordan did not let go of Devon's hand, and Devon took strength from the simple gesture.

"I threw some clothes in here for you," Jordan said, pulling a few items out of the duffel bag. "They're not much, but I've got some more stuff in the back of the truck. The cabin's not big, but it's comfortable. At least, I think so."

"It's lovely," Devon said, and she meant it. The home was wood from top to bottom, a deep cherry color that was rich and warm. The large front room included both the kitchen and living area, and a large stone fireplace that was clearly more than just decorative flanked one end of the room. A chocolate-brown leather sofa adorned with a purple-and-blue afghan faced the fireplace, the couch serving as a natural break between the living room and kitchen. Two large bookshelves sat astride the fireplace, every inch of them packed with books. A small television sat on a table in one corner of the room, as if it was an afterthought. In the other corner, a wingback reading chair sat in front of the window, and Devon could imagine spending an afternoon tucked into it, her legs curled up beneath her, reading some delicious novel. A surprisingly spacious bathroom held both a shower and an invitingly deep claw-foot bathtub. The bedroom was decorated in various shades of blue, a four-poster bed dominating the space. Devon thought the cabin was the personification of Jordan: strong yet soft, no-nonsense but never boring, understatedly elegant and infinitely compelling.

Jordan gave Devon's hand a light squeeze and then finally let it go. Devon's hand still tingled everywhere their skin had touched. Jordan set the clothes on the bed.

"Well, uh," Jordan started, seemingly having trouble finding her words. Devon thought she was adorable. "You should get some sleep," Jordan finally said, starting for the door.

Realization hit Devon then. "I'm not taking the bed."

"Yes, you are," Jordan responded, flashing a dazzling smile.

Jordan's kitchen looked as if a bomb had gone off, without the fire damage. Broken glass was everywhere. Henry could discern at least three different types: the remains of a vase, which lay smashed on the floor in a pool of water near the dining table, its flowers withering at the center of the debris; what appeared to have once been a drinking glass, which had seemingly exploded upon impact against one of the kitchen walls; and the shattered ruins of the sliding glass door.

Henry stood at the edge of the kitchen, waiting for the Mobile Crime Unit detective to finish photographing the room. Much of the glass from the sliding door had landed outside the house as Billy had crashed through it, but splinters still covered the kitchen floor, twinkling like a million tiny stars with each flash of the tech's camera.

And there was blood. A small spray raced up one of the kitchen cabinets. Droplets beat an irregular pattern from the middle of the kitchen to the sliding door. Crimson lined the edges of some of the larger shards of glass near the doorframe. They had also found another small spray pattern in the grass just outside the door.

From the blood trail, and from what Jordan had told him, the events reformed in his mind like a storyboard. The blood would be Billy's, or at least most of it would be, Henry was sure. The red painting the cabinets and kitchen floor was from the broken nose Jordan had given Billy, the staining of the door glass from Billy breaking through it, and the pattern outside from the gunshot he had apparently suffered at Jordan's hand. It wasn't enough blood to indicate anything more than a scratch, but Jordan had hit him just the same. She had really done a number on him. Henry had to smile at that.

The tech finished taking pictures and a different detective began dusting for prints. Henry knew they would find none. But they had Billy's blood now, which would help them put him away later. Unfortunately, it would do nothing to help them catch the bastard.

Henry heard a set of heavy footsteps behind him. He turned to find Captain Buchanan standing at the kitchen threshold, eyes wide.

"My God," Buchanan said sadly. "I got a call that a PBP detective's house was broken into and there was an altercation of some kind. When I realized it was Salinger...are they okay?"

"They're okay," Henry answered.

"What happened?"

He led Captain Buchanan through the crime scene and the events as he knew them. They ended up standing in front of the bullet hole in the frame of the sliding glass door, the bullet having already been collected as evidence. Buchanan traced the hole with a latex-gloved finger.

"Where are they now?" Buchanan asked.

"Somewhere safe," Henry answered. "I don't know exactly where. Jordan didn't say. She's being understandably cautious."

"You two were right to hold this one close. But even so..." Buchanan trailed off, looking again at the remains of the kitchen. "How did he find them so fast?" he muttered, almost to himself.

"Our best guess is he followed us," Henry said, his tone revealing only a fraction of the remorse he felt.

"Followed you? From where?" Buchanan's voice rose in disbelief, then crashed back down in realization. "From the police station."

"He must have been at the diner watching for her. When he saw us put Devon in our car, he followed and waited. Then he followed us again." Henry still had a hard time believing it. It wasn't that unusual for a perp to lurk at a crime scene, but it was highly unusual for one to follow the cops from the crime scene to another location, let alone to a second. Then again, everything about this case was highly unusual.

"That takes a distressing level of patience."

"And skill. I saw nothing between the station and the house. If he was tailing us, he's damn good."

Buchanan's forehead was lined with concern. He looked toward the front of the house. "He could be out there now."

Henry had thought of that. "I've got a couple of unis out front keeping an eye on the crowd, looking for anyone suspicious. But we don't have much of a description beyond middle-aged white guy."

The captain snapped off his gloves. The sound cracked through the air like twin gunshots.

"Maybe it wasn't a tail. What about the phones?"

"It's a possibility, though I don't think so. But we'll have to be careful from now on."

"You're in touch with her, then?"

"Yes." Henry didn't need to explain that the next time he heard from Jordan, it would be from an anonymous disposable phone. He knew his partner too well to expect anything less.

"Good," Buchanan said. "Keep it to yourself. He's too good, and we're flying blind. He knows us, knows our tricks. The fewer who know where your partner is, the better. What's your next step?"

"More digging. We need to figure out what makes this guy tick. We'll check the hospitals, though I don't think he'll show up there. There isn't enough blood to indicate he was badly wounded, sadly, plus he's too smart for that. Maybe he'll make a mistake"—Henry huffed in frustration—"but we can't just wait for him to turn up again. We've got to figure out how to find him before he finds Jordan and Devon."

CHAPTER FIFTEEN

The normally quiet street was busy for such an early hour. Besides the four police cars, police van, and two unmarked cars with red lights set atop their roofs, much of the neighborhood had come out of their homes to see what all the fuss was about. Some were clustered in small groups on both sides of the street, whispering animatedly as they watched the cops go in and out of the house with various cases and red-striped evidence bags. No doubt they were coming up with all manner of theories as to what had happened in the predawn hours to elicit such a response.

A group of about twenty rubberneckers had gathered up the courage to come in closer. They were just beyond the police tape on the sidewalk directly in front of the house. A cop was posted on the other side of the tape, looking bored, there to ensure no nosy neighbors trespassed too closely. Billy had lurked at the edges for a while, just another gawker wondering what had happened, before insinuating himself into the crowd near the police barricade.

He moved cautiously among the onlookers, taking care to keep at least a foot between the person standing next to him and his tender left biceps, discreetly bandaged beneath his jacket.

The witch had winged him. It was little more than a graze, but it stung like hell. And it pissed Billy off more than it hurt. A few inches over, and the bullet would have hit a lung or worse.

After everything had gone to hell—he still wasn't sure how that cop had gotten the upper hand and shot him—he had sprinted to his car and raced back to his motel to care for his wounds. He'd dealt with the gunshot first, cleaning it out and staving off the bleeding before bandaging it. The broken nose had been a bitch to reset, but the bruising around his eyes wouldn't come in for at least another day, he knew from experience. Between the ice and the ibuprofen, it hadn't swelled too badly. Then he'd spent the next half hour picking tiny shards of glass out of his arms, which had taken the brunt of him crashing through the door, and cleaning those cuts. His arms looked like he'd taken a cheese grater to them, but with the jacket on, no one was the wiser.

All in all, most of his injuries were well hidden. Still, Billy pulled his ball cap down a little lower over his forehead, trying to keep his face at least partly shadowed. It wasn't uncommon for people to come back to the scenes of their crimes—policing 101—so he didn't want to draw any excess attention.

He knew it was a risk, but it wasn't as if he had any real choice. He had no idea what had happened to Maddie and the cop after he had fled. And the dog. That damn dog. Billy had had no indication there was a dog in that house before he'd entered. He'd become vaguely aware of the barking during the fight with the cop. Then she'd pulled her gun on him and he'd heard the monster charging down the stairs, and that had been it. Billy had expected to feel the dog's claws at his back and teeth piercing his skin before he made it to his car, but neither the weight nor the bite ever came.

Regardless, he'd had to come back to the house. It was his only link to wherever his daughter had gone. For all he knew, Maddie was now locked down in a bunker somewhere, five feet of steel and a hundred cops standing between them. If that was the case, he would never get to her now. And yet, somehow he didn't think it *was* the case.

If nothing else, God wouldn't have brought Billy so close to coming face-to-face with her, at last, only to take her away from him again. Hadn't Billy been a faithful servant all these years? Hadn't he done everything He had asked of him? He had tested Billy, certainly, measured him, challenged him, but Billy had met every test, overcome every obstacle to fulfill the Lord's will. Surely he had been deemed worthy by now? Surely he would finally be allowed to address his greatest mistake, his single failure in a lifetime of service?

No, the Lord would not do this to Billy. There was another answer, another path forward. All Billy had to do was look for the signs.

❖

Jordan sipped her coffee, watching the sun burn off the fog along the tree line. The cabin was situated halfway up the mountain, along an old mining road that got very little use anymore. There were fewer than a dozen homes on the whole mountain, and she knew many of the owners, mostly families who had owned their places for generations and who only used them now for vacations. There were a few who lived there year-round, an older couple who had built their lives on the mountain and a fiftyish former literature professor who had retired from the University of Pittsburgh to write her long-planned but never-completed first novel.

They, like Jordan's family and the rest of the mountain's residents, owned substantial parcels of land. Coal mining had been big in the area in the '30s and '40s, but by the mid-1950s, the seam had started to run dry. Then one of the mines had collapsed, killing eleven men and landing the mining company in a public relations nightmare. The company, which owned the whole mountain and much of the surrounding area, closed up shop a few years later and sold off the land at rock-bottom prices, eager to move out of the area. A handful of people, including Jordan's grandfather, had bought up large acreages, agreeing to keep the land as undeveloped as possible.

Jordan walked over to the kitchen to double-check her inventory. She'd unloaded the boxes she'd placed in the SUV the morning before. It was a lucky stroke she'd been planning to relocate up here—they had some clothes, towels, and bed linens. Unfortunately, Jordan had not packed any food, and the cupboards were pretty bare. A few cans of soup, a box of crackers that had most likely gone stale, some bottled water, and coffee were all she really had. She would need to get supplies.

She heard a door creak and Max's softly padding steps. He was at her side in an instant, nuzzling her hip. She bent down to give him a good-morning rub.

"Did you sleep well, boy?"

"He did," Devon said as she walked into the room. "Although, did you know your dog is a bed hog?"

Jordan laughed. "He's just a good snuggler, aren't you Max?" The dog puffed out his chest as if to dare Devon to dispute it. Jordan stood and turned to Devon. "Did you get any sleep?" Devon looked radiant in the soft glow of morning, her hair loose at her shoulders, her skin still flushed from sleep. Jordan's heart fluttered.

"A little. You?"

Jordan shrugged noncommittally, but Devon wasn't buying it.

"I told you to take the bed."

Jordan hummed a nonresponse, turning to pour Devon a cup of coffee. Devon *had* told her to take the bed, but she hadn't been about to put Devon in the front room, so close to the only entrance to the cabin. And she didn't dwell on the surge of chivalry that had made her insist when Devon had protested.

"We could always share," Devon suggested.

That thought put images in Jordan's head that had no business being there. "I intend to be between you and anything that might come through that door, so I'll keep the couch."

Devon let the matter drop.

"I'm going to need to run down to the general store, pick up some supplies," Jordan said, changing the subject. "Unless you're a big fan of stale saltines?"

Devon wrinkled her nose in a way Jordan found absolutely adorable. "Not particularly."

"Mel's opens early. I won't be gone long," Jordan said, moving toward the door.

"You're leaving me here?" The plaintiveness in Devon's tone pulled Jordan up short. "Sorry," Devon said quickly, her cheeks staining red. "I don't mean to sound so whiny."

Jordan's heart flipped at Devon's embarrassment, and the fear she imagined lay beneath it. She should have considered how Devon would react to the idea of being left alone after all that had happened.

"You'll be safe here," Jordan said, stepping closer. "He didn't follow us, and there's no way he could have found us." Jordan nearly added *already* but wisely held her tongue. No need to stoke Devon's fear any further.

"Even if he knows who I am, there's no way to connect this cabin with me. The deed isn't listed under my name or my mother's. It was my grandfather's place, and he left it in a trust to my mother. The deed is still in the trust's name. I'm planning on buying it from my mom soon." Jordan thought she saw a question, or maybe two, in Devon's face, but whatever it was went unasked. "Besides," Jordan added, "you'll have Max here to protect you." The dog sidled up to his master, as if confirming the vow.

"It's not that," Devon said, shaking her head. "I'm sure you're right. I just…"

Jordan said nothing, giving Devon space to find the words.

Devon exhaled heavily. "I just don't want to be alone, I guess. Not that Max isn't great company," she added a little nervously.

"I think the fewer people that see you, that know you're up here, the better."

"I get that. But who will know? Whoever is in the store, I suppose. How many people can that be at this hour?"

Devon wasn't wrong. The reality was, few people lived in the area, especially this time of year. It was a very small community, but that smallness was exactly what Jordan was worried about. "You'll stick out like a sore thumb."

"What, you mean you don't bring girls up here every weekend?" Devon teased, an obvious attempt to defuse some of the tension.

"I've never brought anyone here," she said quietly. "Except Henry and Max."

She watched Devon process the admission. Jordan wasn't sure why she had said it, but now it was out there, hanging in the air. What was it about this woman that made Jordan reveal herself so readily?

Devon seemed to be weighing her response, but in the end she let the moment gracefully slide. Jordan was relieved. Mostly.

"I understand your thinking, but I still want to come with you," Devon said, turning the conversation back to its beginning.

Jordan was torn. Her original reasons for wanting to leave Devon at the cabin remained, but in truth she didn't like the idea of letting Devon out of her sight.

As if sensing the direction of Jordan's thoughts, Devon said, "The safest place for me is by your side."

Jordan considered the possibilities, weighed the evidence, and relented. "All right, I guess Max gets the cabin to himself for a while." Devon smiled brightly, like a child who had just conned her way into staying up an hour past bedtime. Jordan nearly laughed. Max padded over to the fireplace, flopping down in front of it with a satisfied sigh. Jordan did laugh then. The dog was entirely too smart for his own good.

Twenty minutes later, they pulled up to Mel's General Store. The store was nestled at the base of the mountain, sitting at the crossing of the road up the mountain and the road that traveled past it. It reminded Devon of the old storefronts in *Little House on the Prairie*, complete with a hitching post in the front for tying up horses.

On the way there, Jordan had told Devon a little about the region's history and residents. They were deep within Somerset County, a sparsely populated area in the midst of the Appalachian Mountains. In the summer, this part of western Pennsylvania was full of hikers, campers, and other vacationers looking to enjoy nature. But this time of year, the region was left mostly to the locals. Mel's made most of its money from the summer tourists, Jordan explained, but it was also the only real store for nearly thirty miles, and so it was the lifeblood of the mountain's permanent residents. Internet access was nonexistent up on the mountain, which meant no online shopping, and so if you needed something—anything—you went to Mel's. If Mel's didn't have it, they could get it.

A bell chimed as they entered, announcing their arrival. Devon found that the inside of the store matched the outside's throwback charm. Items for sale were displayed on wooden crates and large tables. The walls were lined with antique signs ranging from gas station logos to soda ads to a hand-painted one that read: *Mel's has everything. If you can't find it here, you don't need it.*

Devon half expected everything to be caked in a layer of dust, but she quickly realized that fear was unfounded. Although items— everything from camping equipment and automotive supplies to clothing and groceries—were packed into every available nook and cranny, the store was immaculate and well ordered. Mel's really did seem to have everything.

"Well, Jordan Salinger, as I live and breathe," a deep feminine voice purred from the back of the store.

Devon searched out the face behind the voice. A striking woman with long fiery hair glided up one of the aisles toward the counter. She was perhaps in her early thirties, with porcelain skin and emerald eyes so bright they practically glowed.

"Hi, Mel."

"You haven't been by lately," Mel said, coming to rest directly in front of Jordan. Devon noticed the way the redhead fit herself to Jordan's body, not quite touching but every curve aligning so close, Devon thought, that Jordan must have felt the heat radiating from the woman's skin. Mel reached out and lightly stroked Jordan's forearm. Devon cringed inwardly. "I missed you."

"Been busy," Jordan said with a smile. She stepped back slightly, so subtly that most might have thought it was an unconscious move. But Devon knew that nearly everything Jordan did was purposeful. Apparently, Mel knew that, too, her sexy grin faltering a little. Jordan gave Mel's arm a quick squeeze. "It's good to see you, too, Mel."

That appeared to placate Mel, her grin returning to its earlier strength. "What can I do you for?" Devon had a sudden and unfamiliar urge to slap the woman.

"We need to stock up," Jordan said, ignoring the blatant come-on.

"We?" For the first time, Mel noticed there was someone else in the store besides Jordan. Devon smiled at her and gave a goofy little wave, cursing herself as she did so. Mel did not smile back, and Devon found herself feeling even more like a child, one who had just been targeted by the playground bully.

"Yeah," Jordan said, turning toward Devon in a clear invitation. Devon came up beside her. "Melanie Davies, meet Sabrina West. Sabrina, this is Mel."

Although they had come up with her name and backstory before leaving the cabin, Devon still felt weird hearing Jordan call her Sabrina. Given how many names she had gone by over the years, the irony was not lost on her. Although she had been Devon James less than a year, she found she had grown attached to the identity, especially over the previous twenty-four hours.

Devon offered her hand to Mel. "It's nice to meet you."

After a few beats, Mel accepted the handshake. "Likewise," Mel drawled, "Sabrina."

"Sabrina's an old friend of mine from college," Jordan said, beginning to fill in the story. She and Devon had agreed to keep things as simple as possible. Not too many details, just enough to circumvent any questions.

"Funny," Mel said, folding her arms across her chest. "You've never mentioned her."

The challenge was clear. Devon wondered if Mel would treat anyone Jordan brought here this way, or if it was something about her in particular. She couldn't help but hope it was the latter.

"Funny," Devon shot back sweetly, knowing Jordan was watching their interplay with interest, "Jordan never mentioned you, either."

"Yes, well"—Jordan coughed—"Mel, Sabrina needed to get away for a while, and I thought the cabin would be a good place for her to do that."

"Oh?" Mel asked blandly.

Jordan lowered her voice, as if imparting a confidence. "Bad breakup."

Mel's focus shifted back to Devon and she played her part, lowering her eyes slightly and nodding. She had never thought herself much of an actress, though she supposed she had been acting most of her life, taking on roles she couldn't leave on the set at the end of a day's filming. For nearly a decade, her life had depended on her ability to act.

Mel seemed to relax a little, apparently believing the performance. "Oh, that's too bad, honey," she said, her voice sickeningly sympathetic. "Men can be such bastards."

"So can women." She lifted her chin defiantly, making the double meaning of her words as clear as possible.

Mel blinked slowly. Then she did something unexpected. She smiled.

"Ain't that the truth," Mel said with a laugh. Devon figured their pissing match wasn't over, but they had reached a détente of sorts. Jordan seemed to breathe a little easier now.

"So, what do you need?" Mel asked.

"A little bit of everything, I'm afraid," Jordan said.

"My specialty," Mel said with a wink meant as much for Devon as for Jordan. No, their pissing match was definitely not over.

Over the next few minutes, the three women loaded up several boxes with foodstuffs, plus a large bag of kibble for Max. Devon noticed Mel listing their items in a large, worn spiral notebook before they carried the boxes and dog food out to the car. They returned inside, and Jordan walked over to the camping section. Devon chose to take the opportunity to see if she could find some underwear. Jordan had packed a few items from her own closet for Devon, and they were good on the basics—except for undergarments. She didn't relish the idea of wearing Jordan's underwear. It just seemed too…personal.

Mel came up beside Devon. "Didn't pack much, did you?" Devon hadn't realized the woman had been watching her.

"Um, no. The trip was a little…unexpected."

"It's good for her," Mel mused. Devon looked at Mel, found her watching Jordan from across the store. She turned back to Devon. "To have company. Friends."

Devon was taken aback by the unexpected revelation, and the tenderness of Mel's words. It was clear Mel was interested in Jordan, that perhaps they even shared a romantic past, however fleeting. But now it was also clear to Devon that the redhead had real feelings for Jordan, feelings that—no matter how inconvenient—Devon shared.

"She's been alone for a long time, hasn't she?"

Mel nodded knowingly, and appreciatively. "I've known Jordan for years, since we were both kids. Her parents used to bring her up here in the summer, back when my dad was running this place. She was very close to her father and mother both, but especially her dad. After he died, I think Jordan walled off a part of herself."

It was a pain Devon understood all too well, not for Billy, certainly, but for her mother. It was a loss Devon never spoke of, that she had buried down deep.

"Then, after the shooting, she changed. She shut down, locked everyone out. Even those she let in, Henry and her mom, could never really touch her. Then Caroline left, though she was gone long before the shooting, if you ask me."

Devon nodded as if she knew the details. She desperately wanted to know what had happened to Jordan that day, to understand the terrible events that had scarred her so deeply. She wanted to understand about Caroline, about the disdain that dripped from Mel's voice when she said that name. But Mel said no more about any of it, and Devon knew she could not ask without giving herself away. So she asked the one question she could.

"And you?"

"And me, what?" Mel asked. Devon did not respond, knowing full well that Mel had understood her question.

"Ah, yes, and me." Mel sighed wistfully, the longing plain on her face. She opened her mouth to say more but then shut down, seemingly thinking better of giving herself away completely, though Devon thought she already knew.

She picked up a pair of white cotton briefs and tried to hand them to Devon. She was redirecting the conversation. Devon let her.

"You have anything a little less grandmotherly?" Devon asked, eyeing the panties suspiciously.

Mel laughed. "Afraid not. I can order something for you, but it will take a few days, maybe longer." She held the underwear out to Devon once more. "Guess you'll just have to make do with these. Not like anyone besides you will be seeing them, right?"

Devon did not take the panties. "That's okay, I'll just go without," she said a bit saucily, leaving Mel's question hanging unanswered as she walked over to Jordan. She threw an extra sway into her hips for good measure.

Devon held no illusions about her relationship with Jordan, but Mel certainly didn't need to know that. Despite their awkward introduction and the unanticipated jealousy the woman inspired, Devon found she liked Mel. But that didn't mean she was about to back down where Jordan was concerned, even if she had absolutely no claim on her heart.

Mel followed Devon to where Jordan was weighing the merits of folding knives. The blades brought the real world crashing back down.

"What's your preference?" Jordan asked Mel. Mel pointed to the one in Jordan's left hand and Jordan returned the one in her right hand, picking up a second knife like the one Mel had chosen.

"I need one more thing," Jordan said. They walked up to the counter. "One of those disposable cell phones you have in the back. And it needs to have Bluetooth."

Mel eyed her questioningly. "What's going on?"

"Nothing. My cell's been a little on the fritz," Jordan covered smoothly. "Want to have a backup just in case. Don't want to get stranded on the road somewhere with no phone."

Mel didn't appear to be convinced, but she nodded and retreated to the back room. She returned with a cheap disposable phone in a clear plastic case.

"Number's inside the packaging," she said, adding the phone and knives to her notepad. "Probably not a bad idea with the storm coming in."

"What storm?" Jordan asked.

"Arctic front, probably will be here forty-eight hours from now. They're still not sure about the totals, but they're saying it could be as much as a foot, probably more up the mountain."

Jordan groaned. "I better get that woodpile stacked, then."

"Hmm," Mel hummed, grinning like the Cheshire cat. Devon knew exactly what was running through the woman's mind, since it was the same delicious image that had popped into her own head. Devon scowled, which only made Mel grin further. "Want me to put this all on your account?"

"Do you mind?" Jordan asked.

"For you, never," Mel purred. She pulled out another book from beneath the counter, this one a leather-bound ledger that looked like it dated back to the '50s. Mel flipped pages until she found one with Jordan's information at the top. Then she added the total to the bottom and dated it.

"When are you going to get a computer like everyone else?" Jordan joked.

"Never," Mel exclaimed, as if the very thought was an affront. "It was good enough for Dad, and it's good enough for me."

"You're just like Henry," Jordan said with a laugh, "scared of anything with a microchip."

Devon watched the easy interplay between the two women and thought they really would make a good couple. That did not sit well with her.

Mel slapped Jordan's arm playfully. "I am nothing like Henry. I have an iPhone, an iPod, and a laptop at home. They just have no place in this store. There's something to be said for tradition, you know."

"That there is," Jordan said. She turned to Devon. "I'm sorry I didn't ask. Did you see anything else you needed?"

"Not a thing," Devon said sweetly, resting her hand on Jordan's shoulder. "Better to go without."

Jordan looked at her questioningly, but a squeeze of Devon's hand silenced her. Devon saw Mel's smile fade as she was reminded of their earlier conversation, just as Devon had intended. Devon savored the tiny victory.

"It was nice to meet you," Devon said.

This time Mel offered a handshake and Devon accepted, although Mel squeezed her hand a little harder than necessary. "Likewise. I hope you have a pleasant stay."

"I'm sure it will be," Devon said, and she could practically feel the daggers Mel threw at her back as they exited the store.

Chapter Sixteen

Jordan's first order of business upon reaching the cabin was unloading the car and feeding Max who, although normally something of a snob about his food, wolfed down his bowl of kibble with gusto. Her second order of business was to dismantle her cell phone, ensuring it could not be traced, and to try out the new disposable phone. After freeing the phone from its plastic packaging with her new knife, she went outside to make the call. It wasn't that she didn't want Devon to hear the conversation, but cell reception inside the house was spotty at best. She dialed the main station number instead of Henry's cell.

"Lieutenant Wayne," Henry answered once the call had been transferred.

"It's me," Jordan said simply.

"Jordan?" Henry asked, his voice dropping. "Are you guys okay?"

The relief she felt at hearing her partner's voice surprised Jordan. "We're fine. Getting settled."

"Are you where I think you are?" Henry asked.

"Yes. I took the long way." Henry laughed. Having gotten lost himself a time or two on the maze of roads leading to the mountain, Jordan knew he understood what she meant.

"So you weren't followed."

"No, we weren't." There was no way to be one hundred percent certain of that, but Jordan was positive nonetheless. "Do you have me on the caller ID?"

She heard the phone rustling and knew Henry was checking for the number of her new cell phone on the phone's display on his desk. "Last four are zero five two four?"

"You got it."

"I asked…get me…phone…should have…today—"

"Henry, hang on, you're breaking up." Jordan stepped farther away from the cabin, toward the woodpile and chopping block where she would be spending some quality time once she ended the call. The woodpile was definitely too low, with only a couple of days' worth of fuel. "Say again?"

"Is this better?" Henry asked.

"Yes, much. Sorry. You know how the cell service is here. Probably will get worse the next few days. Word is there's a snowstorm heading this way."

"I heard. I keep telling you landlines are better," he said in his fatherly tone.

"This coming from the man who doesn't know how to check his voice mail," Jordan shot back.

"That's not true. It's the damn ringer I can't seem to get to work right. Stupid phone always ends up on silent or vibrate." Jordan laughed. Henry turned the conversation. "How are you holding up? Really."

"I'm fine. A little beat-up and sore, but fine."

"I don't just mean physically."

Jordan sighed. "I'm fine. Honestly. I want to get this guy."

"And we will, Jordan. You have to know that."

"I do." And she really did. One way or another, they would get him. She just prayed no one else got hurt in the meantime. "You come up with anything yet?"

It was Henry's turn to sigh. "MCU is still working on it, but so far, no prints. There is some blood, and I'm presuming it's all his?"

"It is," Jordan said. "I thought I hit him."

"You definitely did, though the splatter makes me think you probably just nicked him, I'm afraid."

Jordan swore under her breath. She'd been hoping she'd hit something more vital.

"You did good, Jordan. Once we get the DNA back, we'll run it through CODIS, hopefully match it up to some of his other handiwork."

"That's great for trial, but won't do anything to help us catch him," Jordan said, her voice rising in frustration.

"It's what we do," Henry said. She knew he wasn't trying to placate her. "I've confirmed what Devon told us yesterday. The DeKalb investigation was a real hack job. You wouldn't believe it, Jordan. DeKalb focused on Devon from the beginning and never looked into Billy. They didn't even really investigate."

"Damn." Jordan was frustrated once more by the incompetence of the people who should have protected Devon all those years ago.

"There's more," Henry said. Jordan heard him shuffling the phone again. When he spoke again, his voice was hushed. "There's a warrant out for her."

Jordan said nothing. She didn't need to. They both knew where they stood on the matter.

Henry's voice returned to its regular volume. "It would really help if we knew where Devon has been for the last ten years. *Who* she's been. There's a reason she kept moving all those years."

"He's been on her trail." But Jordan knew there was more, things Devon hadn't told her. "I'll talk to her about it today. E-mail me what you've found so far. I need to get inside this bastard's head."

"Will do."

"And Henry? Be careful, okay? If he found us last night because he followed us to the house, he could follow you again."

"I know, and I will. Keep your head down."

"Always."

❖

At some point during Henry's conversation, Lawson had returned from the store with his new cell phone.

"It's ready to go," Lawson said, handing Henry the unwrapped phone and a slip of paper. "That's the phone number."

"I hate these things," Henry grumbled, looking it over. "Bad enough I have to carry one, but now I have two."

Henry tried to work his way through the phone's menu, but it was maddeningly different than his regular phone. "How do I add a contact?"

Lawson took the phone back. "Give it to me. What do you want to program in?"

Henry handed him his notepad with Jordan's new number. "Put it in and forget it, understand?"

Lawson nodded, hit a few keys, then handed the phone back to Henry and showed him how to access the phone's contacts. Henry noticed Lawson had programmed the number under Holden Caulfield instead of using Jordan's name. Henry grinned at the reference before sticking the phone in his breast pocket.

He picked up the stack of paper on his desk, including his notes. "Can you get these to Jordan? Do that techy thing you do to get them into an e-mail?"

Lawson chuckled. "You mean PDF them? Yeah, I can do that."

"Did we get anything from Roscoe yet?" Henry asked. Lawson shook his head. "For Pete's sake!" Henry picked up his desk phone and began dialing.

"Who are you calling?" Lawson asked.

"A friend who maybe can put some pressure on that sheriff's office."

"Coleman," a gruff voice answered on the first ring.

"Hey Carl, it's Henry."

"I thought you were dodging me," Coleman said, his voice instantly lightening.

"I wasn't."

"So you've got it then?" Henry could hear the giddiness in Coleman's voice. It wasn't something Henry heard often, just when Henry lost a bet.

"My signed, near-mint, 1967 copy of *Whisper Not* by the one and only Ella Fitzgerald? Yes, I have it."

"You mean *my* signed, near-mint, 1967 copy of *Whisper Not* by the one and only Ella Fitzgerald, don't you?"

"When I give it to you, yes," Henry said grudgingly. "But for now, she's still mine."

"I told you not to take the bet," Coleman said with a laugh. "So are you just calling to make arrangements, or do you have something else to discuss?"

"Something else. We've got a murder investigation going on here, Carl, and I need your help." He rarely asked for help and knew that would get Carl's attention.

"How can I help you?" Coleman said, suddenly all business.

Henry filled in the details of the case, Devon's history, and everything they had learned.

"Is your partner okay?" was the first thing Coleman asked when Henry was finished.

Henry appreciated that. "She's fine. Banged up, but fine. Listen, I need that personnel file from Roscoe and the case file from the fire investigation."

"I'll see what I can do," Coleman said. He went silent for a moment, then asked, "Do you need a parachute?"

Henry had known FBI Special Agent Carl Coleman for nearly forty years. They had met near the end of Vietnam, both green seventeen-year-olds in a foreign land trying to not get their heads blown off. Their CO, a grizzled veteran at the ripe old age of twenty-two, used to assess the risk level of missions based on what a person needed to survive a fall. *We need a cushion* meant they were in good shape, while *we need a pool* meant they were at risk. *We need a parachute* meant they were in way too deep.

"Almost," Henry said, "and not just for me."

"I'll be in touch."

❖

Devon flipped open the knife and closed it again. It was made to be opened one handed, with a slide of a button and a flip of the wrist. It swiveled smoothly, with little effort. She could appreciate that even as the feel of it in her hand nauseated her.

She didn't like knives. She wasn't comfortable with weapons of any sort, but she *really* didn't like knives. They reminded her of everything evil in her life.

She understood Jordan's reason for giving it to her. Devon had suspected it was meant for her back at Mel's when Jordan had purchased two of the blades. Still, Devon had hoped she'd been wrong.

"It won't come to this, but just in case," Jordan had said, handing her the knife. "It isn't much, but you need to have some way to defend yourself if..."

She hadn't needed to finish the sentence. *If he finds us and gets past Max and me.*

The thought filled Devon with an ice-cold dread. Jordan's unspoken nightmare scenario would only happen if she and Max were dead. It was enough to turn her stomach inside out.

Devon shook off the images filling her brain and set the knife on the kitchen table. She needed some air, the cabin feeling suddenly, violently claustrophobic.

It was another beautiful day. The crystalline blue sky was dotted with puffy white clouds, and a light breeze played through her hair. It was still relatively warm for Pennsylvania in late November, though the temperature had dropped some at this higher elevation and there was a definite bite to the air, the first tendrils of the oncoming cold front.

It was quiet up on the mountain, clear and clean and peaceful, the only sounds coming from the animals rustling through the trees beyond the home and the rhythmic *thwack* coming from around the side of the cabin.

Devon rounded the corner and halted midstep, momentarily dazed. Jordan brought down the ax in a graceful, powerful arc, splitting the log set on the tree stump cleanly in two. She efficiently placed another log upon the stump and repeated the process. Devon didn't have much experience with chopping wood, but she didn't have to be a logger to understand that splitting a log with a single stroke was no easy task.

Jordan had come out here only a half hour earlier to work on building up their woodpile, while Devon had stayed inside to take care of their morning dishes. She had figured it was the least she could do and had thought she'd have plenty of time to finish up and come out to help Jordan before she had gotten too far into her task. But by the large rack of firewood and the dwindling pile of logs, Devon could see she had underestimated Jordan's prowess with an ax.

That, however, was not what stopped Devon in her tracks. Jordan had stripped down to a dark tank top, and the thin material clung to her taut stomach as she raised the ax and brought it back down. Sweat gleamed off her bare arms and chest, the perspiration highlighting the fullness of her biceps, the curve of her muscular shoulders, and the swell of her breasts.

Max sat off to one side, his tongue lolling out of his mouth as if he were the one laboring instead of Jordan. He cast a glance back at Devon, confirming her presence, and then turned back to his job managing his master's work.

Devon's heart quivered in her chest, her mouth going inexplicably dry. Her eyes trailed down to Jordan's firm legs, noting how they strained against her jeans. Jordan turned to grab another log, treating Devon to the sight of her shapely behind encased in denim. Devon swallowed thickly. Although her mouth was dry, another part of her was anything but. She unconsciously clenched her thighs, jolts of pleasure racing to every corner of her body. Her nipples tightened to aching points.

She had not noticed another woman—not like this—in years, perhaps ever. She felt like a voyeur watching Jordan this way, but she could not turn away. Her gaze was transfixed by the magnificent sight before her.

She is utterly gorgeous. And I want her.

Once the words were spoken in her head, she could not dismiss them. Her desire for Jordan was as real as anything she had ever felt in her life. She didn't just care for Jordan, she needed her. Hungered for her. That realization was as surprising and wondrous to Devon as it was unwelcome and frightening.

Devon had never let herself feel this way about anyone. She'd had flings, and friendships of sorts. She had even let herself care for a few people here and there in a guarded way. But Devon understood all too well what would happen if she let herself get too close. They would be taken away, ripped from her life like a page being torn from a book, never to be seen or held or known to her again. Even though she withheld a part of her heart, the loss was always terrible, and she knew, deep down in the place she didn't speak of, if she ever truly opened herself up to a person, it would be her undoing.

This thing she was feeling now for Jordan gave her hope but also terrified her, for it represented the promise of both actual happiness and of the ultimate loss. If she could open herself to Jordan, let her in completely, then she might finally—someday—be loved in return. But loving meant losing, and Devon knew that to lose someone she loved would destroy her.

Wait...love?

It was impossible. It was too soon. It was impractical and complicated and inopportune and illogical and potentially disastrous. And yet she could feel the stirrings of it inside her, cinders searching for the slightest gust of wind to spark them into flame.

She did not love Jordan Salinger. But for the first time, she thought she *could* love. And that scared her far more than Billy ever could.

Devon roused herself from her turmoil and slid her mask into place, the one of friendly passivity that she had worn for so many years, and walked over to Jordan and Max.

"Can I help?" Devon asked, trying to ignore the sexy smudge across Jordan's forehead after she swiped at her brow with her forearm.

"No, I think we're good," Jordan said. She rested the ax against the stump, surveying the woodpile. "We've got enough for at least a week now, maybe more. That ought to be enough."

"I'm sorry I didn't get out here earlier to help you. This is hardly physical therapy for bruised ribs."

"Are you kidding?" Jordan asked, flashing a toothy smile. "I absolutely hate doing dishes. So you saved me from that."

Devon laughed. "I think I got the better end of that deal."

"It's a deal I would happily make again." Jordan returned the ax to the shed at the back of the house, stretching as she walked back.

Devon felt the tingle in her body return at the sight of Jordan's shirt slipping up a few inches above her jeans and the tantalizing strip of golden skin it revealed. A twinge passed across Jordan's face, shifting Devon's focus. "What's wrong?"

Jordan reached her arm across her chest, attempting to stretch out her shoulder. "Nothing. A little stiff."

"Come inside and I'll rub it out for you."

Jordan looked at her a little funny. "It's okay."

"I insist," Devon said, taking Jordan's hand and leading her into the cabin. Max loped behind them and made a beeline for his water bowl once inside. Devon deposited Jordan into one of the kitchen chairs and stepped behind her, beginning to rub her tight neck. The groan that escaped told Devon all she needed to know about whether Jordan liked what she was doing.

She worked both shoulders gently at first, increasing the firmness of her massage as Jordan's muscles loosened up. She tried to ignore how Jordan's skin felt beneath her fingers, or the warmth spreading through her with each moan that passed Jordan's lips.

She slipped the straps of Jordan's tank top and bra over her shoulders to give her better access. That's when she noticed the scar just below her left clavicle. It was actually two scars, one a line that was vaguely crescent shaped, which bisected a puckered circle Devon understood instantly had been caused by a bullet. Her hands stilled. She felt Jordan tense, as if waiting for Devon to pull away. Sadness flooded Devon, for the wound and for whoever had made Jordan feel like it was something to be ashamed of. Devon began her massage once more.

Silence siphoned off all the oxygen in the cabin. After several long minutes, Jordan spoke.

"Last year a woman was shot to death. Wife, mother of three. Henry and I were assigned to the case. We suspected her husband, but we didn't have much more than circumstantial evidence. No witnesses and no gun. We questioned him for hours but eventually had to let him go."

Jordan's voice was low and steady, but Devon could hear the strain of telling it lacing her tale. She lightened her touch, more soothing now than therapeutic.

"Then we caught a break. A drug dealer looking for a plea on another crime said the husband had bought a gun from him a few days before the murder, and then the guy had wanted to sell it back to him a few days later. The dealer still had the gun. It was the right caliber, and there was a single print on the barrel matching the husband. We got our warrant and went to arrest him."

Jordan fell silent, as if working up the courage to tell the rest. Devon continued her rhythmic kneading, easing the pain she could reach.

"Henry took the front and I went around back in case the guy tried to run. He saw me coming and started firing as I approached. Henry came running but we both got pinned down. And then we heard the kids screaming from inside the house."

Devon had to work to keep her fingers from digging too deeply into Jordan's flesh. She could only imagine the terror of those moments for Jordan and her partner, and also for the children.

"They were supposed to be in school, but he'd kept them home that day. The two youngest were crying, but the oldest one—he was only five—he kept yelling *Daddy, stop shooting!* We didn't fire back once we realized the kids were in there. Henry called for backup. Every time we tried to leave or talk to him, he started shooting again. Turned out he'd armed up since we'd released him, had gotten his hands on another handgun and an assault rifle, and he had plenty of ammo."

Jordan's muscles tensed, signaling what Devon knew had to be coming next. She kept her hands moving, supporting Jordan the only way she could.

"SWAT arrived. They ordered the husband out of the house, which shifted his attention away from us to what was going on out front. He had shut all the blinds and SWAT couldn't see in, but Henry and I were free to move. The negotiator arrived. He tried calling out over the bullhorn, but the husband wouldn't respond. Then they tried the phone, but the husband wouldn't pick up. It was just too damn quiet. Something wasn't right, and we all knew it. The SWAT team leader gave the order to breach. We had no time. I managed to get the back door to the kitchen open and Henry and I snuck inside."

Devon realized she was holding her breath and forced herself to relax. She stroked Jordan's arms and back, lending the only comfort she could.

"We finally were able to see into the living room. He wasn't there, but the front door was booby trapped with explosives. Henry tried to warn the SWAT team over the radio, but I was already moving. I rounded the corner and went down the hall—I found him with the kids in a bedroom. He had his arm wrapped around the oldest boy, the gun pressed to his back. The little ones cowered in the corner. I ordered him to drop the gun and then all hell broke loose. It sounded like thunder, and the whole house shook. I heard his gun go off, saw the boy falling to the floor. I managed to get off a shot before I felt his next bullet slamming into me. He was dead before he hit the ground. I passed out."

Jordan hung her head, seemingly finished, seemingly in shame. Devon wasn't about to let that be the end. She rounded the chair, kneeling in front of Jordan and taking her hand.

"You did nothing wrong. You saved two children."

"Two SWAT officers died in the explosion," Jordan said. "The boy—his name was Jacob—died instantly, according to the ME. But he didn't. I saw his face. I watched him as he fell. He was looking at me, looking to me to save him. But I didn't."

"You couldn't have," Devon said, the need to free Jordan from her guilt overwhelming. She lifted Jordan's chin, demanding she look at her. "If it wasn't for you, all three of those kids would have died. The guns, the explosives? I'm no detective but even I can see he'd been planning for them all to die in some asinine blaze of glory. You saved two children."

Jordan stared into Devon's depths, as if searching for some kernel of truth, some tiny scrap of salvation to cling to.

"You *saved* two children," she said again.

"Not everyone sees it that way," Jordan said.

"Well, anyone who thinks you're anything other than a hero has their head up their ass," Devon snapped. "And that includes you."

Jordan barked out a small laugh, still looking for something in Devon's face. Perhaps it was permission, Devon thought, to believe what she was saying. Perhaps Jordan was seeking leave to forgive herself. If it had been within Devon's power to give, she would have done so without reservation.

Eventually, Jordan breathed deeply and nodded almost imperceptibly. It was not acceptance, but it was not rejection, either. Devon thought that whatever it was, it was enough for now.

CHAPTER SEVENTEEN

Devon stood, giving Jordan space. She watched as Jordan rolled both shoulders, and then rotated her left arm experimentally.

"Hey, that's really good," Jordan said, standing. "Were you a massage therapist in a past life or something?"

Devon shrugged. "One of them." She saw understanding reach Jordan's face.

"You know, it would really help if you could tell us where you've been since leaving Illinois," Jordan said cautiously. "*Who* you've been. Henry's working on tracking Billy's movements. If we know where you've been—"

"Then you might find where he's been, too," Devon finished Jordan's thought. She nodded in confirmation.

Devon was once again caught between the urge to tell Jordan everything and the instinct to run. She wanted so desperately to tell her the truth, but she feared Jordan would reject her if she knew, would walk away from her and never look back. She feared it more now than she had even twenty-four hours ago, because now she knew the loss would be so much greater than any she had experienced before. Devon wasn't sure she could survive Jordan turning away from her. She should walk away now, before it was too late.

She sank slowly into a chair, trapped within her indecision. A heartbeat later, Jordan sat down, too, scooting her chair in close. Their knees touched, and she reached for Devon's hand.

"I think the reason you've run so many times is that you were afraid Billy had found you," she said gently. "And I think you were right. I think, at least once or twice, Billy was only a few steps behind you."

Devon nodded slowly, so Jordan pressed on.

"If we can track his movements over the years, discover where he's been and perhaps even what he's done, it might give us some insight into how to find him. At the very least, it will ensure that when we do catch him, we can put him away forever."

"You think he's killed others," Devon said, more statement than question.

"Yes," Jordan answered. "And I think you do, too."

Jordan's simple statement, made without judgment, opened a door inside Devon that she had kept closed for ten years. The question was not whether she had the courage to walk through it—she wasn't ready for that yet—but whether she was brave enough to push it open a little farther. She felt the safety and strength of Jordan's hand holding her own.

"Do you have something I can write with?" Devon asked. Jordan brought back a notepad and pen.

"When I left DeKalb, I had no idea where I was going," Devon said as she began to write. "I took one bus and then another, begging strangers for money to buy my next bus ticket and a little food. I finally ended up in Colorado, and I became Emily Pressman."

Devon kept writing as she spoke. The names of who she had been were burned into her memory, like old friends she had lost touch with along the way but never forgotten. She wrote them down, along with cities, dates, addresses, occupations, and even people with whom she had associated—people Billy might have targeted.

"I found a motel, one of those roadside places that doesn't offer much beyond a bed and a roof over your head, but the rates were cheap and the sheets were clean. I kept waiting for Billy to show up, to come bursting through the door to finally kill me. But he never came. After about a week I had run out of money, but the owner, Mrs. Brindle—the woman who taught me to play cards—took pity on me and let me stay on. One afternoon a couple weeks later, she asked me if I had anywhere else to be. I didn't know what to say. So she handed me a mop and a broom and said I must be bored sitting in my room all day, so I might as well make myself useful."

Devon paused, thinking about Mrs. Brindle, the lady who had given her so much. She could still picture her as if she was standing right in front of her. The carefully coiffed gray hair pulled into a perfect bun each morning, the reading glasses permanently perched on her delicate nose, and those awful floral-print dresses. The more lace and ruffles, the better.

"Nearly two years went by—I'd become something of a permanent resident of the hotel—and I started thinking about trying to get an apartment, but I couldn't bear the thought of leaving Mrs. Brindle alone. Then one day when I was at the market, I had this... feeling. Like someone watching me. I didn't see anything out of the ordinary, and I assumed my mind was playing tricks on me. A few days later, I felt it again out in front of the library."

Devon kept writing but stopped speaking, summoning the courage to tell the next terrible part. The gentle touch of Jordan's hand on her knee gave her the courage she needed.

"I told Mrs. Brindle I had to leave. She took me seriously. I had never told her about Illinois, but she had guessed I was hiding from something. She asked if the thing I was running from had found me, and I told her I thought it might have, and I didn't want anyone to get hurt. She told me I needed to deal with the past or I'd be running forever."

Devon looked up at Jordan, needing her to understand. "She was so kind to me, and I trusted her. She asked me to wait a day, to let her bring the sheriff out. Mrs. Brindle said he would help me, that she would be right there beside me, holding my hand through it all. So I agreed."

"Of course you did," Jordan said, once again without judgment. "You had to trust someone."

"Yes, well, on her way back from the sheriff's office, Mrs. Brindle was killed." The pain of it was still fresh, an open wound that refused to scab over. "If I'd left when I said I would, she'd still be alive."

"What happened?" Jordan asked softly, instantly dousing some of Devon's fire. She needed to get through this. She could finish beating herself up later.

"A deer jumped out and she ran off the road, supposedly. Mrs. Brindle wasn't the best driver, but there were a lot of deer in that area, so she was always extra careful on the highway. Plus, it was the middle of the day, not the usual time for deer to wander out into the road."

Devon half expected Jordan to say, "Accidents happen," or something like it. Except she didn't say it. She didn't say anything. She just waited for Devon to continue, seeming to understand there was more to come.

"The sheriff came by to tell me Mrs. Brindle was dead. That she had no living relatives, but he'd make sure her funeral was paid for if I wanted to make the arrangements. He said Mrs. Brindle had been very insistent that he come by and speak with me. I was so upset about Mrs. Brindle, and I felt so guilty. I was scared, but I needed to honor her request and tell the sheriff everything. That's when I saw it."

"You found a wheat penny," Jordan said without missing a beat.

"Right there on the counter. Mrs. Brindle was meticulous. Everything was always in its proper place. That penny was left where I would find it, and I knew what it meant."

"He had found you."

Devon nodded. "I don't know how he did it, or why. Maybe he cut her brake lines or something. But I knew he was responsible, and that if I didn't run, I would be next. So I made up some story for the sheriff about why I'd needed to talk to him, then asked him to give me a ride into town. I stopped by my room to get my purse and that was it. As soon as he dropped me off, I made my way to the bus terminal and caught the first one out of town." Devon braced herself but saw nothing but compassion on Jordan's face.

"You did nothing wrong," Jordan said, echoing Devon's own, earlier words. "It wasn't your fault."

"I brought Billy there." Devon couldn't help the tears that began to form. "If I hadn't been there, he wouldn't have been, either."

Jordan slipped off her chair and pulled Devon into her arms. "You did nothing wrong," Jordan said again, whispering into Devon's ear. Devon clung to her, trying to absorb the comfort she offered, trying to let herself believe that Mrs. Brindle's death was not her fault.

"You know, it seems to me we both need to forgive ourselves," Jordan said, pulling back slightly. She cupped Devon's cheek, as if willing her to accept the words.

"Easier said than done," Devon responded, a mirthless laugh bubbling up from her chest.

"My father used to say that guilt is like being hunted by a wolf. The best way to escape it is to never have crossed its path. But sometimes, you don't have that option. So when it comes for you, you have to kill it before it kills you," Jordan said. "How about we both agree it's time to kill our guilt, once and for all?"

Still wrapped in Jordan's embrace, with Jordan's hand pressed against her cheek, Devon wanted so much to agree. She wanted to believe that maybe, just maybe, it was possible to escape her guilt. But she also knew there was much more left to tell, terrible things so much worse than this. Things Jordan could never forgive.

"Agreed," Devon lied.

CHAPTER EIGHTEEN

Jordan scanned the files Henry had sent, jotting notes in a small notepad on the table next to her laptop. Devon hummed a wordless tune as she made dinner. Jordan had to smile when she recognized *The Sound of Music*.

She angled her computer screen out of Devon's eyeline. Jordan wasn't trying to hide anything, but she also didn't want to confront Devon with the horrors of the crime scene unnecessarily. Seeing it once was more than enough. Henry's preliminary notes from the diner were unsurprisingly thorough, complete with his impressions of the crime scene and killer. Although she appreciated the insight, she tried to separate his perspective from the facts.

Who am I kidding? I'm a long way past biased.

The photos were especially helpful. She started with the ones from the kitchen. Chuck's death had been messy but efficient. The pattern of the blood spatter on the floor was unobstructed, confirming that Chuck had been killed from behind. The volume of blood combined with the ME's preliminary autopsy results suggested Chuck had died quickly. The depth and precision of the cut across his neck indicated the killer had known exactly what he was doing. There was no hesitation, no second-guessing. It certainly wasn't the killer's first time.

If she, Henry, and Lawson were going to catch Billy, they needed to understand him. They needed to understand who he was, how he was, and why he was the way he was. Knowing these things would help them predict what Billy would do next—and how to stop him. They needed to profile him. And Jordan was very good at profiling.

First step, the crime scene. Jordan called up the ME's preliminary report on Sally. Unlike Chuck, Sally had been killed from the front, with a single stab wound to the heart. Jordan considered that. It took a lot of skill to stab someone in the heart—you needed excellent aim and a lot of strength to get through the chest muscles, tissue, and rib cage in one blow. Death had come mercifully quickly for Sally, as it had for Chuck. Her heart would have stopped beating almost immediately.

And yet, the killer had stabbed Sally eleven more times. They had barely bled—they had occurred postmortem and had therefore been wholly unnecessary, but they weren't done in a fit of rage. Jordan studied the photos of Sally's body and the surrounding area. There was no ripping or tearing to indicate frenzy, and the wounds were fairly shallow—all of which meant the killer hadn't lost control, despite the overkill. He had been restrained and careful. That never boded well.

Something else about the stab wounds nagged at Jordan. She flipped back to the background information Henry had confirmed the day before, skimming through the dates and facts until she found the one that had been nipping at the base of her brain.

November 2000. The month and year of the fire, when Billy killed Devon's mother and supposedly died.

Twelve years ago this month. Twelve years since Devon escaped, to match Sally's twelve stab wounds.

Twelve years, twelve wounds.

Jordan didn't believe in coincidence.

She moved on to the cash register. The drawer had been mostly cleaned out. The killer had left three one-dollar bills and a five sitting neatly in their slots, and two rolls of coins, one pennies and one dimes. Jordan had seen enough stores knocked over to know that thieves often didn't get everything. But the money left in the register seemed too calculated. Not enough value to raise suspicion, but enough to seem like the usual left-behinds.

There had been no signs of forced entry, and the front door was locked when the bodies were discovered. The back door was an emergency exit, the kind with a push bar on the inside which locked automatically when it closed. The killer either had keys or was let in.

Henry suspected the latter, and Jordan agreed. The front door had a bell above it, which would have meant the killer couldn't have slipped in unnoticed, and it was clear to Jordan that Chuck had to have been killed first. It seemed unlikely Sally's murder had been a quiet one, which meant Chuck would have come running—unless Chuck was already dead. So if Chuck was killed first, then the killer had to have come in the back, where Chuck was working. And that most likely meant Billy talked his way into the restaurant and was charming or manipulative enough—or both—to get Chuck to drop his guard.

They had turned up no significant prints, and no physical or trace evidence to tie back to the killer. No fingerprints, no blood other than the victims', no shoeprints or smudges or unidentified fibers. There were only three things that seemed at all out of place, and two of them might not be out of place at all: the wheat penny on the counter, and the fork and plate left in the drying rack.

Henry'd had the plate and fork tested; both had been washed spotless, no trace of DNA left behind. The autopsy reports confirmed Henry's assessment that neither Chuck nor Sally had eaten a piece of pie that morning, which—given that the pie was so fresh it had still been warm when Henry had arrived—could only mean one thing. The killer had helped himself to pie, either before or after the murders. Either the victims—or at least Chuck—had known the killer, and the man had eaten the pie before murdering them, or the killer had killed them and then eaten his pie. Jordan had to acknowledge the former possibility, but the profile she was building told her what the real truth was.

Jordan leaned back in her chair and rubbed her eyes. She glanced over at Devon, who seemed happily focused on preparing their feast of…whatever it was she was cooking. Jordan might have worried, but Devon seemed so darn happy cooking for her. Jordan closed her eyes. The idea that this charming, sweet, resilient woman could share DNA with the man who so coldly butchered two people and then callously enjoyed a piece of pie seemed impossible to Jordan.

The murders of Chuck and Sally were cold, calculated, and efficient. There was no physical evidence left behind, the scene was meticulous and controlled. This killer was experienced, well past his first murder. He was calm and rational and skilled. He wasn't worried about the police or being caught. He was self-assured enough that after he finished his work, he had time and appetite enough to enjoy some pie. He was an organized killer to the extreme, and that made him exceptionally dangerous.

❖

Henry rubbed at his eyes and checked his watch. It was after eight o'clock. He had sent Lawson home more than an hour earlier, threatening the rookie with a monthlong punishment of picking up coffee for the whole squad if he refused. Lawson, knowing full well how persnickety the other detectives could be about their coffee orders, smartly agreed.

He turned back to his computer, scanning Jordan's e-mail once more. Seattle. Boston. Dallas. San Diego. Santa Fe. Memphis. West Palm Beach. Charlotte. St. Paul. Boise. And finally Pittsburgh. Devon had lived in eleven cities in eight years. The longest she had stayed anywhere was eighteen months. Her shortest stay had been in Memphis, where after only five weeks she had run again. Each time she ran, she had to start over. Had to learn a new name. Become someone else.

It had been a surprisingly detailed list. Henry had no idea how she'd been able to keep track of it all, this many years later, let alone lived it without going stark raving mad. He and Lawson had spent much of the afternoon confirming what they could, and they'd needed to create a timeline on a whiteboard to keep it all straight.

Devon had largely been a ghost, which gave Henry an even greater respect for this young woman who had survived so much almost entirely alone. It also saddened him to think of her out there for so many years, constantly looking over her shoulder, knowing that at any moment, Billy might find her.

They hadn't been able to find much about Mrs. Brindle other than some news clippings. There had been no investigation since the sheriff had considered it an accident, so no evidence had been collected, and Henry was sure that car had long ago been sold for scrap. Not that he doubted Devon's story. But short of a confession from Billy, there would never be justice for Mrs. Eleanor Brindle.

After a few minutes of staring at the fuzzy words on the screen, he decided to call it a day. He wouldn't do Jordan or Devon or anyone else any good keeping at it when he was this tired. It was too easy to miss something critical.

He threw on his jacket and headed down to his car. He saw nothing out of the ordinary on the street and was certain no vehicle was following him as he drove home, though he took a few extra turns along the way just to be sure.

His house was dark when he pulled up. He'd forgotten to leave the porch light on again. Ella had always made sure to leave a light on for him, a beacon of love guiding him home no matter how late he arrived or how awful his day had been.

He sighed heavily. It was one of a million little things that he hadn't truly appreciated until she was taken from him. The thought of her made his heart ache.

Henry unlocked his door and entered the darkened house. It was so still now without her. Ella had filled their home with her warmth and laughter, so much so that every room had buzzed with her joyful spirit. Now the house was a mere shadow of itself, as was he. More than anything, he hated the stillness.

Henry emptied his pockets on the counter. It was an old habit Ella had broken him of during their marriage, now returned in her absence. He set down his keys, notepad, pen, wallet, change, and two phones in a haphazard pile, and then hung his jacket messily on a hanger in the hall closet. He poured himself a short glass of scotch and settled into his recliner, hoping against hope that the drink might help his mind to settle down. It didn't work, as he knew it wouldn't. As it never did. The only thing that had ever been able to settle his mind was Ella.

He heard something vibrating in the kitchen. It was his disposable phone. He picked up quickly. "Hey."

"Hey yourself," Jordan answered, a faint smile in her voice. "Rough day?"

Henry chuckled. "Do I sound that bad?"

"You always sound that bad. You got anything new?"

"Not much. I called Coleman, got him working to get us the personnel file from Roscoe and the arson report."

"A little pressure from the feds never hurt." Jordan paused. "What did you have to give up?"

"I don't want to talk about it."

It was good to hear Jordan's laugh. His partner was well aware of his ongoing series of wagers with the agent. They bet on anything: baseball games, horse races, congressional elections, which movie would be number one at the box office Fourth of July weekend. They'd once had a bet over how long a federal government shutdown would last. Henry had won, much to Coleman's chagrin.

"It'll help if he can get it," Jordan said. "Would be good to better understand that period of his life. It'd be even better to have a photo of him."

"Agreed. What about you? Anything new?"

Jordan went silent for a moment and he could hear Max churning up dried grass and leaves, likely racing around Jordan in elliptical paths, always just out of reach at his closest point.

"He's an organized killer. Meticulous and controlled. As long as he stays that way, we'll only find what he wants us to find. The murders of Chuck and Sally, and of Jessica, were coldly efficient, despite their brutality. I would include Devon's mother in that group as well, and even Mrs. Brindle."

"Mrs. Brindle wasn't killed with a knife."

"I know, but look at what we know. All the facts line up with Devon's story—there's not one piece of evidence that conflicts with what she's said."

"Jordan, I wasn't—"

"I know you weren't questioning her, Henry, though it's okay for us to question her. We *need* to question everything. You and I both know there's still more to this yet."

Henry did know, could feel it in his gut, but they would get to that.

"But if Billy caused Mrs. Brindle's accident, then it completely fits. Meticulous, controlled, coldly efficient. They were all a means to an end."

Henry felt a chill run down his spine. "Devon."

"Exactly. All of these murders were about Devon. At first I thought they were about revenge, about making Devon pay because she got away from him and he had to make someone pay, or he just wanted Devon to lose people close to her. And I certainly think there's an element of that here, but these kills were really about protecting himself, about covering up. He's stayed hidden for twelve years. Everyone thinks he's dead—it's how he moves around so easily, how he can keep coming after Devon. And he'd do anything to protect that."

"Anything?"

"He changes his MO. Though he favors the knife, and I believe prefers even more to slit his victims' throats, he is adaptable. He'll kill in whatever manner is required to achieve his goal at any time. With Mrs. Brindle, she had gone to the sheriff, but Billy needed her out of the way to get to Devon—so Billy needed her death to look like an accident. At the diner, Billy killed Chuck and Sally quickly and waited for Devon, but she was late. Sally's wounds were a message to Devon, along with the penny. He was there. He had found her again. He will never stop."

"And he'll do whatever it takes to kill Devon."

"Precisely. Devon is his motivation. His obsession."

"Why?" Henry asked.

"I don't know yet. He's not interested in notoriety. The wheat penny is distinct but subtle, not meant to draw attention, but he feels compelled to leave it. In part, he's telling the cops he's better than them, so good, in fact, that they don't even know about him. It reinforces his delusions of grandeur and his superiority. But I think that's only half the story."

"What's the other half?"

"This coin means something to him. It's his signature, something he's compelled to do—everything else is flexible. Devon said he used to bring her these coins after his fishing trips, which is how she recognized he'd come after her. But *why* did he bring them? What did they signify to him that he needed to share with her then, and why use them now? He didn't leave one at NIU, but he has since then—with Mrs. Brindle, and with Chuck and Sally."

"He's taunting her with it."

"Yes," Jordan agreed. "But I think it's more than that. It's a compulsion. I bet this has something to do with his parents, some kind of familial bond or symbol or meaning."

Henry understood where she was heading. "I'll have Lawson dig into Billy's family in the morning."

"Good."

The line went quiet again, and Henry sensed Jordan hesitating. "What is it? What are you thinking that you don't want to say?"

"You know me too well, partner." It warmed Henry's heart to hear her call him that again. "Five murders in twelve years aren't very many for Billy's level of organization, control, and skill."

Acid crept up into Henry's throat. But he felt almost relieved. His body was acknowledging what his mind had been trying to piece together for days, what had been nagging at him since the beginning. "You think there are others—murders not connected to Devon."

"Yes. I think these are about Billy's mission. But I think there are others motivated by something entirely different. And I think Devon might be the link between the two, whether she knows it or not. She's so haunted, Henry," Jordan said. "She blames herself."

Like someone else he knew. "You'll help her. You'll find the truth."

"I'm afraid to push too hard. She's scared, and not just because she's afraid he'll find us."

"Trust your instincts. You have one of the most intuitive minds I've ever come across. If you think there's more, chances are, there is."

Jordan laughed. "You blowing smoke up my ass, partner?"

Henry laughed, too. It felt good to lighten the mood a little, even momentarily. "Hardly."

Jordan went quiet. Henry could practically hear her mind working, attempting to fill in the blanks. He knew she would drive herself crazy trying to figure it out.

"You two all settled in now?" he asked to distract her.

"Yeah. We picked up some supplies at Mel's this morning."

"We? You took Devon with you?"

A pause. "She can be pretty persuasive."

"I'll bet," Henry said, grinning to himself. Yet another reason he liked Devon.

"What did you tell Mel?"

"That Devon is an old friend from college going through a bad breakup and we're up here for some R and R."

"And she bought that?" Henry knew Mel well enough to know she had a nose for bullshit.

"Seemed to. But even if not, Mel won't say anything. She's no gossip."

"So how did Mel and Devon get along?"

"What do you mean?"

Henry's grin broadened. Jordan was intuitive about everything except how people felt about her. He knew she and Mel had gotten together a couple of times since Caroline left. Jordan saw her as a friend with benefits, but Mel seemed interested in more than a fling. It was a fact to which he knew Jordan was completely oblivious.

"Oh, nothing."

They said their good-byes and Henry settled back into his recliner, picking up his forgotten scotch. He took a sip, chuckling to himself. Despite the gravity of their situation, he allowed himself a few moments to imagine how the sassy redhead had reacted to Jordan bringing the attractive blonde into her store. He had a sneaking suspicion that Devon would not have backed down from that challenge, as formidable as Mel could be.

Henry was no matchmaker, but he couldn't help but think Devon was good for Jordan, that together perhaps Devon and Jordan could both find some peace. And maybe when this was all over, Jordan would finally allow herself to be happy.

Chapter Nineteen

Jordan lay on the couch, finding sleep frustratingly elusive despite her exhaustion. For once, however, her sleeplessness had nothing to do with a five-year-old boy. For the first time since the shooting, she found the burden on her soul was no longer quite so heavy. It wasn't gone, not yet, but it was definitely lighter. And that was miraculous.

She couldn't wrap her mind around it, but somehow speaking of her guilt had started to free her from it. But Jordan knew that talking was only part of it.

Devon, with her soothing touch and gentle reassurance, had helped Jordan reach inside that dark place and pull her guilt out into the healing light of day. That light had pushed back the shadows of shame obscuring her memory, allowing the truth to emerge. She was not responsible for that boy's death, or for the two police officers that had been killed. Jordan could now allow herself to believe that without her actions it was likely more people would have died. None of those children would have escaped their father's gun.

Somehow, Devon had helped her do what others could not. Not Henry, not her mother, and certainly not Caroline. Not that she blamed Caroline, not anymore. They had been drifting apart long before the shooting, even though she hadn't admitted it at the time. Caroline had never been comfortable with the danger Jordan faced as a cop. It had created a wedge between them, one she had ignored. After the shooting, after Caroline's fears were made real, Jordan had been too busy blaming herself, too busy pushing Caroline and everyone else away to care. Another wedge, this one creating a final, insurmountable divide.

No, she did not blame Caroline for leaving. But now she didn't want to keep punishing herself for Caroline, or for the boy, or for any of it. She wanted to forgive herself. The wolf had hunted her for so long, and she was tired of running. It was time to kill her guilt, once and for all. And Devon had given her the strength to do it.

The bedroom door creaked, and she heard Max quietly enter the room. He rounded the corner of the couch and pushed his nose into Jordan's hand.

"What's the matter, boy? Can't sleep?"

He whined plaintively, looking toward the bedroom and then back at Jordan. Now she could hear a faint whimpering coming from the bedroom. Jordan was off the couch in an instant, not fearing an intruder—Max would never have left Devon unprotected—but understanding something was not right.

She pushed open the bedroom door, soft sobs filling her ears. Devon was thrashing, her legs tangled in the blanket, in the throes of some nightmare. Jordan's heart clenched at the sight. She could only imagine the visions tormenting this strong, resilient woman who had survived so much without breaking. She did not deserve whatever wicked dreams had overtaken her mind, just like she did not deserve any of the horrors that had consumed so much of her life.

Jordan did not want to wake her, knowing from experience that being woken from a nightmare could leave her shaken for hours. But she could not stand by and watch Devon's anguish. So she did the only thing she could think of.

Jordan set her gun on the nightstand and slipped quietly into the bed beside Devon, wrapping her arms around her. She gently pulled Devon's head against her lips and began whispering into her hair, soothing words without meaning and yet meaning everything. Devon's movements slowed, her body unconsciously recognizing the warmth of Jordan's and the safety of her arms. Her breathing eased as her body stilled, and she eventually fell into a steady, heavy rhythm.

Jordan wasn't sure how long she stayed that way, holding Devon, keeping the nightmares at bay, but she knew she would stay forever if that was what Devon needed. It was a startling thought but she kept still, turning it over in her mind as she basked in the feeling of Devon in her arms.

Devon was beautiful and brave, strong yet compassionate, full of a humor and spirit that would be alluring in any woman but made all the more remarkable for all that Devon had been through. When Devon smiled at her, Jordan felt like she could do anything. She could walk on hot coals without being burned, swim across the Atlantic Ocean, outwrestle Hercules and outrun Hermes.

Jordan was all too aware how perfectly their bodies fit, lying here with Devon so close. Devon had snuggled into her, molding her body against Jordan's, Devon's every curve locking into Jordan's hollows, as if they were one.

Devon shifted her leg up onto Jordan's. She could feel the warm apex of Devon's thighs pressing against her and a flurry of unbidden images flooded her mind, of heat and skin and smooth and wet. Jordan was suddenly infinitely aware of the swell of Devon's breasts pressing against her, of Devon's hot breath on her throat, her lips only millimeters from Jordan's skin. What it would be like to feel Devon beneath her, moving against her, meeting her thrust for thrust and moan for moan.

Jordan shut her eyes tightly, willing the pictures from her mind, the flush from her skin. This was not the time or the place. Devon was trusting Jordan to keep her safe, and here she was lusting after the woman she was supposed to be protecting. She had a job to do and she needed to stay focused. Devon deserved that much.

Jordan slipped from the bed, careful to not break the peaceful sleep that had finally overtaken Devon. Max, who had followed Jordan into the room and taken up watch beside the bed, now jumped up onto it, as if knowing that was where he was needed. He settled down beside Devon, not touching her but close enough Jordan was sure Devon would be able to sense him.

"You're a good boy, Max," Jordan whispered. He rested his head on his paws, blinking up at Jordan before settling into his own restful slumber. Jordan retrieved her weapon and headed to the doorway. She lingered there, taking in the way Devon's hair gleamed in the moonlight filtering in through a gap in the window drapes. She looked like an angel, and to her, Devon was one. And she would do whatever it took to keep her safe, even if that meant putting aside her own needs.

In another life...

❖

Billy was not a happy man. Since the debacle at the house, there had been no sign of Maddie or her gallant Detective Salinger. Yes, he knew Salinger's name now, and Lieutenant Wayne's, courtesy of some nosy neighbors at the crime scene.

After midnight, Billy had gone to a run-down Internet café to learn more about his quarry. Lieutenant Henry Wayne, thirty-year veteran of the Pittsburgh Bureau of Police. Widower, no children, no ties of any kind to be exploited. Numerous commendations over his career, with an impressive arrest record and an even more impressive rate of conviction for cases he investigated. Promoted to lieutenant following the Dubois hostage incident. A formidable opponent, to be sure. Billy liked that.

Then there was Detective Jordan Salinger, the hero cop of the Dubois affair. She was the wild card. On the force for ten years, a detective for five. Out on medical leave after getting shot. Saved two children, killed Dubois. One child dead, along with two cops. The media had hailed her as a hero and, after an internal affairs investigation, so had the Pittsburgh Bureau of Police. She had been offered a promotion and a raise, pretty much anything she wanted, but she turned it all down. She had also turned down all requests for interviews: *Detective Salinger could not be reached for comment.*

A champion of the people, who eschewed her celebrity status. Interesting. Definitely a wild card.

It would make her downfall all the more satisfying.

That was, of course, assuming Billy could pick up their trail. He needed to catch a break, but so far, he had nothing.

Billy felt like tearing the steering wheel from the dashboard and beating someone to death with it. Instead, he took in a deep lungful of air and released it slowly, calming his inner rage.

My God, why have You forsaken me?

No, God had not forsaken him. The Lord was testing him, testing his faith. Like Abraham, like Job, he was being tested and his faith would be rewarded. He just had to be smarter. Bolder. Nothing good ever came from waiting. In order to see the sign, he needed to look for it, not wait for it to appear.

He had not been able to find anything that would point him to where Salinger might have taken Maddie. An easy hack of the local tax records showed the house belonged to Salinger's mother. Her father had died many years earlier, so that was no help. The mother, though, might have potential if he really got into a jam, and if he could find her. So far, there'd been no sign of her, either. And there was no other property he could find attached to either Salinger or her mother, at least not in Pittsburgh. When he had time, he would broaden his investigation.

He laughed at that. *Investigation.* Funny how he still thought like a cop after all these years. Of course, the skills he had learned at the sheriff's office had come in handy. One of these days, he'd have to find a way to thank them. Another lesson his momma had taught him: always say thank you. Maybe he'd make an anonymous donation to their softball team, if they still had one. Get them some new uniforms or something.

The one thing he did know now was why Salinger had behaved as she had that first morning outside of the police station. She probably hadn't been back to the station since the shooting. She was afraid. And that might certainly be something he could exploit.

Sometimes Billy thought he should have gotten a degree in psychology, though he had read enough books on it over the years that he figured he had earned an honorary one, at least.

He had read plenty of books about serial killers, too, and one thing Billy was sure of was that he was no mere serial killer.

Such a mundane term, and so inadequate to describe his work.

Billy's was a much higher calling than simple murder. He was a purifier of souls. What serial killer could say that and mean it, honestly?

He had not planned to kill his wife when he had. It had not been her time, and it was his greatest—his only—mistake. Billy was meticulous about his work, planning every detail, calculating every variable. From his very first kill, Billy had always been in control.

His wife had been...impulse. And Maddie had been failure. A failure he was finally going to rectify.

One way or another, the endgame was near. Maddie was his greatest hunt, and in the end, he would fulfill the Lord's plan. In order to do that, though, he needed to find her. And he would need to be bold.

CHAPTER TWENTY

Devon awoke feeling better rested than she had in ages. She knew she had been tired, but was surprised at how well she had slept. It was unusual for her to sleep through the night. She often woke up multiple times, almost always with a nightmare fresh in her mind. She tended to remember her dreams for days and months, even years, afterward. This morning, however, she had no nightmare lodged in her brain, nor any dream. Instead, she had only the fleeting feeling of being held.

She found Jordan in the kitchen making pancakes, the ever-present gun tucked into the holster at Jordan's hip. It was so domestic, apart from the gun. So almost normal. She nearly laughed, especially once she saw the flour coating Jordan's shirt and the big gob of batter clinging to her hair.

"What time is it?" she asked instead, suppressing her laughter. It would be terribly impolite to make fun of the woman who was trying to make her breakfast.

"About nine," Jordan said, flashing a smile at Devon over her shoulder. "I'm making pancakes."

"I see that," Devon said, standing beside Jordan now. She reached up and picked the batter out of her hair.

Jordan considered the gooey smear in Devon's hand. "Guess I should say I'm trying to make pancakes."

Devon leaned over the skillet, her hand naturally finding its way to the small of Jordan's back. The pancakes actually looked surprisingly delicious, considering the mess. "Smells fantastic," she said, turning back to Jordan. She noticed that Jordan had stopped moving and was staring at her, unblinking.

"What's wrong?" Devon asked. Then she realized where her hand was. "Oh, sorry, I…" she sputtered, stepping back and dropping her hand.

Jordan appeared to shake herself out of a trance. "No, it's fine," she said quickly. She flashed Devon a grin. "Hungry?"

Devon nodded and sat down at the table, which was already set. What in the world had possessed her to touch Jordan that way, like they were lovers cozied up in a bungalow instead of refugees hiding from a madman? It had felt so natural, so right. The intimacy of it frightened her.

The pancakes were, in fact, delicious and the breakfast conversation was light, with none of their earlier awkwardness. But the heat from Jordan's skin lingered on Devon's hand, unsettling her.

After they finished, Jordan made a move to wash the dishes, but Devon beat her to the sink. "We had a deal, remember?"

Jordan nodded, stretching as she stepped out of the way.

"Do you need another rub?" Devon asked as she scoured the frying pan.

"I'm okay," Jordan said.

Devon wasn't buying it. "You're not a superhero. And sleeping on that couch isn't doing anything for your injuries."

Jordan didn't respond.

"You can't spend another night on the couch," Devon said. "Not in your condition."

"What am I, eighty-three?" Jordan joked. "The couch is—"

"Is *not* where you're going to be sleeping tonight. You're taking the bed, and I don't want to hear another word about it."

Jordan, seeming to finally understand that she could not win this argument, relented. "Fine."

Devon nodded, knowing full well this discussion wasn't over. Which was fine with her. She would win in the end. She finished rinsing the last plate and turned to Jordan, picking up where she'd left off. "How are your ribs?"

Jordan looked like she might brush Devon off, but instead she lifted the side of her shirt. Devon stepped closer, reaching out to trace the tender flesh. The bruising had settled into a deep purple, but the edges had started to recede, turning a sickly yellow. Jordan inhaled sharply at the touch, and Devon snatched back her hand. "Sorry."

"No, it's not..." Jordan floundered. "You didn't hurt me. You never could."

Devon digested the words. They filled her with a sudden warmth, even though she knew Jordan was so very wrong. "Have you been icing it?"

"Every night," Jordan said.

"And what about your head?"

"Bump's nearly gone. See?" Jordan said, tilting her head down for Devon to take a closer look.

Devon stepped closer, gently parting Jordan's hair and feeling the area with her fingertips. Jordan was right. The swelling had subsided considerably.

"And what about this?" Devon asked, her fingers finding Jordan's cheek. The bruising there was not as bad as Devon had feared it would become. She caressed Jordan's cheek with infinite care, unable to stop herself. Jordan nuzzled her face into Devon's palm. She thought she heard Jordan moan, but it didn't sound like pain.

"It's fine," Jordan said huskily. She searched Devon's face. "Better now."

Devon found herself caught in Jordan's orbit. Gravity drew her closer, and she found herself unable—and unwilling—to escape. She focused on Jordan's lips, so full, so inviting. She knew she should stop, should pull back before she did something she would regret, but Jordan wasn't pulling away, either, and Devon couldn't stop thinking about what it would be like to taste those lips, just once.

And yet, even though they were now just inches apart, so close she could feel Jordan's breath, Devon found the strength to pull away. Her fingers trailed down Jordan's face and she took a step back. Jordan looked at her, dazed.

"I'm going to draw you a bath," Devon said, her voice deep and uneven. She tried to settle her heart. "I saw some Epsom salt in the bathroom." She didn't wait for a response, fleeing the room.

She couldn't deal with her feelings, the almost-kiss, so she focused on Jordan's bath. She ran the water, pouring a generous helping of the salt into the claw-foot tub. It didn't take long to fill the tub with steaming water. Devon imagined Jordan in the tub, soaking out a hard day's work fixing up the cabin—a thought which did nothing to steady her racing pulse.

Devon shut off the water and took a few moments to compose herself. This was about Jordan, not her libido. But oh, how she wanted to kiss her.

She found Jordan still standing where she'd left her in the kitchen, still looking shell-shocked. "Your bath awaits, milady," Devon said lightly. She threw in a curtsy for good measure, trying desperately to move them past what had almost happened. She hoped Jordan would follow her lead.

"Why, thank you, fair maiden," Jordan finally said, bowing. Devon relaxed slightly. Jordan passed her in the hallway, nodding ever so slightly as she passed, as if to say that she understood. That it was okay. That Devon hadn't ruined anything.

When the bathroom door closed, Devon sank against the wall. Max trotted over and sat next to her, and they both contemplated the now-closed door.

"What am I going to do, Max?" she whispered. Max turned, studying her. Then he licked her cheek. "Oh, you think I should have kissed her, huh?" Devon said, ruffling his fur. "I'm not sure that would help anything."

Max cocked his head to one side.

"I don't even know if she feels anything for me."

The shepherd chuffed.

"You think she does?"

Max chuffed again.

Devon leaned her head back against the wall. She was having a conversation with a dog. A very intelligent dog, but a dog nonetheless. She was finally losing it. As if he had heard her inner thoughts, Max pawed at Devon's leg, demanding her attention.

"What?"

He licked her cheek again, reaffirming his earlier point. Devon stroked his head. "I'm scared, Max. I've done terrible things, things I haven't told her. I know I have to tell her, but I'm going to lose her when I do."

Max climbed into Devon's lap, covering her legs with his body. They stayed that way for a long time, long enough for Jordan to finish her bath. The sight of her, emerging from the bathroom freshly scrubbed, hair glistening, a towel barely covering her from breast to upper thigh, nearly did Devon in.

"Good bath?" she choked out, failing miserably to hide her desire.

"Great bath," Jordan said, grinning. She stretched, making the towel slip dangerously low across her breasts.

Devon stared, transfixed.

"Should I go put some clothes on?" Jordan asked.

Devon tore her gaze from Jordan's chest. Jordan's eyes sparkled mischievously.

Is she flirting with me? Devon felt suddenly lighter, despite the weight of Max still across her lap. *Two can play at this game.*

"That depends," she said, rising. Max amiably scrambled off her lap. She leaned one shoulder against the wall, crossing her arms confidently. She raked her eyes down and back up Jordan's body. "You need any help?"

Jordan's mouth parted and she swallowed thickly. "Um, that's okay," she croaked, "I think I've got it." She quickly retreated into the bedroom and shut the door.

"Well, would you look at that," Devon said to Max. He looked at her approvingly. "Maybe there's hope for us yet."

Jordan dressed slowly, pondering how the tables had turned so quickly. She had been flustered by what had almost happened in the kitchen, though not because she hadn't wanted the kiss to happen.

Dear God, how she wanted to kiss that woman.

But Jordan knew, as she had known the night before, that the time wasn't right. She didn't want to take advantage of Devon, and they had bigger things to deal with than her raging hormones.

But then Devon had touched her. First, it was Devon's hand against the small of her back. Then, it was Devon's fingers trailing fire along her abdomen. By the time Devon had touched her cheek, she was powerless to resist. She hadn't been able to stop herself from seeking more contact, from turning into the warm touch of Devon's hand. She had watched the change in Devon's eyes as they found Jordan's lips, felt the hitch in Devon's breath as she leaned in closer. If Devon had kissed her, Jordan would have let her. Not just let her. She would have kissed her back.

But Devon had not kissed her, had instead pulled away, leaving Jordan breathless and wanting. Then she had run and Jordan had let her, even though all she wanted to do was pull Devon close and kiss the hell out of her.

When Devon tried to dispel the awkwardness between them, Jordan had followed her lead. But though the bath did wonders for her aching body, it did nothing to soothe her aching heart.

She absolutely ached for Devon James, that much was clear to her now. And perhaps, just maybe, Devon felt the same. The thought both delighted and terrified her.

We can't do this. Not now. Not yet.

It was scary, what she felt for Devon. But it was also exhilarating. She had not felt this way about anyone in a long time, not even about Caroline, maybe not ever about anyone. And if Devon felt the same? She didn't know for certain, but she understood now that it was a risk she was willing—that she needed—to take.

If she was going to take on the wolf, then she might as well take on the whole pack. All her guilt, all her doubt, all her fear. And the biggest fear of all was that she was unworthy of love.

But she had seen something in Devon's face when they were standing so close that looked a little bit like the possibility of love. And if Devon could love her…well. Devon was the most amazing person she had ever known.

Jordan was filled with a hope she had never known, along with a renewed determination to protect the woman who held her heart. And when all this was over, she would find the courage to go after what she wanted. And what she wanted was Devon.

She'd had no intention of flirting after her bath, but when she saw the effect her half-naked body was having on Devon, she couldn't help herself. She'd flirted.

Boy, had that backfired on her. That woman was a world-class flirt.

Jordan smiled to herself. When this was over, there would be payback. Oh yes, she would see to it that Devon was deliciously, wickedly paid back.

She dressed and went in search of Devon. She found her outside playing with Max.

"You shouldn't be out here by yourself," she said, grinning despite her disapproval.

"I'm not by myself, I'm with Max," Devon said, laughing as Max jumped for the stick in her hand. Devon launched the makeshift toy off near the tree line, the shepherd giving merry chase.

Jordan watched them for a few minutes, Devon laughing, Max's tail wagging furiously, and found herself content. It was not a feeling to which she was accustomed, but one she thought she could definitely get used to.

She pulled out her cell and dialed Henry's disposable cell.

"Hey, partner," Henry said, picking up immediately.

"Hey."

"How are things?"

"All's quiet here," Jordan said. "How about you?"

"Finally got the case files from Roscoe."

Jordan's heart quickened. "Well?"

"I haven't had a chance to read them yet. Literally just pulled them off the fax when you called."

"What in the hell are you talking to me for, then?"

Henry laughed. "Because you called me."

"Oh. Right. Well, get to it and call me back."

"What? Jordan...breaking..."

Jordan moved farther out from the house. "Better?"

"I seriously hate these phones," Henry growled.

Jordan looked up toward the sky. A blanket of gray had replaced yesterday's puffy white clouds and brilliant blue. "It's only going to get worse."

"Seriously. What if I can't get ahold of you?"

"If you can't get through, call Mel's," she said, and gave him the number. "She can get a message to me."

"She tell you anything else?" Watching Devon with Max out in the grass, running around like she didn't have a care in the world, Jordan wanted to believe there was nothing left to tell. But her heart suddenly felt as heavy as the leaden sky, and she knew what it meant.

"No. Not yet. I'll let you know."

"Okay," Henry said. "Now stop bothering me and let me get some police work done."

"See ya, partner."

She disconnected the call, pushing aside the gloom that had invaded her soul, and went to join Devon and Max.

Henry and Lawson took turns reading through each of the three files. The first was Billy's personnel file from the Roscoe sheriff's department. It seemed incomplete to Henry. For one thing, there was no photo of Billy, which he had been counting on.

Assholes probably couldn't be bothered to send it.

The second and third were better, the report from the house fire and the autopsies of the two bodies found in the ruins. For whatever Coleman had done to get these reports, he was grateful.

Henry waited as Lawson finished reviewing the files. Lawson closed the final jacket, frustration evident.

"Well?" Henry asked, wanting to see if Lawson had picked up on what he'd seen. The rookie did not disappoint.

"The female vic seems a match for Marie Montgomery, but that most definitely wasn't Billy's body in that house. You'd have to be blind to miss it."

Henry nodded for Lawson to continue.

"Personnel file has Billy at six foot, same as Jordan said. But the autopsy has the male vic at five nine. He didn't magically shrink three inches in the fire."

"Go on."

"Then there's the fracture at the base of the skull. Devon hit him in the side of the head, so there might have been a fracture there. But where'd the fracture in the back come from?"

Henry nodded again.

"And finally, there's the time of death. The medical examiner put TOD at two weeks prior to the fire, at least. How in the hell could Roscoe have missed that?"

"They didn't want to see it," Henry said. "It's easy to miss things you don't want to find."

"Bastards."

Henry wholeheartedly agreed. "Both bodies were found in the basement, along with half the house. The explosion from the propane tanks really did a number."

"Yeah, but look at this." Lawson opened the fire investigation report and flipped through the pages. "The fire burned hotter in some places, and they found traces of accelerant in nearly all the rooms, but especially in the basement."

"Theories?"

"It almost looks like arson," Lawson said, leaning back in his chair. "But they ruled it an accident, that it started in the kitchen near the stove, which is consistent with what Devon said."

Henry didn't understand it, either. He had no doubt about the veracity of Devon's story. But the house fire didn't make sense.

"Autopsy shows Marie's throat was cut," Lawson said. "Bastard sliced deep. Damn near decapitated her."

"Lot of rage," Henry said.

The personnel file was thin. No commendations, no citations. Nothing really good or bad. By all accounts, Billy was just an average cop. The only two notations of interest were that Billy used all his vacation time, and he seemed to excel at picking locks.

"No wonder he had no problem getting into Jordan's house," Lawson said.

Henry saw the captain in his office. Now that the feds were involved, he needed to loop in Captain Buchanan. He scribbled Coleman's e-mail address on the list of cities and dates he'd gotten from Jordan and handed it to Lawson.

"Do me a favor, e-mail Coleman and see if he can get a photo of Billy from the sheriff's office. It's about time you and he got to know each other, anyway. Send him this list and Jordan's preliminary profile. I think she's right—Billy's killed more than the people we know about. Six to one, at least a few of those cities and time frames correspond with unsolved murders."

❖

The cold finally got the better of Devon and Jordan, putting an end to their outdoor fun. They each lugged in an armload of wood, and Jordan quickly set about starting a fire.

"That happened fast," Devon said, blowing on her hands to thaw them.

"It does that up here, even without a storm coming," Jordan said, setting up the logs. Within minutes, she had a healthy fire going.

It drew Devon in. "Oh, that's heavenly," she said, rubbing her hands together and holding them close to the fire.

"I can pull over a chair if you want."

"No, that's okay." Devon noticed Jordan hung back from the fireplace. "Aren't you cold?"

"Nah. I've lived in Pittsburgh all my life. I'm used to it." Jordan retreated into the kitchen and called out, "I've got tea or hot chocolate. Or I can make more coffee?"

Devon could barely contain a moan at the thought of hot chocolate. "Always chocolate."

Jordan laughed. "A woman after my own heart."

Feeling a bit warmer, she followed Jordan into the kitchen. "How's Henry?"

"Good," Jordan said. "He just got Billy's personnel file from Roscoe, and the report on the fire and the autopsy. He's looking them over now."

"Good, good," Devon said absently, talk of Billy instantly dampening her mood.

"Devon?" Jordan asked, immediately picking up on the change. "What is it?"

"Nothing," Devon said, shivering. "I hope there's something useful in those files."

Jordan eyed her for a moment but didn't press. "Hopefully. I don't expect much from the personnel file, but perhaps from the others. Maybe it will at least give us some idea as to whose body burned up in that fire."

It was a question Devon had long pondered. There had been no one else in the house that day, apart from Billy, Devon, and her mother. She'd tortured herself for years, knowing Billy was alive, knowing he hadn't burned, knowing she had no proof anyone would believe.

"Devon?" Jordan said gently.

"Huh? Oh, sorry," Devon said, coming back to the present.

"Where were you?"

"Oh, I was just…thinking."

The kettle whistled and Jordan took it off the burner, setting it to the side. She turned back to Devon, stepping closer.

"What were you thinking?" Jordan asked softly.

Devon started to speak, but shook her head. *Don't do this. Please, don't make me tell you.*

Her silent plea went unanswered.

"I need to ask…" Jordan hesitated. "What haven't you told me?"

There it was, the question Devon had been dreading. A heavy stone settled in her stomach. The time had finally arrived. Jordan had asked, and as much as Devon wanted to, she would not—she could not—lie. Not to Jordan.

God, please don't let her hate me.

She was about to speak when someone knocked at the door.

CHAPTER TWENTY-ONE

Jordan's gun was drawn and in her hand before she could even think. She pushed Devon behind her, aiming the gun at the door. But Max wasn't growling. In fact, his tail was wagging expectantly.

"Hello? Anybody home?" a familiar voice called out.

Jordan holstered her gun and shook her head. She turned to find Devon still staring nervously at the door. "It's okay. It's just Mel."

Devon visibly relaxed. "Well, that was a heart attack I didn't need."

Jordan chuckled and opened the door.

"I just couldn't stay away," Mel said. Jordan stepped back to allow Mel into the cabin. "Oh, hey, Sabrina."

It seemed to take Devon a moment to realize Mel was talking to her. "Hey, Mel."

"Hello, Max," Mel said, scratching the dog's head. For once, Max was uninterested in the affection, focusing on the bundle in Mel's hand.

"Is that what I think it is?" Jordan asked, her mouth already watering.

"Ever the detective," Mel said, pulling the red-and-white checked cloth off the treat with a flourish. "I was baking this morning and remembered how much you *loved* my apple pie, and I just couldn't let you go without."

Mel was certainly turning on the charm this morning, Jordan thought. *Huh.*

Max was still sniffing at the pie. Jordan shooed him away and he went, reluctantly, and lay down in front of the fire. She turned to Devon to tell her she was in for a treat and was taken aback by the stiff set of Devon's jaw.

"Sabrina—do you like apple pie?" Jordan asked hesitantly. She had no idea what in the world was going on. They had all seemed to get along fine yesterday.

"Actually, I prefer cherry," Devon said with a smile full of ice. She stepped closer. "Far more succulent."

"Yes, well, I add cinnamon," Mel said, also stepping closer, "and Jordan likes her pie a little spicy. Don't you, Jordan?"

So they were not, in fact, actually talking about pie. Jordan suddenly felt like a prize bull at the county fair. *Oh boy*.

"I, uh, like both?" She needed to get out of this without hurting Mel. They'd been friends for many years, and Jordan had few friends. She'd thought they were on the same page, friends with benefits, just two lonely people seeking comfort and pleasure in each other's arms. Apparently, she'd been wrong.

"Hmm, that's new," Mel said dismissively, setting the pie on the table. She grabbed a knife and plates from the kitchen. "Jordan, how about I serve you up a piece of my pie so you can see what you've been missing?"

Jordan glanced nervously at Devon, who was biting the inside of her cheek.

"You want some, dear?" Mel asked Devon with a honeyed smile laced with vinegar. Jordan thought Devon's head was going to explode.

"Certainly," Devon said, laying on the charm. "If you're giving it away."

Jordan watched the escalating sexual brinksmanship play out with a mix of horror and resignation.

"Mmmm, so good." Mel moaned between bites, sounding a bit like—no, exactly like—she did when they were in bed together. *Oh dear Lord.*

Jordan chewed nervously. It really was good pie, not that she could admit that. She watched Devon from the corner of her eye, smiling sweetly around mouthfuls.

After the third bite, Devon set down her fork and delicately wiped the corners of her mouth with her napkin. "Not bad," Devon said. "I can see why Jordan might have liked it, once upon a time."

She leaned into Jordan and set her hand on Jordan's bare forearm, trailing her fingers back and forth. Jordan shivered.

"But now that I'm here, I'll have to serve you up my cherry pie. It just melts in your mouth."

She couldn't stop staring at Devon's lips. Vaguely she heard Mel set down her fork and scoot back her chair.

"It seems your tastes have changed, Jordan," she said with obvious disappointment. Jordan dragged her gaze away from Devon and up to Mel, who tilted her head contemplatively. "But I suppose sometimes change is good."

She gave Devon a little nod and excused herself, shutting the door behind her with a soft click. Jordan stared at the closed door, wondering what exactly had just happened. Devon was scraping her plate—with some force—into the trash can.

"Devon?" Jordan brought her own plate over to the counter. "You want to tell me what's going on?"

Devon said nothing, taking her plate over to the sink. She jabbed at the faucet, turning it on. "Nothing's going on."

Jordan was mystified. The temperature in the cabin had plunged thirty degrees in an instant. Her head was spinning. She felt her ire rising. "Something is most definitely going on. I'm not an idiot."

Devon's shoulders sagged. "No, you're not," she conceded. She shut off the water but didn't turn. Jordan waited. Finally, Devon tried to brush past her, but Jordan blocked her path.

"Let me pass," Devon said, staring at the floor.

"Look at me," Jordan said. Devon refused.

"Please, look at me," Jordan said again, but her plea fell on deaf ears. Devon tried to push past her again, but this time Jordan grabbed her arm.

"Let go of me," Devon ground out.

"Not until you tell me what's happening here," Jordan said, her voice rising.

Devon tried to pull away, but Jordan held firm, taking care not to hurt her. "Devon, please talk to me." She tried again to pull away, but Jordan wasn't about to let go. "Damn it, Devon, talk to—"

The words died on her tongue as Devon's lips crashed into hers.

❖

The front desk area was crowded when Billy walked in, people pushing and yelling and generally making asses of themselves. There seemed to be two gangs, judging by their tattoos, which was unlikely to end well. It usually didn't.

Billy waited his turn behind the unruly mob, scratching at his unshaven face. His skin itched, one of the many reasons he hated growing facial hair. He preferred to be clean-shaven, but sometimes he had to sacrifice for his mission. He had dyed his hair that morning, nothing too drastic, but a few shades darker than normal. He wore a pair of jeans, a button-down shirt, and a Pittsburgh Penguins jacket and hat. The key to disguise, Billy had learned over the years, was to blend in.

Coming to the police station was a first for Billy, but it was a necessary risk. Besides, he wasn't too concerned. Billy Dean Montgomery was a dead man. The cops were chasing a ghost.

The shouting match at the front desk had escalated to the point that several officers had stepped in to keep the peace. They led the two groups into the recesses of the building, presumably to separate corners, if they were smart. He approached the front desk with a shy smile and a shake of his head.

"Busy day, huh?" he said, offering the cop behind the desk a *What can you do?* shrug.

"Yeah," the cop said dejectedly. "I'm supposed to be off this afternoon. Got tickets to the Pens game."

Billy whistled. "Gosh, I'd hate to see you miss that. Hope you're able to go."

The officer smiled. "Me, too. Now, how can I help you?"

Billy looked around as if he was nervous and leaned over the desk. "Well, see I might know something. About those murders. At the diner?"

The cop's eyebrows lifted. "What do you know?"

Billy looked around again, like he was afraid. "It may be nothing but…I figured I better come in. Is there a detective I can talk to?"

The cop called over another officer. "Hey, Frank. Take this guy back to Lieutenant Wayne. It's about the diner murders."

The cop named Frank directed Billy upstairs, back to the bullpen. Billy called, "Thank you and good luck," to the cop behind the desk as he followed. Frank led him over to a chair next to an empty desk.

Perfect.

"You need something, Frank?" another man asked, one who seemed vaguely familiar to Billy. He searched his brain, coming up with it. He'd seen this man at the diner, talking to Wayne and Maddie.

Damn.

"Yeah, this guy needs to see Lieutenant Wayne. The diner."

"He's in with the captain. I can take it."

Frank shrugged and left.

"I'm Detective Lawson. How can I help you, Mr....?" He waved Billy over to the chair next to his desk. Billy sat down uncomfortably.

"Collins. Jack Collins."

"All right, Mr. Collins. What can I do for you?" Lawson asked.

Billy needed to adjust, and quickly. He fidgeted in his chair. "Well, I think I might know something. About who did it."

"Go on."

"Can I get a glass of water?"

"Of course." Lawson walked over to the cooler Billy had spotted on the far side of the room. He didn't have much time. He casually looked around the room, quickly scanning the desk he had initially been brought to, but was disappointed. The desk was clean.

Time to make another adjustment.

He turned his eyes back to Lawson's desk. The man was a neat freak. No open notes or messages. His computer screen showed the city's seal. He noted a stack of files in a basket at the far corner of the desk, but it wasn't like he could just go pawing through the man's files out here in the open.

Damn it.

Lawson brought back the water, and Billy gulped it down.

"It's okay, Mr. Collins. Just relax."

Billy nodded. "It's just so awful what happened. To Sally and Chuck. They were good people."

Lawson nodded encouragingly.

"I couldn't believe it when I heard," Billy continued. "How's the waitress? Devon?"

Lawson's eyes narrowed. "What do you mean?"

Billy backpedaled. "I heard she found them. Such a nice girl. Works mostly in the morning, so I don't know her very well. I'm usually a dinner guy. Best meatloaf in the city."

Billy waited while Lawson considered him. Sweat started to trickle down his spine. He'd been too forward, and this cop was too suspicious.

Damn it. Damn it.

"She's fine," Lawson said eventually, betraying nothing.

"Good, good," Billy said.

Lawson leaned forward in his chair. "What do you know, Mr. Collins?"

"Like I said, I usually go the diner in the evenings. I was there the night before the…well, before. A little later than usual. And there was this guy. At the counter. He didn't seem right."

"Can you describe him?"

Gotcha. "Yeah, sure. I didn't get a good look at him at first. His back was to me, and he left a while before me. But when I left, I saw him clear as day. Up the street, under a lamp. He was watching the diner. I had to walk right by him to catch my bus."

"What did he look like?" Lawson asked again.

"About my height. Not real bulky, kinda lean. Short hair. Hard to tell the color under the streetlamp but it looked sort of light brownish. Real shifty eyes."

Lawson began scribbling onto a notepad.

"He kinda looked at me funny. When I passed him." Billy swallowed hard, putting on a show. "I don't know if he did it, but I'm kinda scared. That he'll find me or something."

Lawson looked up at him. "Don't worry. We can protect you."

Billy did his best to look relieved. "Oh, that's good. Like one of those witness protection kinds of deals? Like on TV?"

"Something like that."

"Put me in one of those safe houses?"

Lawson's pen stopped moving. "You know, I'd like to have Lieutenant Wayne hear your story." Lawson pushed back his chair. "He's the one running the case."

Billy had overreached. He replayed the bullpen's layout in his mind, figuring his way out. His left hand inched closer to the heavy stapler on Lawson's desk. He knew he could reach it and knock Lawson upside the head before the man would have time to reach for his gun.

"Hey! Put the weapon down!"

Billy's head jerked up at the commotion erupting behind him. Suddenly officers were running, guns drawn.

"Shit!" Lawson yelled, reaching for his gun. Billy turned. The two groups he'd seen earlier must have gotten a little too close to each other. Lawson headed into the fray.

Billy knew this was his chance. God had opened the door.

He bolted from his seat and flew through the station, down the stairs, and out the front door. He didn't stop running until he reached his car three blocks away.

CHAPTER TWENTY-TWO

K issing Jordan was beyond anything Devon had imagined. What's more, Jordan was kissing her back.

It had been impulse, without thought, driven by her anger and her hunger. She was not angry with Jordan—how could she be, for she had no claim on her—but with herself. For letting Mel get to her, for pushing, for revealing her desire so openly, for embarrassing herself so completely.

She had wanted to run, but Jordan hadn't let her. She was coming apart, unable to tell Jordan how she felt despite having already revealed herself. She was a broken thing, damaged beyond repair, lost beyond all hope of salvation.

But Jordan, fearless, valiant, bullheaded Jordan, refused to back down. Refused to let her go. Refused to let her run.

And Devon had kissed her.

Just as she had been unable to stop herself from challenging Mel, so too was she now unable to stop this kiss. The first touch of Jordan's tongue had been her undoing. The floodgates had opened, and she was powerless against the wave that came crashing through it.

Her arms twined their way around Jordan's neck, no longer held by Jordan's hands. Jordan pulled her closer, crushing their bodies together, wrapping her strong arms around Devon. Their mouths met over and again, nipping, sucking, tongues slipping over and around.

Heat and wet. Inferno and storm.

Jordan moved against her, walked her back until she was pressed between the counter and Jordan's body. Trapped, though Devon had no thought of escape.

Jordan held her tightly, one hand slipping to the swell of her backside while the other wound its way up into her hair. Devon had never felt so wanted and so safe.

She heard Jordan groan gutturally and desperately wanted to hear her make that sound again. She tugged at Jordan's neck, crushing their bodies together, their breasts, their stomachs, their thighs. She couldn't get close enough.

She began to rock involuntarily, a slow roll of her hips against Jordan's. She felt Jordan's leg slip between hers, giving her something to grind against. *Oh God.*

And there was that groan again, reverberating through Devon's body like a string being plucked, the hum of it shaking her to her core. It jarred her back to consciousness.

She couldn't do this. Not without Jordan knowing the truth.

Willing all her strength, Devon broke their kiss. Jordan blinked slowly, hair sexily tousled, lips temptingly swollen. Devon nearly began their kiss anew. The rakish grin on Jordan's face was not helping matters.

Slowly, painfully, she extricated herself from between the counter and Jordan's arms, putting some space between their overheated bodies. Her heart still pounded, the sound beating time in her ears. She had never, ever, been kissed like that. And she feared she never would be again.

"I have to tell you something," Devon said unsteadily.

Jordan looked at her in disbelief. "Now?"

"Now," Devon confirmed. "Before I lose my nerve."

Jordan read the shift in Devon, seeming to understand that whatever Devon was about to say, it was bigger than what was happening between them. "Okay," she said, holding out her hand. "But we are going to talk about *this*"—gesturing between them—"later, right?"

"If you want," Devon said, unable to commit to a conversation she knew Jordan might not want later.

"Oh, I want," Jordan said cheekily. It made Devon smile.

Jordan led her to the sofa and sat beside her, giving Devon space without distance. Devon tucked her knees to her chest, something she hadn't done since she was a little girl.

Devon searched for the words but didn't know where to begin. A Bible verse, one of the few she knew, popped into her head. *"And I only am escaped alone to tell thee."*

"Book of Job?" Jordan asked, surprising Devon. She nodded. If she had the opportunity to still know Jordan years from now, the woman would never cease to surprise her.

Max, who had been lying dejectedly in front of the fire since Jordan had forced him away from the pie, took up a new spot at the floor next to Devon. She took strength from his presence at her side.

"I haven't told you everything. About Billy. About me."

Jordan's expression remained the same. Open. Concerned. Understanding. "I know."

Devon smiled weakly. "I know you know. But you don't know."

Jordan eased back slightly. "You can tell me anything."

Devon prayed that was true.

"I told you Billy used to go on these fishing trips when I was younger. I always wanted to go, but my mom wouldn't let me." Jordan nodded. "That was mostly true, but it wasn't the whole truth."

Devon searched Jordan's face for some change, some hint of betrayal, but it wasn't there.

It would come soon enough.

"On my thirteenth birthday, Billy announced he was taking me on his next fishing trip. I was so excited. My mom seemed surprised, and maybe even a little concerned, but that didn't matter to me. All that mattered was Billy was finally letting me go with him. Things had been tense around the house for a while, and I always thought it was my fault, that I'd done things to make Billy mad. So when he said he wanted to take me along, I just knew everything was going to be okay. Mom helped me pack a bag, and we were off. We drove for hours, north into Wisconsin. Billy wouldn't tell me where we were going, only that it was one of his favorite fishing spots. It was already getting dark by the time we got there. Billy checked us into a little motel, some dive off the interstate. He said if this trip went well and I liked it, we'd camp out under the stars the next time. I thought we would just go to sleep, but after we dropped off our bags, Billy said we should walk down to the bar up the street, get a bite to eat. I'd never been in a bar before, but Billy said it was okay, so off we went."

Devon took one last glance at Jordan and then shifted her gaze to the sofa, knowing the next time she looked at Jordan's face, it would be full of contempt.

"There was this woman, young, pretty. She sat next to us at the bar. She seemed nice enough, said she was just passing through. I was so tired and just wanted to go to bed, but Billy insisted we stay and keep the woman company. Her name was Sheryl. Eventually, Sheryl paid her tab and got up to leave—said she had a few more hours of driving to go that night. Billy said it was time for us to go, too. There wasn't anyone else left in the bar except for the bartender, the cook, and us. Billy insisted we walk Sheryl to her car, since it was so late. She agreed. He put gloves on as we were walking. I remember thinking it was odd because it wasn't that cold out. When we got to her car, Sheryl turned to thank us. That's when Billy pulled out his knife."

Devon shuddered at the memory but forced herself to keep talking. She closed her eyes, unable to bear having them open for the next part. Unable to bear the chance of seeing Jordan turn against her.

"He held the knife to her throat and pulled a bandana out of his back pocket and told me to put it in her mouth and tie it behind her head. I was so scared. I just stood there, holding this bandana, crying. He told me to get it together, but I kept on crying. He backhanded me. I fell to the ground. I couldn't get up, couldn't make my body move. He yanked the bandana out of my hand and told me he'd do it himself. Once he'd gagged her he shoved her into the front seat of her car. He slid in next to her and told me to get in the back. I still couldn't move. Then he looked me in the eye—the same look he'd given his buddies at that poker game. I got in."

Devon hugged her knees in tighter, warding off the cold chill of memory. She felt like throwing up. She felt thirteen again.

"We drove off into the woods. There was this run-down shack deep in the trees. He dragged Sheryl out of the car and into the shack, and told me to follow. The only thing inside was this old, rotten bed, with handcuffs hanging from the four corners. He chained her up and told her that no one was around for miles, so no one would hear her if she screamed. He said that if she behaved herself, then it would all be over soon. Then he took me back to the motel."

Tears pricked at her eyes but she closed them tighter, keeping the tears locked behind her eyelids. She would not let them fall until she was done. She would have plenty to cry about then.

"Back at the motel, he told me how disappointed he was in me. That I'd failed a rite of passage, one he'd passed when he was thirteen. He hadn't cried. He hadn't said no. God demanded, and I would obey. I couldn't stop crying. He grabbed my arm and twisted it behind my back, told me I needed to get my act together. It hurt so much. Then he locked me in the bathroom for the rest of the night. I heard him go out for a while, but then he was back. I was so scared, I didn't make a sound. At the crack of dawn, we went back to the woods. I was afraid of what would happen to Sheryl, but I was more afraid of Billy. I should have tried to run, to call for help, to do something. But I didn't. I just got in our car. Sheryl's car was gone."

Devon began rocking herself. She felt Max sit up beside her, nudge her arm with his nose, but she ignored him. She didn't deserve comfort. She didn't deserve anything except scorn, and disgust, and hatred.

"He unlocked Sheryl's handcuffs and brought her outside. He pushed his knife into my hand and said in order to earn my place by his side, I had to offer up a sacrifice to the Lord. I had to hunt her down and deliver her to God. Then he told her to run. She did. But I just stood there. Everything started spinning. The last thing I remember is Sheryl running into the trees and Billy chasing after her. I blacked out. When I woke up, Billy had dragged Sheryl and me out beyond the shack. He was sitting on a rock, staring at me, a shovel in his hand. He didn't say anything, just watched me. It reminded me of an eagle, cocking its head back and forth, studying its prey. Sheryl was lying there staring up at me. Her throat was cut."

Devon rocked harder now, and the tears leaked out no matter how hard she shut her eyes against them. She began to hyperventilate but reined her breathing in just enough to finish the story.

"He made me bury her. Dig the hole and cover her with dirt. When we were done, he told me if I ever told anyone, he would do the same thing to my mom and to me. Mom was asleep when we got home. He put me into bed. He set a single wheat penny on the dresser, and I finally understood what it meant. What it had always meant. The next day, he told Mom I'd gotten sick on the boat, fallen and hit my head. That explained the bruise on my face and why we were back early. For days, when my mom wasn't looking, he'd just stare at me, like he was trying to figure out if I was going to tell. Once, he slid his finger across his throat. Like I could ever forget. I never told, and I managed to avoid going with him again for two years. Then one day he said he was taking me camping. My mom said no. And he killed her. And I started running."

Her tears fell freely now, her terrible truth revealed, at last. She had helped Billy commit murder. She had done nothing to stop him. Her mother, and who knew how many others, had died because she hadn't been strong enough to stand up to him.

Jordan hadn't made a sound since Devon had begun her confession. She could still feel her there on the sofa, watching her. With every fiber of her being Devon feared what she would read on Jordan's face. The revulsion. The loathing. The unmitigated disgust. Devon couldn't bear it, but she knew she had to face it. She owed Jordan that much.

And so Devon opened her eyes and blinked away her tears. But what she saw was nothing she could have ever expected, or even hoped for. Jordan was crying, gazing at her with such compassion that Devon was sure it had to be a mistake. She was sure this was the ultimate cosmic joke, for her to see this woman looking at her this way, only to have it ripped away, replaced by the abhorrence she so rightly deserved.

When it didn't happen, when seconds turned to minutes and Jordan just kept looking at her with tenderness and understanding, Devon crumbled.

"You need to arrest me," she said. "Take me to jail, lock me away forever."

"No," Jordan said evenly.

"Yes!" Devon cried, rising to her knees. "I didn't stop him. I helped him kill Sheryl. I buried her. It's all my fault."

"No," Jordan said again in the same voice as before.

"Damn it, what in the hell is wrong with you?" She fell into Jordan, beating her fists against Jordan's chest. "I killed my mother. *I killed them all.*"

Devon cried and pounded Jordan's chest, exhausting herself within minutes. She felt Jordan's arms around her, pulling her closer, giving her sanctuary from herself. Her weeping subsided into hiccupping sobs, her tears soaking Jordan's shirt.

She buried her face in the crook of Jordan's neck, her body wrapped within sheltering arms. Jordan's lips went to Devon's ear, and she began to whisper, "You were only a child. You didn't have a choice. It's not your fault."

Over and over, Jordan said the words, for endless minutes like a mantra, or maybe a prayer. Devon felt the words sing in her ears and sink into her skin, filling up the dark place that had held this misery for so long. And as she cried herself out, and as Jordan held her, she found herself starting to believe.

❖

Henry yanked open the door, the captain hot on his heels.

"What in the hell is going on?" the captain yelled.

At least five people were in handcuffs, and another was spread-eagled over a desk, being frisked.

Lawson holstered his weapon. "Property dispute, if you can believe that," he said. "But one of them had a knife."

The captain went to sort things out.

Lawson pulled Henry to the side. "Hey, I got this guy over here, says he might have seen Billy the night before the murders."

"What?"

"Well, he didn't use Billy's name, but he described someone who matches the description Jordan gave us. But…"

"But, what?"

"Something's not right about this guy." Lawson glanced over his shoulder back toward his desk. "Shit, he's gone."

Henry took off for the front door, practically knocking two cops over as he ran. He skidded to a stop on the sidewalk out front, frantically scanning the area. Nothing. Lawson came up behind him.

"Damn it, I shouldn't have walked away."

Henry was panting heavily. He wasn't made for running anymore. "S'okay." He caught his breath. "Let's go back inside, and you can fill me in."

If Lawson noticed how out of shape Henry was, he didn't mention it, for which Henry was grateful. He felt embarrassed enough.

Back inside, Lawson filled him in on his conversation with Mr. Collins. "I don't know, Henry. He seemed too interested, you know? In Ms. James. In witness protection."

A sick feeling rose up from Henry's gut. "What did Mr. Collins look like?"

"Maybe six feet, brown hair, beginning of a beard, about one eighty…" Lawson faltered. "Son of a bitch."

Henry's gut twisted.

"Lieutenant Wayne?" One of the uniforms approached and held out a piece of paper. "This came in for you over the fax."

Henry stared at the paper. He handed it to Lawson. "This look like him?"

"Holy shit," Lawson muttered, sinking down into his chair. "Twenty years older, a little bigger, hair a little darker—yeah, that's him."

It was Billy's photo from Roscoe. Coleman had come through again, only this time, ten minutes too late.

"Was he alone at your desk?" Henry asked suddenly.

"It was only for a—"

"Check your desk," Henry said, scanning his own. "See if anything's missing, anything's even a hair out of place."

Neither man touched anything. Henry saw nothing out of the ordinary. Neither did Lawson.

"Get MCU up here. I want these desks and chairs dusted for prints, and I want this room swept for bugs," Henry said. Lawson picked up the phone on a neighboring desk. "Michaels! Get over here!"

The cop who had brought Henry the fax jogged over. "What do you need, sir?"

"Go pull the surveillance tapes for the last thirty minutes," Henry barked. "Get them down to the techs."

"What are they looking for?"

Henry turned to Lawson, who answered. "White guy. Late forties to early fifties. Pens cap and jacket. He was sitting at my desk less than ten minutes ago."

"I'm on it," Michaels said and ran off.

Once Lawson was off the phone, Henry led him over to the far side of the room. They watched in silence as the MCU techs dusted Lawson and Henry's desks and searched for listening devices. They pulled dozens of prints but found no bugs.

Henry flopped down into a chair. They'd had him. They'd had him right here and had let him get away.

"I am so sorry," Lawson said, head in his hands. "So sorry."

Henry was angry, but he didn't blame Lawson. Not really. How in the hell could he—could they—have known Billy would walk right into their police station. In all his years of police work, he had never heard of something like that happening. It was brazen. It was reckless. It was—

"Desperate."

"What?" Lawson asked, dropping his hands. Henry looked at him, a smile tickling the corners of his mouth. "Desperate. He had to have been pretty damn desperate to come here."

Henry started to laugh. Lawson looked at him like he was losing his mind. Maybe he was.

"He came here looking for information. He doesn't have the damnedest clue where Devon and Jordan are. Which means they're safe, for now."

Lawson was starting to get it. "And if Billy's desperate enough to come here—"

"Then he's getting reckless enough to make a mistake." And Henry would have to be ready for him.

CHAPTER TWENTY-THREE

Jordan sat by the window, watching Devon sleep. She had held Devon for what felt like hours but could never be long enough, telling her over and over it wasn't her fault. Trying to make her understand. Pleading with her to believe.

My God. My God.

Everything clicked into place. This was the missing piece, the reason Billy was so obsessed with Devon. He'd planned to make her his protégée, to have her continue his work, his legacy, like someone—probably his own father—had done when he was thirteen. And she'd rejected him. Billy's ego couldn't take that kind of blow. He would hunt her until the end of time, for her continued existence was a repudiation of everything he was.

More than that, Billy wasn't just murdering people as a means to an end on his quest to kill Devon. He was a serial killer in the truest sense, complete with his own killing ground. If he'd been killing since he was thirteen…Jordan could barely comprehend it. Organized serial killers liked to kill within their comfort zone but were cautious enough to know better than to kill in the area where they lived. Jordan figured Billy had searched for and found his spot in Wisconsin not long after the family had settled in Illinois. He likely had a spot somewhere in or near West Virginia as well.

But Billy had been on the move since his "death," hunting his daughter. He might have set up another killing ground somewhere, one that he could return to from time to time, but Jordan doubted it. Billy had proven himself adaptable, had evolved over the years into something different. Something more cunning, more terrifying. Cross-country serial killers were rare and nearly impossible to catch. Billy's path was tied to Devon's, his MO flexible, his signature subtle, and Jordan would stake money that Billy did not have a particular type of victim other than people who wouldn't easily be missed, which would have made it nearly impossible for law enforcement to see a pattern over the years.

On top of all that, Billy thought he was killing for God. His mission wasn't just about killing Devon; it was about *killing*, period. Best case scenario, he was a brutal, deliberate serial killer with delusions of a mission from God and an unresolved need to warp his daughter to mirror his narcissistic sense of self.

The things this beautiful, broken soul had been put through. Had survived. And when she found Billy—and Jordan would find him—she would kill him. There would be no trial, no plea agreement, no defense attorney convincing a judge or jury that Billy was crazy.

Billy was crazy, no doubt about it. But Jordan refused to allow that to be his excuse.

Jordan believed in the rule of law, believed in the legal system and, God help her, even in the right of every person to be represented by counsel. People deserved to get a fair trial, no matter what they'd done.

But Billy was not a person. He was a rabid animal. A monster. And the only thing he deserved was to be put down.

If that made her a murderer, she couldn't care less. Let the ACLU come after her. Let her be prosecuted. It didn't matter. Nothing mattered, except freeing Devon from this psycho's grasp. From being hunted. She was tired of waiting. It was time to kill the wolf. But that meant she had to set a trap.

A plan began to take shape in her mind. They needed to draw him out. Lure him in. Unfortunately, traps required bait, and the only bait Billy was interested in was Devon.

Jordan ran her fingers through her shorn hair. Could she do this? Put Devon at risk? It wasn't fair. She should just take Devon and run, leave Billy and everything else far behind. They could build a new life together somewhere, just the two of them. She could keep Devon safe. She could love her.

But Billy would find them. Somehow, someday, he would track them down and destroy anything they'd built. He would burn it to the ground, razing entire city blocks if he had to. His destruction knew no bounds, his cunning, no end.

And what of Henry? And her mother? Billy would find them and kill them, too, just out of spite. To cause maximum pain. She couldn't take them with her. She couldn't protect them all.

God. Help me. Please.

She rested her chin in her palm and watched Devon sleep. She had been utterly, bodily exhausted when she had finally finished crying. Years worth of pent-up tears, of agony and regret, would do that to a person.

She heard Devon's words in her head, begging Jordan to arrest her, pleading with Jordan to condemn her, demanding that Jordan hate her. But Jordan could not hate her. Or condemn her. And she certainly wasn't about to arrest her. Devon had done nothing wrong. She had done nothing but try to keep her mother, keep herself, safe.

Devon was a victim, just like all of Billy's victims. She had helped bury that body under duress, stayed silent under threat of harm to herself and to her mother. She had been abused, mentally and physically. And she had seen firsthand what Billy was capable of.

No jury on earth would convict Devon, even if there was a prosecutor stupid enough to bring charges.

Jordan's heart swelled. She was falling in love with Devon James. There was no doubt about it now. And she would do whatever it took to protect her, or die trying.

The phone at her hip vibrated. Not wanting to disturb Devon's much-needed slumber, she silently called for Max, grabbed her coat, and went outside.

"Tell me you're having a better day than I am," she said, half in jest, half in despair.

"I wish I could," Henry said, sounding despondent.

"What's wrong?"

Henry told her about Billy coming to the station. The line cut out on and off, but she got the gist. All the air fled from her lungs. They'd had him, and he'd gotten away. He'd been there, and—

"Does he know where we are?" Jordan asked, panicked.

"No, no," Henry said. "He didn't get anything."

"What about bugs. Are you—"

"Checked and cleared. He got nothing, I swear." A pause. "I'm sorry, Jordan."

"It's okay."

"I'm so, so—"

"Henry? You still there?"

"I'm here."

Damn phones. Jordan kicked at the browning grass. Max sat a few steps away, watching her talk to Henry.

"You couldn't have known," she said and meant it. "It's not your fault." She could hear Henry digesting the words. "Really," she added. It was enough. "Okay."

Billy was no longer stable. He was growing bolder, more reckless, which meant he was devolving. He was more likely to make a mistake, but he was also infinitely more dangerous. They needed to take advantage before it was too late.

"I think we can use this," she said.

She could practically hear Henry smiling over the phone. "Exactly what…was thinking."

She needed more time to think. To plan. And she needed to tell him Devon's story. She started to speak but thought better of it. This was not a conversation to be had over the phone, especially one cutting in and out.

"We need to do this face to face," she said.

"How?"

"Technology is a wonderful thing, my friend. I can get it set up on my end. I'll e-mail Lawson the details. Eleven o'clock."

They disconnected. By tomorrow, the storm would be coming in and the phones would be shot to hell. But Jordan knew one way to get uninterrupted service. She didn't like the idea of leaving Devon alone, but it was safer.

Jordan bent down and Max trotted over.

"You're going to be in charge tomorrow, buddy. And Devon's not going to like it one bit." She stroked Max's neck. "If he comes anywhere near her, you rip out his fucking throat."

Max seemed to understand. He growled.

Chapter Twenty-four

Devon lay awake, unable to sleep any longer. Jordan's arm was wrapped securely around her, and Devon thought there couldn't be a safer or better place in the entire world. Max lay curled up on the rug at the foot of the bed, not seeming to mind having his sleeping spot taken away. There just wasn't room for the three of them.

Jordan once again had planned to sleep on the couch. But Devon refused to give in. She'd thumbed the shadows beneath Jordan's eyes, telling her that, as gorgeous as she was, two nights without real sleep were starting to show. When that hadn't worked, Devon had played her only real card: she didn't want to be alone. To that, Jordan had acquiesced.

She studied Jordan's face, tracing her features, memorizing every curve, every line. She still had a hard time accepting that Jordan had not pushed her away. She still wasn't sure she didn't deserve to be cast aside. But Jordan had been relentless. From the moment she had started pounding Jordan's chest right up until she'd fallen into an exhausted sleep, Jordan had refused to allow Devon's demons to get the better of her. Each time she felt her guilt rising up, Jordan had been at her side, with gentle touches or soothing words.

You were only a child. You didn't have a choice. It's not your fault.

She had slept on the couch for two hours, long enough for day to give way into evening and for Jordan to make dinner and talk to Henry. Billy had been at the police station. She could barely wrap her mind around it. Jordan had told her over dinner, had held her hand to help keep the tremors that overtook her at the news at bay.

After dinner, they had sat on the couch, a fire crackling in the fireplace. They had discussed Billy and what his going to the station might mean, and Jordan told her she planned to head down the mountain to use Mel's broadband to videoconference with Henry.

Her initial reaction to *that* news had been less than ladylike. She'd actually snorted. Jordan had known better than to laugh and had soothed her with a kiss.

Jordan shifted in her sleep, her arm tightening around Devon's back, pulling her closer. She snuggled in, taking solace in Jordan's warmth. She smiled to herself, recalling the almost comical events leading to them actually getting into bed. Jordan had taken Max out for one last walk and Devon had made her way to the bedroom. She'd turned down the sheets on the far side of the bed and then stopped, waiting. She wanted Jordan in her bed, wanted it in more ways than one, but when the moment was nearly upon her, her stomach was twisted in knots.

She knew she was being foolish. They were both adults. They could share a bed without…

Not that she didn't want to make love to Jordan. She did want that. She wanted that very much. But everything was so new, still so jumbled in her mind. She just needed a little time.

She'd felt Jordan in the doorway, looked up to find her there, and nearly burst out laughing. Jordan was looking at the bed like it was covered in mousetraps.

Oh, thank God.

Jordan's nervousness soothed her, giving her strength, erasing her apprehension. She rounded the bed and held out her hand, which Jordan took instantly.

"So it wasn't just me, then?" Jordan asked, grinning.

"Nope."

Everything was different after that. They'd changed into their sleepwear—Jordan in the bathroom, Devon in the bedroom—and slid into bed easily, without disquiet, like it was the most natural thing in the world. Jordan had been asleep within minutes, and Devon took comfort in her rhythmic respiration. But as comfortable as she was, as right as it felt to be lying here in Jordan's arms, Devon found sleep elusive.

The day had been a tornado of emotions, spinning her around, twisting her inside out and back again. She had reached the heights of passion and the depths of despair in a single afternoon. At the center of it all had been Jordan, comforting her, loving her, making her feel things that only hours ago she had thought she had no right to feel. She could only pray this feeling wouldn't be taken away from her.

❖

Billy paced his motel room, clenching and unclenching his fists. He couldn't afford any more mistakes, and trashing his room, while satisfying, would definitely be a mistake.

He had gone to the police station seeking answers, and he had found only suspicion. Suspicion and failure.

He was not used to failing. He was not used to taking such risks, risks that found no reward, like footsteps without purchase in the sand.

And yet he had beaten them, hadn't he? He had been there, right *there*, within their grasp, and he had escaped. He had beaten them at their own game, shown them how foolish they were, and how powerful was the will of the Lord.

They grope in the dark without light, and he maketh them to stagger like a drunken man.

Job 12:25 made him feel a little better, as it spoke of just how blind the police could be with God on his side. They had nothing. They knew nothing.

But he had still failed. He was confident the surveillance cameras had not gotten a good image. He was too smart for that, the cap pulled low—but not too low—on his head, his face angled away from the cameras just enough to block their view without anyone knowing he was doing it.

Billy was no rookie.

But Detective Lawson had seen his face. He had counted on not arousing suspicion, counted on the cops being charmed by his manner, lulled by his story, seduced by their own eagerness to solve their case. That's what cops did. They wanted the easy answer. It was how Billy had stayed dead all these years, how he had evaded detection, despite Maddie's attempts years ago to convince the police he was alive and killing.

But Lawson had been skeptical and Billy had pushed too hard, his own eagerness getting the better of him. The answers had been there, *right there*, within his reach. And now, he had nothing. He had no idea what to do next.

"Lord, please. I need a sign. I have looked, but I do not see. Forgive my weakness, my failings. I am at your mercy, Lord. I need your guidance."

But there was only silence. The radiator hummed in the corner of the room, mocking Billy with its ambivalence.

He fell to his knees, clasping his hands together, eyelids slamming shut. *"When thou passest through the waters, I will be with thee,"* Billy prayed, *"and through the rivers, they shall not overflow thee: when thou walkest through the fire, thou shalt not be burned."*

Billy pressed his clutched hands to his forehead, willing God to hear him. *"Neither shall the flame kindle upon thee."*

He repeated the last line over and over, faster and faster, rocking back and forth on his knees until the words and the world whirred by him at a million miles an hour, hurtling him through time and space and destiny unfolding, until all was light and heat and the absence of sound.

God. Please.

A door opened. A path revealed itself.

He heard a distant scratching, and he was flying again, ripped from the light back into darkness. He opened his eyes and heard the sound again.

He opened the room's only window and an orange tabby leapt up onto the ledge from the fire escape. It stared at him, its head tipped to the side.

"Mrow."

Billy picked the cat up by the scruff of the neck, examining it. It hung limply from his hand, permitting his inspection. He walked over to the bed and folded the cat into his arms, beginning to stroke its fur. It purred like a freight train.

"Awfully cold out there," Billy murmured. "You're probably hungry."

He set the cat down on the bed and walked over to the small table in the corner of the room. The cat watched him fish a can of tuna from a plastic bag but stayed on the bed, even once Billy had cracked back the lid. He set the open container on the floor in the center of the room, waiting. The cat did not move.

"Well, come on now," he cooed. "You must like tuna. All cats like tuna."

The cat hopped down from the bed and stalked over to the can. It sniffed twice and then dove in, seeming to enjoy the feast. But halfway through, the cat stopped. It looked up at Billy, and then over toward the closet.

"What is it? You smell a rat?"

The tabby looked up at him again and then scampered over to the cracked closet door. It nudged the door open a little farther, just enough for it to slip inside. It made no sound.

Puzzled, Billy walked over to the closet and opened the door fully. There sat the cat, squarely in the middle of the closet floor, looking up at him expectantly.

"Mrow."

What an odd cat.

"Don't you want your dinner?"

The cat came out of the closet and nudged the door closed with its head. When it was open only a crack again, it slipped back inside.

Billy opened the door once more to find the cat in exactly the same spot as before.

"Mrow."

At last, Billy understood. He had done this before.

"Hear, O Lord, when I cry with my voice: have mercy also upon me, and answer me," he quoted reverently.

The Lord had shown him the way. He knew what he must do.

CHAPTER TWENTY-FIVE

Jordan's unconscious mind began the torturous climb toward wakefulness. Light crested over her body, warming her skin. Not light. Flame. Enveloping her, folding over and under her. Within her. From within. From without. Scorching. Thick. Powerful.

She tried to blink away the fog, but the exquisite sensations washing over her body clouded her brain, a barrier between her and full awareness. She could not think. Only feel. A soft, firm weight on her chest. On her thigh. Sultry, languid breath on her neck. Her head turned, lips seeking the source of the whisper against her skin.

They found what they were searching for.

Full. Silken. Moist.

She moaned.

The first touch of her tongue against Devon's was a live wire zapping her body, and she was instantly, gloriously awake.

Awake, and kissing Devon.

Awake, and full of wonder.

Devon met Jordan's moan and opened her mouth farther, welcoming her in. Devon's lithe body slid against hers, moving more fully over her, and Jordan grasped her hips, pulling her the rest of the way. Devon's thighs squeezed Jordan's hips, rocking slowly, ever so slowly.

It was hell.

It was heaven.

Jordan's eyelids fluttered open. Devon's sky blue eyes, now dark as the ocean, watched her. Devon flicked out her tongue, catching Jordan's lip with its tip.

Jordan groaned and dove back in. She caressed Devon's thighs, so soft, so smooth. Her fingers slipped beneath the hem of Devon's nightshirt, traced the edge of Devon's panties. Devon's hand slipped into Jordan's hair, tugging, demanding. Their tongues clashed, dueling for dominance, for surrender. Wanton. Hungry.

Jordan's hands found Devon's ass. She cupped the supple flesh, pulling Devon ever more tightly against her body. The thin cotton barrier of Devon's underwear was maddening, and she had to fight to keep herself from ripping the panties away. She skimmed her hands up Devon's back beneath her shirt, delighting in the way the taut muscles moved under silken skin. Then her hands slipped down, down, down beneath Devon's panties. She squeezed her flesh, rubbing and circling, fingers pressing and clutching. Devon released a moan from deep in the back of her throat into Jordan's mouth before thrusting her tongue deeply inside.

There was something niggling in the back of Jordan's mind, some vague invader telling her to slow down, that this wasn't the time—something about time and needing to…but oh, Devon was moving again, kissing her, sucking on her bottom lip, and Jordan was so wet. So, so wet.

She flipped Devon over onto her back, pinning her beneath her weight, sliding her thigh between Devon's legs, pressing, thrusting. They moved as one, skimming and surging, skin grown slick from the heat between them. Jordan's shorts had ridden up to bare her upper thighs, her tank top bunched to just below her breasts. She wanted to feel Devon's skin against her stomach, needed to feel their passion-slick bodies gliding over each other with nothing between them.

Devon's questing hand made her lose focus as it brushed Jordan's breast, then closed around it. She deftly flicked Jordan's nipple.

"I need you inside me," Devon gasped. She nipped at Jordan's neck, laving the skin she'd just bitten. She exhaled hotly in Jordan's ear, traced the shell of it with her tongue, tugged at the earlobe with her teeth. "Please."

Oh God.

Jordan was helpless to resist. She shifted slightly and trailed her hand down, pushing past the thin cotton, her fingers tickling the edge of soft curls. Devon inhaled sharply, spread her legs wider, pulled Jordan's head down to claim her lips again.

Jordan felt the earth move. It took her several moments to realize it wasn't her doing.

Catching her breath, she pressed her forehead to Devon's. "I'm gonna kill him."

Devon kissed the corners of her mouth. "You can't kill him," she said. "He's a good boy."

Jordan turned her head. Max was standing on top of the bed beside them. He barked. "He's a fucking cock block is what he is," Jordan grumbled.

Devon laughed, the sweet sound taking the edge off Jordan's frustration. She caressed Jordan's cheek, turning her head. She took Jordan's lips once, then again, less urgently than before but just as passionately. She leaned back into the pillow.

"He probably just needs to go out," she said with a glance at her watch. "It's nearly nine."

Jordan hadn't realized they had slept so long. She couldn't remember the last time she'd had so much sleep.

"Yeah, well," she said, rolling up and out of bed, "he needs to learn to take himself out."

Devon laughed again. It was a sound Jordan would never tire of hearing.

Now that his humans were up and paying attention, Max bounded off the bed and darted out of the room toward the front door.

Jordan yanked a pair of sweats from the dresser and pulled them on over her thin sleep shorts. She tugged on a sweatshirt and grabbed a pair of socks. She couldn't really be mad, but damn, Max's timing absolutely sucked.

"Hey, it's okay." Devon stood before Jordan and caught her before she could sit on the bed. She took Jordan's face in both her hands and kissed her soundly. The socks fell limply from Jordan's fingers, her arms wrapping around Devon's waist. The kiss was intense but unhurried, telling Jordan everything she needed to know.

This is for real. She doesn't regret it. This is only the beginning.

Whatever excuses Jordan had made before for holding back were just that: excuses. They were distinctions without meaning, barriers without reason. The hesitancy Jordan had felt before about giving in to her feelings, the conviction to not get involved until the danger was over, vanished at Devon's touch. They were already involved.

Jordan leaned back, brushing an errant hair from Devon's face. "You okay?"

"Other than the interruptus of our coitus, I'm fantastic."

Jordan chuckled. "How'd I get so lucky?"

Devon traced Jordan's cheek and gave her a soft, brief kiss. Then she slipped out of Jordan's embrace.

"Hey, where are you going?" Jordan whined.

Devon laughed. "You have a dog to walk. And I have a shower to take." She sashayed—actually *sashayed*—over to the door. She flashed Jordan a seductive smile over her shoulder. "And as for lucky, you ain't seen nothing yet."

Jordan's heart stopped as Devon peeled her shirt over her head, stretching her arms high and thrusting out her chest, and flung the shirt at her. It fell helplessly to the floor, Jordan unable to do anything but stare at the curve of Devon's breast peeking at her from the side. Devon slipped Jordan's robe off the hook on the back of the door and slid into it. She tied the belt loosely at her waist, the flaps of the robe gaping just enough to give Jordan a tantalizing hint of flesh.

"If you're good, perhaps I'll leave you some hot water," Devon taunted. Jordan didn't respond. She wasn't sure she'd even blinked. "Well, maybe a cold shower would be better for you."

With a flip of her hair, she was gone, leaving a stunned Jordan in her wake.

Damn, that woman can flirt. Lucky me.

Devon sighed as the water cascaded over her skin. While the steamy spray was doing nothing for her overheated body, it still felt amazing.

Wow, that woman could kiss.

Devon's hand wandered down, tangling in the curls Jordan's hand had only skimmed. She throbbed at the memory. She could still feel Jordan's hands upon her, touching her, pressing into her. She longed to feel those hands again, caressing her. Stroking her. Making her come.

Her fingers traced her sex, dipped inside, found the pool of wetness that was all Jordan's doing. She flicked her index finger over the tight bundle of nerves, just once, and she nearly orgasmed.

She had never felt like this before. No one had ever made her feel like this.

So erotic. So carnal. So wanted.

Knowing that Jordan wanted her, and that she wanted her despite her past, despite what she had done, shredded the last of Devon's doubt. She was falling in love with Jordan, wholeheartedly, overwhelmingly, absolutely and completely. Mind, heart, body, and soul.

Devon shivered, moving her hand away from temptation and reaching for the shower gel. Self-gratification wasn't what she wanted, no matter how much her body thrummed. She wanted Jordan. She would wait for Jordan. Hopefully, she would not have to wait too long.

Disappointed as she was with the abrupt end to their activities, she was also relieved. The videoconference was set for eleven, and it was already after nine. They would have had to stop even if Max hadn't interrupted, or else they would have had to rush, and Devon had no intention of rushing. She wanted hours. She wanted days. She wanted to start and end and begin again, to hear Jordan cry out her name and then beg her for more, to shudder and shake by Jordan's hands and mouth and tongue and then do it all over again, over and over until they collapsed from sheer exhaustion.

Devon's eyelids slammed shut. The thoughts running amok in her brain were not helping. She soaped her body and washed her hair, trying to think of anything but Jordan. It proved impossible.

She dried off quickly and slipped back into Jordan's robe. She smelled Jordan's perfume, sandalwood and vanilla and something entirely, uniquely Jordan, and it made her shudder. In the bedroom, she slipped into jeans and a blue V-neck sweater. These clothes did not smell like Jordan, for which Devon was grateful. She needed to focus, and she couldn't do that while her head was filled with her almost-lover's scent.

She found Jordan in the living room.

"Leave me any hot water?"

"A little," Devon said. She walked into Jordan's outstretched arms.

"You smell good," Jordan whispered, kissing Devon's neck. Devon hummed, her temperature rising at the first touch of Jordan's lips.

"You better cut that out," she playfully admonished, leaning back to gaze at Jordan, "or we're going to be late for the meeting."

Jordan's face paled.

"What?" Devon asked.

"You're not going."

Devon stepped out of Jordan's arms. "What do you mean I'm not going?"

"You're going to stay here with Max."

Devon crossed her arms. She wasn't sure what incensed her more—the idea of Jordan going without her, or that Jordan had made this decision for her like she was some preschooler in need of daycare.

"Listen, I just think it's better this way," Jordan said in a rush. "Safer. There's no sense in taking unnecessary chances, and you leaving this cabin is unnecessary."

"Seriously, Jordan? What possible risk could there be in me going with you?"

"Billy could be there," Jordan said, like it was the most logical thing in the world. It only angered Devon further.

"Really?" Devon said hotly. "And how would he know you're going to be at Mel's at eleven o'clock. ESP? Henry doesn't know that's where you're going. Hell, even Mel doesn't know!"

Jordan started to speak, but Devon wasn't finished.

"And if by some crazy chance Billy is there, you…what? You thought you'd just leave me here while you face God knows what out there, by yourself?"

"I won't be by myself. Mel—"

"Not what I meant, and you know it."

Jordan roughly ran a hand through her hair. "I don't know what you want from me here."

Jordan's plaintive expression doused some of Devon's fire. She stepped closer and cupped Jordan's cheek. "I know you want to protect me, but this is my life. It's all a crapshoot. All I know is that, whatever happens, I want to be by your side. Don't make decisions for me. Don't treat me like a child."

Devon stood silently as Jordan searched her face—for doubt? for hesitation? But Devon was resolved. It was time for her to stop hiding. She wanted—she *needed*—to take control of her own life.

"Okay."

Devon kissed her. "Good. Now, do you want to tell me about this plan of yours that you were concocting last night?"

"I will, I promise. Let me get showered and I'll tell you in the car. Okay?"

❖

Jordan pulled into the parking lot at Mel's. A light snow had begun to fall on their drive in, the granules so fine they were barely visible, the first gasps of the threatening winter storm. Jordan knew it wouldn't be long before the weather turned wicked—a knowledge clearly shared by the locals, for the parking lot was empty.

Still, Jordan took no chances. She was vigilant as they exited the car, taking Devon's hand and ushering her quickly inside. Her other hand fell to the gun at her hip. It was almost unthinkable that Billy would be here, but he had surprised them more than once. She swiftly scanned the room, her focus landing on Mel, whose smiling face slipped to confusion as Jordan ushered Devon inside and locked the front door behind them, flipping the *Open* sign to *Closed*.

"Jordan?" Mel asked from behind the counter. "What's going on?"

"No one else is here, right?" Jordan asked, ignoring Mel's question.

"It's just me. Haven't had anyone in all morning. Storm's coming," Mel said slowly, her forehead creasing. She looked from Jordan to Devon and back again. "What's going on?"

Jordan left Devon standing next to Mel and quickly checked out the back storeroom, making sure the back door was secured. Satisfied, she returned to the front counter next to Devon. Mel had her arms crossed and was tapping her fingers impatiently. Jordan knew that look. Mel didn't like being ignored.

"Jordan—"

"Mel, I'm sorry for barging in here like this."

"For heaven's sake, spit it out already!"

"We need to use your Internet."

"You swoop in here like the damned Secret Service because you need to use my *Internet*?"

Jordan tried to interrupt, to explain, but Mel was having none of it.

"Don't even try it, honey, because I'm not buying. I've known you too long for that. I've let it slide until now, but don't think for one second that I bought this whole bad-breakup-college-friends-getaway thing. And now you barge in here, hand on your gun, locking the door, clearing the place like you're Linda Hamilton in *Terminator 2*. So I'll ask again. What is going on?"

Jordan looked to Devon, who nodded her assent. Mel's discretion had never been a question to Jordan, but it hadn't been Jordan's story to share. Now the endgame was near, and Mel was no fool.

"It's a very long story, which I promise to explain when this is all over. But this"—Jordan took Devon's hand—"is Devon James, she's been running from her serial-killer father for more than a decade, and a few days ago he killed two people at the diner where Devon works, and he nearly killed me, and now we're hiding her while we try to stop him."

It sounded insane to Jordan, like some crazy movie plot dreamed up by a sleep-deprived screenwriter who'd lived on nothing but coffee and peanut butter for days, and she was living it. She could only imagine how it sounded to Mel.

Mel stared at Jordan, unblinking. Her eyes shifted to Devon, then back to Jordan, then down to Devon's hand, which was clasped firmly in Jordan's. Jordan didn't even remember taking it.

Finally, Mel spoke. "Well, holy shit."

Devon burst out laughing and Mel followed suit, breaking the tension in the room. Jordan felt her own laughter bubbling up. As usual, Mel had a way with words.

"Promise me when this is over…" Mel said, trying to catch her breath, "the three of us will get bombed off our asses and you'll tell me everything."

"Absolutely," Devon answered for them. "I'll need a good blackout by then."

"Atta girl," Mel said approvingly.

"Linda Hamilton, huh?" Jordan asked.

"I always had a thing for her," Mel answered with a sad shrug.

The implication made Jordan wince. She at once understood that Mel's feelings for her ran deeper than she had ever suspected.

"Don't worry about it," Mel said, as if reading Jordan's mind. She offered a bittersweet smile. "Seems like you found what you really needed. I'm glad for that. You've been alone too long." Mel turned on her heel before Jordan could respond. "Now then," she called over her shoulder, "why do you need this broadband of mine?"

She led them to her PC and brought the screen to life.

"We need to talk to Henry face-to-face but can't risk an in-person meet."

"Gotcha. Do whatever you need to do. I'll be up front if you need anything."

Jordan stopped her. "Mel, I…thanks."

Mel tilted her head. "You're okay? You said he—"

"Yeah, I'm fine."

"Do you think he'll come up here?"

Jordan knew Mel wasn't worried for herself. Another pang of guilt worked through her at the thought she might be putting Mel in danger.

"I hope not. But I'm going to e-mail you his photo. It's old, but I want you to be careful."

"Always am. You just watch your own fine ass."

With that, she was gone. Jordan looked over at Devon, who was grinning. "What?" she asked, a little surprised Devon wasn't displaying any jealousy, faux or otherwise.

"She's right," Devon said, her grin broadening. "You do have a fine ass."

Jordan rolled her eyes, willing away the flush she could feel rising. Now was not the time. She glanced at her watch. It was nearly eleven.

She logged into the website. Devon sat next to Jordan so they were both in the webcam window. At precisely eleven o'clock, Henry and Lawson's faces filled their screen.

Henry was disturbingly punctual. Ella had once told Jordan that Henry had arrived two hours early for their wedding because the newspaper had said there was a 10 percent chance of rain showers on their wedding day, and he was afraid the road might be slippery.

"Jordan," Henry said, his eyes matching the relief in his voice. "It's good to see you two."

Seeing Henry filled Jordan with an unexplainable peace. She hadn't known it, but she had desperately needed to see her partner's face. "You, too."

Jordan recognized one of the police station conference rooms. "You're secure?"

Lawson spoke. "We're hardwired in and alone. We won't be overheard or interrupted."

"You've got a plan?" Henry asked.

"The outline of one, yes. But there's something we need to talk about first." Jordan felt Devon stiffen beside her. They had talked about this in the car, and Devon had agreed Henry and Lawson needed to know everything about Billy and about her, but that didn't make the telling of it any easier for Devon.

Jordan wrapped her arm around Devon's shoulders, uncaring what she was revealing to Henry and Lawson. If Devon was going to bare her soul, then Jordan was damn sure going to hold her while she did it.

"It was my thirteenth birthday..." Devon began, recounting every terrible detail, omitting nothing.

"We were right about him, Henry," Jordan said once Devon had finished. "He's been killing for years.

Henry addressed Devon first, his eyes brimming with compassion. "It wasn't your fault, Devon." Lawson nodded his agreement. Devon sagged into Jordan, some of the anxiety leaving her body.

"I'll give this to Coleman," Henry said.

"Tell him to look in Wisconsin through 2000, then nationwide."

"I've already given him the cities Devon's been in and corresponding dates."

"Yes, but we need to go back further. He's been killing for nearly forty years. His MO changed twelve years ago. What he does now isn't his preferred way to kill—he's fighting his instincts. He's driven to hunt, and to do it well, without rushing or worrying about discovery, he needs someplace he knows and is comfortable. The Wisconsin bodies will be different from the ones over the last twelve years. They'll be clustered and buried. He'll have taken his time selecting his prey, stalking them, killing them. After 2000, he was killing outside his comfort zone. He picked victims of opportunity, which made him more vulnerable to detection, so he'd be more cautious, more controlled. Those earlier victims, the ones he thought no one would ever find, those are the key."

"He might have left evidence behind," Henry said, understanding.

"Precisely."

"We need to look around West Virginia, too," Lawson added. "Billy's father was a Baptist preacher, a good God-fearing man who also happened to head up the local branch of the KKK."

Jordan leaned back in her chair, taking in the news. It explained so much. Billy was raised by a violent man who taught him to fear God. To Billy, God and violence were intrinsically linked.

Devon laid her hand on Jordan's thigh, as if seeking strength.

"He and Billy's mom were both murdered when Billy was in his twenties. The cops tied the murders to a power struggle within the Klan and disbanded the chapter. But here's the interesting thing— Billy's parents both had their throats cut, and wheat pennies were found pressed into their hands."

Devon sucked in a ragged breath. Billy had murdered his own parents. It was unimaginable, and yet it made perfect sense.

"The West Virginia cops didn't know what to make of the coins, figured it was just some weird KKK thing," Lawson said.

Jordan covered Devon's hand where it lay on her thigh, trying to ease the weight of Devon's family history as it settled on her shoulders. It was a terrible burden to carry, but Jordan was determined to lighten the load any way she could. And the best way to do that was to end this, once and for all.

"Billy is not your typical serial killer," Jordan explained. "He's not seeking notoriety or fame. In fact, he's gone out of his way to avoid it. He faked his own death so he'd be freer to move, he adapts his MO to fit his needs, and he utilizes a signature that can be easily misinterpreted or overlooked. He believes God has chosen him for greatness, and so he has a significant ego, but because his mission feeds his ego, it isn't easily challenged. Normally we could focus on attacking his success as a killer, but that won't work here. There is one thing that will, though."

"Devon," Henry said.

"Yes," Jordan said. "Billy is obsessed with Devon. Her very existence undermines his elevated status in God's eyes and mocks his mission to kill. He must end her life in order for his own to have meaning. He made a mistake by letting her get away, and all these years she has taunted him by continually slipping out of his grasp. He has to correct his mistake, and he'll do anything to achieve that goal."

"So how do we use that?" Henry asked.

"We need to go public," Jordan said, "tomorrow."

"Tomorrow?" Lawson questioned. "How?"

"We leak it to the press that we're focusing on one suspect in the diner murders, and that we have a key witness. We give them Devon's name, and that the suspect may be linked to other murders around the country. We also leak the attack at my house."

That seemed to startle Henry, but he said nothing.

"When the story breaks, the bureau will have to hold a press conference to deal with the fallout." It had happened before. Details would get out about an investigation, the press would demand answers, the brass would be embarrassed, and then they'd be forced to hold a press conference to clean it up.

"We put the captain up there to make a statement and take questions. The press will have a field day with the serial killer angle, and the inability of the PBP to properly protect the witness, and the captain will have to respond. He'll say the FBI is taking over, that Devon has been uncooperative, and that the FBI is taking her into custody. We'll need Agent Coleman up there for confirmation."

"Shouldn't be a problem," Henry said.

"We plant a question with one of the reporters—Why hasn't Devon already been turned over to the FBI, given the PBP's incompetence?—and the captain will get defensive, saying something about Devon not being a prisoner and having until now resisted working with the FBI."

She hated talking about Devon this way, like she was an impediment to the investigation, but Devon's reluctance and fear would help sell the story to the reporters and, more importantly, to Billy.

She glanced at Devon, who was staring straight ahead. Jordan squeezed her hand. *You still with me?* Devon gave a nearly imperceptible nod.

"We put Henry up there, too, but don't let him speak. He'll be acknowledged as the lead detective, but it will be clear he's not happy about turning over his star witness or the case. He needs to look surly."

"I can be surly," Henry said.

The mental image almost made Jordan laugh. She had never in her life seen Henry look surly. It would be a stretch for him for sure, but she knew he would pull it off.

"You will help seal the deal. If you're pissed about turning Devon over, then it would make sense you'd insist upon conducting the transfer personally. And Billy will follow you."

"What if Billy sees through it all?" Lawson asked. "There are a lot of contingencies in this plan."

They had reached the part Jordan hated. "He won't. Because Devon will be at the police station, and Billy will see Henry putting her in the car." Devon was the ultimate bait, and Jordan knew that no matter what Billy might suspect, the sight of Devon would override all rational thought. He'd hunted her too long, had her slip from his grasp one too many times. "We'll do it here. I can give the FBI the layout. Let them take point on the takedown."

Jordan wanted to kill Billy, to put a bullet in his brain and watch the life bleed out of him, but she set aside her desire because this plan was the only way to assure Devon's safety—even though it put Devon in harm's way. Her only perverse comfort was that Pennsylvania had the death penalty, as did the feds. Jordan opposed the death penalty— there were still too many innocent people being put to death in America. Despite her faith in the legal system, Jordan believed the death penalty needed to be abolished until they could find a way to ensure that only the guilty were put on death row. Billy was the exception to Jordan's rule. He deserved to die, and Jordan would be sure to be sitting in the front row when they gave him the needle.

"It's a solid plan," Henry said. He met Devon's eyes. "How do you feel about this?"

Devon squared her shoulders, determination evident. "I want this over. I'll do whatever I have to do."

"You're a brave woman," Henry said.

Devon shook off the compliment.

"It's true," Jordan said, tipping up Devon's chin. "You're the bravest woman I've ever known."

Jordan searched Devon's depths for acceptance. Devon nuzzled Jordan's hand.

She was overcome by the need to take Devon home, to hold her and kiss her and love her and never let her go. Instead, she brushed her thumb across Devon's lips, a kiss by proxy.

"We'll get this done," Henry vowed. Jordan wished she could do more, but it would be up to Henry and Lawson to lay the trap.

CHAPTER TWENTY-SIX

The weather had worsened considerably during the two hours they spent at Mel's, the fine granules of snow replaced by thick flakes, heavy and wet. Devon watched them assault the windshield as they drove back up the mountain to the cabin. The windshield wipers could barely keep up, and Jordan was driving much more slowly than on the way down.

"I think we're heading back just in time," Jordan said lightly. Devon stared ahead, lost in her thoughts. "Hey? You okay?" Jordan asked. Devon heard her concern.

"I'm fine." She sounded as unconvinced as she felt. Jordan said nothing, but Devon could feel the tension between them. Jordan most likely assumed she was scared, and she was, though not for the reasons she was sure Jordan was thinking.

She wasn't afraid of being used as bait. She actually welcomed it, the chance to take the offensive, to put herself on the line just as Jordan and Henry and Lawson were. Just as Mrs. Brindle had, even unknowingly. She hadn't realized it before, but she had longed for the opportunity to finally do *something* other than run. Other than hide from Billy. Hide from herself.

She needed to play a role in her own salvation, needed it almost as much as she needed Jordan. And that was what scared her.

Not her need, but the potential for loss.

She had a feeling. More than fear. More than apprehension.

Something was going to go wrong. She knew it with sick, unshakeable certainty. And it terrified her.

She could not bear the thought of Jordan being hurt. Being killed. She knew it would break her. It was selfish. It was self-absorbed. But it was true. Losing Jordan would destroy her.

She could feel Jordan glancing at her, trying to read her, trying to understand, but she couldn't speak. She was paralyzed, buried beneath the crippling dread of the inevitability of what was to come. Of what would be taken.

Billy would win, and not because he drew a knife across her throat. He would win by murdering Jordan and, with her, Devon's soul.

Jordan reached out to her, and the world swam back into focus. They were back at the cabin. Jordan turned to her, but Devon was already getting out of the car. She stumbled inside, past a startled Max, and dashed into the bathroom, slamming the door. She fell to her knees and her stomach convulsed. She retched violently, but nothing came up. She waited, her insides heaving, but still there was nothing.

"Are you all right?" Jordan asked through the closed door.

"I'm fine," Devon said, trying to sound stronger than she felt.

She heard Jordan shuffling just beyond the door and could imagine the debate being waged over whether she should leave Devon be or come in. She prayed Jordan would leave.

A few minutes later, her prayers were answered by Jordan's retreating footsteps. She heard the front door open and close. She breathed a little easier.

She didn't know how to tell Jordan this, to explain. She needed to warn her, to call this whole thing off, to tell Jordan to forget it and her and Billy and just let her go.

But she knew her too well. Jordan would never let her go. Jordan would not walk away from her. Jordan would follow her to the ends of the earth, to the depths of hell and back again, to save her from Billy. From herself.

Devon rose on shaky legs, gathering the courage to face her unflinching, relentless defender.

She took another moment to brace herself, to prepare for the fierce determination she knew she would be met with, and then opened the bathroom door.

Jordan was waiting for her in the center of the living room, waiting for Devon to come to her of her own volition, in her own time. Of course she was.

"I took Max out," Jordan said lamely, giving Devon a few extra moments to gather her thoughts. Max looked up at her from his bowl, happily chowing down on his kibble.

"A little early for his dinner," Devon commented absently. It seemed like a safe place to start.

Jordan shrugged. "I didn't want us to be interrupted." She fell silent then. Waiting. Always waiting. Devon thought Jordan would wait for her forever.

Devon stepped closer, just out of Jordan's reach. "I'm sorry."

Jordan's hands flexed at her sides, as if she was struggling to keep from reaching out. "You're scared. I get that. If you don't want—"

Devon stepped closer still, settling two fingers over Jordan's lips. "That's not it."

Jordan said nothing. She kissed Devon's fingers, a move of comfort which only enflamed. Devon felt her blood come alive at the simple act. She fought to control it, needing to tell Jordan. Needing to convey the depths of her feelings. Of her fear.

"I don't want to lose you."

"You won't," Jordan said with certainty, warm breath teasing Devon's fingertips. She shivered. She was quickly losing the battle for control.

"I couldn't bear losing you," Devon said urgently, tears forming now, unbidden.

"You won't," Jordan declared again, her hand tangling in Devon's hair. "It's going to be okay. I prom—"

Devon replaced her fingers with her lips, kissing away the vow she feared Jordan would be unable to keep. Billy was too strong, too cruel, and the universe took too much delight in torment.

Her tears fell freely as they kissed, loosed by the immensity of her swirling emotions. She was caught between love and loss, exhilaration and panic. Touch and taste and want and need and devastation and hope collided, overwhelming her. She could not fight it anymore. She did not want to fight it.

"I promise," Jordan said between hot kisses, the vow now made. This time, Devon didn't stop her. She pushed into Jordan's body, reveling in her strength, her certainty. She took Jordan's resilience, subsuming it into herself, unable to steal what was so freely given. It would be okay because it had to be. Because she deserved it to be. Because they both did.

Devon lost herself in Jordan. Her hands against Devon's face, her tongue plundering Devon's mouth. She felt herself being backed down the hallway toward the bedroom, her feet moving automatically to follow Jordan's lead. The backs of her legs bumped into the bed, but—good God—Jordan was lifting her sweater now, warm fingers raking her sides. Her nipples puckered from the cold room and Jordan's touch in equal measure, Jordan's hands smoothing over newly bared skin, making her shudder and shake.

"I've got you."

Jordan fused their lips together, her palms licking fire across Devon's belly and breasts, grasping and pressing. Devon reached for Jordan's shirt, desperate to be skin to skin. Jordan shucked it over her head and reached for Devon again, bringing their bodies into blissful, scorching contact.

Jordan roamed across Devon's flesh, first with her hands, then with her mouth. She kissed Devon's neck, her chest, nipping and sucking her way down to Devon's breasts. Her mouth latched onto Devon's nipple through thin cotton and Devon cried out. Not content with even this flimsy barrier between them, Jordan yanked the still-clasped bra down to Devon's waist and brought her lips to Devon's naked breast.

White heat exploded behind Devon's eyes as Jordan sucked first one sensitive tip, then the other. She laced her fingers behind Jordan's neck, clinging desperately, barely able to remain upright at the onslaught of Jordan's mouth.

"Oh God," she breathed as Jordan plucked a nipple with her teeth. She felt Jordan smile into her breast, enjoying the effect she was having on Devon's senses. Devon wanted to turn the tables, to make Jordan feel even half of what she was feeling, but she couldn't. She couldn't do anything but hang on for dear life and give herself over to exquisite sensation.

Jordan released her breast and returned to Devon's mouth, a welcome invader set upon conquest. She felt Jordan's hands at her waist, felt her zipper being lowered one agonizing tooth at a time. A hand slid down into her jeans, into her panties. There was no teasing, no uncertainty, only firm fingers slipping into wetness, at last.

"Oh God," Devon voiced again, panting. Her knees buckled, but Jordan was there to catch her. She guided Devon down upon the bed, fingers stroking now, skating over her swollen flesh. Devon surged upward, her hips rising, following. She whimpered when Jordan withdrew but was soothed by soft lips against her cheek.

"I'm not going anywhere," Jordan whispered. She slid off the bed, taking Devon's jeans and panties with her. "I just want to feel you."

Devon lay helplessly entranced as she watched Jordan peel off her remaining clothes. She climbed back onto the bed, straddling Devon, then reached around and unfastened the bra still trapped around Devon's waist, removing the final barrier between them. A needful sigh escaped her as their nude bodies at last made contact. Jordan's fingers found Devon again, gliding over her, into her. She writhed beneath Jordan, her breath falling in heaving gasps.

Jordan entered her over and over, fingers flexing, surging, pulling. Devon moaned into Jordan's mouth, Jordan's tongue matching the cadence of her thrusts. Jordan drove into her, pushing her higher and higher. A thumb brushed her swollen, aching tip, jolting her senses. She was flying now, soaring up into a cloudless sky, unencumbered by gravity or fate or time.

Jordan slipped to her ear, whispering words Devon barely heard but which her heart understood instantly. "I love you."

Devon's body exploded into a million supernovae, the infinity of light and the absence of sound, shooting stars hurtling toward sweet oblivion.

Night had dressed the day in its cloak, shielding it against the raging storm. Jordan listened to the wind howl beyond the window. It could not penetrate here, within the sanctuary of this room. Devon was wrapped tightly around her, her skin warm against Jordan's back, her arm snug around Jordan's waist. Jordan found she liked being held by Devon. It made her feel loved.

They had made love throughout the afternoon and evening, stopping only for Jordan to let Max out sometime before nightfall. She returned to their bed—for she couldn't now think of it any other way—and they began again. Jordan felt a blush staining her cheeks as she thought about the countless times—and ways—they'd made love. Devon's head buried between Jordan's thighs. Devon riding her hand, breasts swaying in the moonlight as she came undone. On their knees, pushing into each other, watching each other come.

Jordan felt herself stir at the memory. She could scarcely believe she wanted Devon again so much, so soon. She was an insatiable thing, wanton and craving, needful and greedy. She turned in Devon's arms, intent upon making her desire known. But one look at Devon's angelic face, so serene, so unguarded, and Jordan couldn't bear to wake her. Her love grew effulgent, lighting the darkest corners of Jordan's soul.

She had told Devon she loved her. She wasn't sure if the words had been heard, but she couldn't wait to tell her again. It didn't matter if Devon wasn't ready to say them, too. There would be time enough for that. Jordan would make sure of it.

She brushed golden hair back behind Devon's ear and kissed her forehead softly. Devon stirred but did not wake, burying her face in Jordan's neck. Jordan's eyelids felt heavy, and though she wanted nothing more than to watch Devon sleep for hours, she fell into a deep slumber full of wondrous dreams.

❖

Henry flicked on the entryway light, not bothering to turn on any others. He had lived in this house long enough to know his way around in the dark. He slipped off his jacket and hung it on the hook on the inside of the closet door, not bothering with a hanger or even opening the door all the way. He was too tired for such civility.

He dropped his keys on the counter, emptied his pockets, set down his gun, and poured himself a drink. He sank down into his chair. Same ritual, different night.

The plan was coming together, but there was still so much to be done. He had finally called it a day around nine, telling Lawson to come back rested by five. Lawson had chuckled good-naturedly. A few hours at home weren't exactly optimal for resting, but he was far too tired to complain.

It was a good plan, Henry mused. It wasn't perfect—there was no way it could be—but it was well thought out and it was their best chance. If everything went well, by this time tomorrow Billy Dean Montgomery would be locked in a cage, Devon would be free, and maybe Jordan could find happiness at last. Or maybe she already had.

Henry smiled at what he had seen during their online meeting. The casual touches, the way Devon leaned into Jordan, the way Jordan kept glancing at Devon to make sure she was okay—Henry was no fool, but a blind man could have seen what was going on between the two of them. It looked to Henry a lot like love. He hoped he was right.

I'm keeping my promise, Ella. There's hope for her yet.

Henry glanced at his watch. He could just e-mail Jordan to give her the update on their little plan, but he wanted to hear his partner's voice. Something told him she wouldn't mind.

He stood and stretched, feeling the satisfying pop of a vertebra slipping back into place. He went to the kitchen and picked up the disposable cell, dialing the programmed number. He listened to it ring once, twice.

Come on, Jordan, pick up.

By the fifth ring, it was pretty clear his call would go unanswered, and that Jordan had not set up voice mail.

As he listened to the seventh ring, his other phone began skittering across the counter.

"What the hell?" he cursed, fumbling to grab the vibrating phone while wedging the disposable between his ear and shoulder. He managed to grab the other phone and was working to flip it open when the disposable started to slip. He juggled both phones for what felt like minutes but was probably only a few seconds. When he finally got a firm grip on the infernal devices, both calls had disconnected. Of course.

He blew out a frustrated breath. "Stupid phones," he groused. He looked at the caller ID on his cell. Coleman.

About time he called back.

Henry shifted both phones to one hand and pulled a glass from the cupboard and filled it from the tap. He downed the water in two long swallows. The house phone began to ring.

Now what?

He took a step toward the wall-mounted phone but stopped. Something wasn't right. He felt a presence, menacing and dark. The air trembled in its wake. There was someone behind him.

Adrenaline coursed through him. His mind raced through the possibilities in milliseconds. His gun was on the counter two feet away. He could reach it. He had to.

He took another step toward the phone, then whirled, reaching for the gun. The pain came before his mind registered the blade coming toward him. It was a strange pain, intense but fleeting, replaced by a thick, wet warmth, like slipping beneath the surface of a perfectly heated bath. He felt it again on the other side of his neck, but it barely registered. He was heavy yet light, leadenly weightless as he floated to the ground.

Billy rose, standing over him, smiling.

"Hello, Lieutenant Wayne. We meet at last."

Henry lay on the floor, his strength melting away. Billy swam in his vision. Henry clung to consciousness, but he knew he was losing blood. So much blood. He fought against it, but it was no use. He was done. His fight was over, but Jordan's was just beginning. He only hoped when the time came, Jordan would put a bullet in Billy's brain for him. With his last ounce of will, he prayed that God would watch over his friend and give her the strength she would need to finish this. Then the world went dark.

Ella, baby...I'm coming home.

CHAPTER TWENTY-SEVEN

Billy watched the life drain from Wayne's body, running down his chest, pooling beneath him. He found it satisfying that the cop's last sight on this earth would be of the man who'd killed him.

One down, two to go.

The ringing stopped. The only sound now was Wayne's faint, wheezing gasps. He had watched Wayne's eyelids quiver, flapping like a bird with a broken wing as the man fought desperately to keep them open. Now they were closed.

Billy had been careful to not go too deep; he didn't want the blood spraying him in the eyes.

Billy knew a dozen ways to kill a man, some painful, some less so; some fast, some excruciatingly slow. When he hunted, he didn't care if he was covered in blood by the end. Wayne was different. Sally had been different, too, but for another reason. Sally had been a message. That kill had been wholly unsatisfying.

Salinger, too, would be different, but he knew he would find it entirely satisfying.

He turned his attention to what he had come for. Wayne's cell phone. The disposable one.

He had been intercepting Wayne's calls for two days, but not one had been from Salinger. More than that, not one call Wayne had received or made in that time had divulged anything of importance. He'd realized fairly quickly that Wayne and Salinger had ditched their regular phones in favor of something that couldn't be intercepted.

Smart. That's why he had gone to the police station, but he'd been foiled there. He wouldn't be foiled this time.

He retrieved the two phones from the floor, eyeing them in turn. He opened one, a fairly expensive model by the look of it, even if it wasn't a smartphone. He scrolled through the menus until he found its phone number, confirming it was the one he'd been intercepting for the past two days. He set it on the counter.

He eagerly looked at the other phone. It was a cheap plastic thing, nothing special. The screen was shattered, probably from falling to the hard tile. He hit a few buttons, but nothing happened. It was dead. He stared at it in disbelief. Then he threw it at the wall in a rage, smashing it to pieces.

He had nothing now. He stumbled into the living room, sinking into the recliner he'd watched Wayne lounging in earlier. He closed his eyes and prayed.

"That the Lord thy God may show us the way wherein we may walk, and the thing that we may do."

When he'd first arrived at the house, he'd searched it carefully but thoroughly. Every drawer, every cabinet. The computer, the trash. He'd found no clue as to where his Maddie had been taken.

Billy repeated the prayer in his head, willing God to show him the way. He walked the house in his mind, the bedrooms, the bath, down the stairs, through the kitchen and den and into the living room. He searched his memory for something, anything, he might have missed. His thoughts returned to the closet where he had hidden.

The closet.

He stood and turned. The sleeve of Wayne's coat hung mournfully in its final resting place. He approached it slowly, letting the anticipation build. He slipped his hands into the outside pockets. They were empty. His hope faded. He pulled one side away from the door, feeling for an interior pocket. He felt something square and firm. He reached inside and pulled out a small notebook.

Billy cradled it in his palms like it was a fragile crystalline egg. He sat on the sofa and laid the book down on the coffee table. He flipped open the first page, then the next. Wayne's handwriting was atrocious, but Billy could make out enough to understand the notebook contained some of Wayne's notes from the investigation.

The shorthand scrawl didn't reveal much, though Billy could see they knew more than he had anticipated.

As he neared the end of the book, he began to grow despondent. He had found nothing that would help him find Maddie.

He turned another page. He stared at a name and phone number. Someone named *Mel*.

He heard a buzzing from the kitchen. He found Wayne's phone—the one he hadn't smashed, the one that was useless to him—vibrating on the counter. It went quiet again, but a minute later a soft ding alerted that a message had been left. He picked up the phone, curious. He held down the one key.

"Hey, Henry, it's Carl. I tried your home phone, too. Maybe you're sleeping. I'm sure you need it by now. Listen, everything's in motion. We should be there about eight tomorrow. That should give us enough time to coordinate everything. I'm bringing the whole team. Once you tell us where we're doing this, I'll send most of the team on to set up their positions. I'll keep a few guys back for the press conference. We can line 'em up in their FBI jackets, put on a good show."

The man on the phone chuckled.

"This guy is a goddamn psycho. I've got at least sixteen unsolved murders matching the MO and signature over the last twelve years, spread out across the country. Plus we've got a couple more up in Wisconsin that date back further—hikers stumbled upon the bodies after some mudslides. I bet we find a whole bunch more, and that shack. No one caught on to the penny before, but we've got his ass now. There's DNA from Wisconsin. We're going to string him up from the rafters. Call me if you're still up. Otherwise, I'll see you tomorrow."

The message ended. Billy stood frozen in disbelief. They were putting it together. There were more for them to find, more from his early days when he'd been far less careful about DNA or other physical things. They knew. And they were laying a trap.

Billy looked down at Wayne. There was no more wheezing breath. They would come looking when Wayne didn't show up to work. He set the phone back on the counter. He was running out of time.

Billy entered the den and moved the mouse of Wayne's computer, waking it. He opened a web browser and searched the phone number. A single entry came up.

Mel's General Store.

Billy leaned back in the chair, his mind racing. His sight fell on the framed photos on the corner of Wayne's desk. An older woman, presumably Wayne's dead wife, smiled at him through dusty glass. Next to it sat a picture of Wayne, Salinger, and that damn dog on a porch. A porch of a rustic-looking cabin.

The signs were always there, if you only looked. They had always been there, all the way back to when he was thirteen, the night his pa had brought him out to the field. It might have been different had he not seen the sign. He'd had no idea that night, when Pa had brought him to the others in their resplendent white robes, what he was in for. Then they'd brought the man out from the car trunk, his hands bound behind his back, his bare torso as black as night, and Billy still had not understood. Two men helped Pa into the deep crimson robe of the Exalted Cyclops, his face gleaming in the light of the bonfire.

"Billy, it is your time," his pa had said. "Time to join us in the brotherhood. Time to take your rightful place by my side."

Pa had held out a large hunting knife, so big Billy could barely close his fingers around its hilt.

"To earn your place, you must offer up a sacrifice to the Lord. You must hunt down the beast and deliver it to God."

Billy held the knife, still unsure. And then he saw it, the golden eagle atop the banner of his pa's chapter of the Ku Klux Klan. It was the sign the Lord had promised him when he was eight, and Billy knew what he had to do, what he was called to do.

Billy looked at the man on the ground, the man staring back at him, pleading silently, and Billy felt nothing except the power of the Lord flowing through him. The Lord wanted him to kill this man—and he was a man, not a beast, his father was wrong about that—and deliver him up to Him.

Pa kicked the man to the ground and shouted at him to run. And after a moment, the man ran. But Billy was faster. He sprinted after the man, propelled by God's will and grace, and he leapt onto the man's back, bringing him down, the lion taking down the gazelle in darkest Africa. He rolled the man onto his back so he could see his face. Soundless words formed in the man's throat, but Billy cut them out with a single swipe of his blade across the man's neck.

It was over so fast, Billy wasn't sure if it was enough. Over the next few years, he honed his craft, knowing the Lord's will of purification required more than simple death. It required patience, and fear, and eventually the end of physical life. Billy learned to hunt, learned to ensure that his prey suffered, not through torture but through the terror instilled by the hand of God. Suffering was the only way to salvation.

Billy hit print and snagged the map as it came off the printer. He returned to the kitchen and picked up Wayne's gun. Billy had never used guns in his work, but he made an exception this time. Salinger had that dog, after all, and it would help him keep control of the detective and Maddie once he found them. He liked the idea of using Salinger's partner's gun against her. He found it had a certain poetry.

It was almost time. Time to help his Maddie find the salvation she had been running from all these years.

He turned off the lights and opened the front door. He was surprised to find it snowing.

CHAPTER TWENTY-EIGHT

It was dark when Jordan awoke. She struggled to adjust, shapes slowly coming into focus. Her pillow. The nightstand. Max's head.

The shepherd's muzzle was inches from her, and now she could feel his warm breath on her face. He looked up at her sorrowfully, in that way of his that said, *Human, it's not fair for you to ignore me this way. Look at me. I'm skin and bones* or *ready to burst* or *oh, so lonely and in need of love. You may commence with my feeding* or *walking* or *rubbing now.* To emphasize his point, he whined pitifully.

"Whazzit?" a sleepy voice mumbled behind her.

"Nothing, baby. Go back to sleep," Jordan said. She tried to slip from Devon's arms without disturbing her further, but it was no use. Devon's arms tightened reflexively as Jordan moved.

"Where do you think you're going?" Devon murmured, her voice dropping to a sexy purr. Jordan shivered. She allowed herself to settle back against Devon's body.

"Max needs to go out." A pang of guilt told her she was right. She had let him out once in the evening, but she'd missed his usual ten o'clock excursion. She'd been a bit…distracted and had forgotten all about him.

Max sat back on his haunches, still eyeing her. He voiced his displeasure that she hadn't yet gotten up. She was a very, very bad human, indeed.

Devon grumbled something unintelligible, but Jordan got the gist. She wasn't happy about leaving their bed, either. She lifted

Devon's palms to her lips, depositing tender kisses. "Sorry, baby, but I've been unfair to him. I promise I'll be back before you know it."

Devon reluctantly acquiesced, though it was under protest. "He needs to learn to take himself out," she said petulantly, echoing Jordan's words from the previous morning. It made Jordan laugh.

"Yeah, well, it's not his fault you fucked me into a coma. Not that I'm complaining," Jordan said, flashing Devon a wicked grin.

She moved to get up but Devon pulled her back and rolled on top of her, pushing Jordan's hands into the pillow above her head. Soft breasts danced centimeters above her skin, swaying seductively as Devon held her down. Devon's thighs burned Jordan's skin, the wet heat radiating between them setting Jordan's body aflame.

"You better not be, because I've got plans for you." Devon kissed her, hard and deep. She tried to pull her hands free. She wanted to touch, to feel satiny skin and firm curves, but Devon was relentless. She tightened her grip, lacing her fingers between Jordan's, pressing them deeper into the pillow.

"Oh yeah?" Jordan asked breathlessly as Devon's lips trailed down and up her neck.

"Oh yeah," Devon murmured. "I want to kiss you," she said, punctuating her words with taunting brushes of her lips against Jordan's mouth. Jordan raised her head, seeking to deepen the kiss, but Devon pulled away, just out of reach. Jordan flopped back against the pillow and Devon followed her down, her mouth against Jordan's ear.

"I want to suck you," she whispered, sending chills racing along Jordan's spine. Devon slid down Jordan's body, releasing her hands, swiping Jordan's breast with her tongue before wrapping her lips around a hardened nipple. Jordan's body went rigid, her back bowed, as Devon sucked. Her hands wove into Devon's hair, pressing her closer, demanding more.

But Devon was still in charge. She gave Jordan's breast a final flick and then worked her way back up to Jordan's ear. "I want to make you come so hard."

Jordan could barely remember her own name, let alone anything else. All she knew was Devon. Her mouth. Her body. Her breasts. Her tight, wet heat when she—

"How long are you going to make poor Max wait?" Devon chastised, rolling off her lover and leaving Jordan confused and panting. Devon propped her head in her hand, a smug smile of satisfaction gracing her lips.

Jordan shook her head, trying to clear the lust still coursing through her. She rolled to her feet, the chilly predawn air helping to cool her blood. "You are very, very naughty."

"You have no idea, Detective," Devon said, greedily drinking in Jordan's naked form.

"That's not helping," Jordan accused, full of humor.

"I know." Devon's grin was positively lascivious.

Jordan didn't bother with underwear. She slipped into her jeans and threw on a sweatshirt, glancing at her watch. "Seriously, babe, it's way too early for us to be up. Why don't you go back to sleep and I'll join you soon."

"Okay," Devon said with a yawn. She snuggled beneath the covers. Jordan took in the sight of Devon looking up at her, willful and wanting. She could never tire of this woman.

Max was already out the door, and Jordan followed.

"And Jordan?" Devon called after her as she reached the doorway. She turned. "I love you, too."

The last remaining brick in the wall around Jordan's heart disintegrated, pulverized by the weight of her love. She had never felt so much peace.

❖

As soon as she heard the front door close, Devon threw back the covers. She slipped into Jordan's robe and went to the kitchen. She had just enough time to get breakfast underway before Jordan came back. They had certainly burned up enough calories through the afternoon and night to warrant a cooked meal. Besides, for what Devon had in mind, her lover was going to need her strength.

She pulled out what she needed from the cabinets and refrigerator, whipping up the pancake batter. She smiled as she envisioned the surprised look on Jordan's face when she returned. She shivered at the thought of what would come after. It amazed her how just thinking of her lover's touch could arouse her like this.

She replayed their lovemaking. Sultry, vivid memories washed over her. She could still feel Jordan's fingers on her body, could smell their combined scents. Jordan was a passionate lover, equal parts wicked and playful, but also tender and considerate. She had taken Devon to the heights of pleasure with knowing hands, deft strokes, and a probing tongue.

She shook off her lustful thoughts. Jordan would be back soon enough, and they would pick up where they had left off. They had plenty of time before they had to go back to Pittsburgh.

❖

The world was bathed in white. Max bounded through the drifts, leaving doggy-sized divots in the pristine snow. Jordan followed, her legs sinking into fresh powder at least a foot and a half deep, and it was still falling. The flakes descended in thick clumps, the wind whipping around what it could.

A few feet ahead, Max bounded gleefully through rolling drifts, biting at snowflakes as they fell. He had absolutely no interest in doing his business, despite his earlier pleading.

"Come on, boy," Jordan urged, her words muted by the wind. Max ran in ever-expanding circles around her, delighted by the wonderland of white.

The snow was a wall around her, blocking out the world. Her visibility was reduced to a few feet, the cabin no longer visible. Max circled at the edges, a dark form weaving in and out of the limits of her vision. He yipped excitedly as he ran, but it sounded muffled and far away, obscured by the snow and wind.

Suddenly, Max skidded to a halt, his ears perking. Jordan caught up to him, noting the tension in his lean body. She heard him growl, low and menacing. Her blood ran cold.

"Come on, boy," she said, reaching for his collar. Something was out there. Something dangerous. She couldn't see anything, hear anything, but she trusted Max's heightened senses. They needed to get back to the cabin. Back to Devon.

Her fingers were inches from Max's collar when he bolted out into the storm.

"Max, no!" But the shepherd was already gone. Jordan reached for the gun at her hip, but her hand closed around air. Her gun wasn't there. It was on the kitchen table, forgotten.

Max was barking now and snarling, the sound breaking through the muted curtain around her, echoing off the snow. She pulled the knife from her pocket, flipping it open. She stepped toward the sound but an agonized yelp halted her.

No. Oh no.

She started to backpedal. She needed her gun. She needed to—

A form, low and dark, raced toward her. Her heart filled with hope. Max was okay. He was coming back. He—

The form resolved into a man and then she was flying through the air, knocked off her feet by the man crashing into her. She lashed out as she fell, swiping with her blade, making contact. She crashed into the ground, the force driving the air from her lungs. She gasped as the man wrenched back her wrist, forcing the knife from her hand. Jordan balled her left fist and punched at the side of his head, trying to knock him off. The blow dazed him, but not enough. He punched her. She felt rather than heard a crunching sound. Stars exploded in her head. She felt him leaning back, but she could not move. She blinked rapidly, trying to clear the haze. Her vision returned, and it was filled with Billy. She saw the silhouette in his hand too late to react. He plunged the knife into her abdomen.

The pain was excruciating, exploding throughout her body, a thousand volts electrocuting every nerve and synapse. Jordan struggled for air. Billy sat back on his haunches, his lips curled into a thin sneer. She waited for the final, killing blow, struggling to keep her mind clear.

Devon. God, Devon.

Billy leaned closer. "Hello, Detective Salinger," he growled, his putrid breath invading her nostrils. "It's so nice to finally meet you."

His smile was menacing. He pressed his palm against her wounded flesh, and Jordan cried out.

"Hurts, doesn't it?" Billy slid a gun out from beneath his jacket. She recognized it immediately, the familiar name on the muzzle screaming at her.

The gun had been her gift to Henry. She'd had the name Shirley engraved on the side, an old joke between them after they'd watched the movie *Airplane*. Another wave of pain seized her, this time born of despair.

"I thought you might recognize it," Billy said smugly. He regarded the weapon for a moment. "I thought I'd have to use this on you, or on that dog of yours. But the weather made that impossible. I prefer it this way, anyway. This will be much slower for you. More painful. And pain is the path to salvation."

Wind swirled around Billy as he stood, like flames whipping about the devil.

"If you're wondering why you're not dead yet, it's because I don't want you to be. I want you to have plenty of time to consider your failure."

He stepped over her, toward the cabin. She lifted her arm and clutched at his jeans. He stared down at the hand weakly clinging to his pants leg. He shook his foot, Jordan's sticky hand falling limply to the snow.

"Now you just lie there like a nice girl. I won't be long. The last thing you see in this life will be my darling daughter's cold, lifeless corpse."

A strangled sob caught in Jordan's throat. She tried to scream, but her lungs made no sound. She stared up into the falling snow as she felt her life leaving her.

❖

The batter finally ready, once Devon had stopped distracting herself with thoughts of Jordan, she heated up the skillet. She poured three pancakes into the pan, the aroma filling the kitchen.

Not that making pancakes was a herculean effort, but besides providing nourishment to fuel their immediate future, she wanted to do something nice for Jordan. Something unexpected. Something that might, even in the smallest way, support her declaration of love.

She had told Jordan she loved her. She had never said that before, not romantically. She hadn't said the words at all in over twelve years. The last person to hear them had been her mother.

And look how that turned out.

Devon shook off the old habit. She would not be afraid any longer. She would not sabotage this precious, wondrous love with insecurity and doubt.

She heard heavy boots stomping beyond the door, the sound lifting her heart instantly. She flipped the first batch of pancakes, a familiar thumping in her chest at the opening door. She heard it close and turned expectantly. The world flipped upside down. The spatula slipped from her fingers, clattering to the floor.

"Hi, baby," Billy said. "Daddy's home."

The summer sun caressed Jordan's skin as she lay on her back watching fluffy white clouds float lazily across the perfectly blue sky. Something about the sky felt familiar. The color of it spread a delicious warmth throughout her body, but she couldn't pinpoint the exact reason.

Long, cool grass tickled her neck and the backs of her legs. A light breeze played in her hair. She couldn't remember the last time she'd felt so relaxed.

"Whatcha doin', kiddo?" Her father's deep, melodic baritone filled her ears. She had always loved the sound of his voice.

She shielded her eyes against the sun's glare. Her father was standing over her, smiling. She smiled back.

"Nothing really," she answered. "Just watching the clouds."

He flopped down beside her with an exaggerated effort that made her laugh. He could be a real goof. He stretched out beside her in the grass, mirroring her position.

It felt so good, being next to each other this way, being close. She treasured this time together. She loved her father very much, though she knew she didn't tell him often enough.

He pointed up at one of the clouds. "See that one there? Doesn't it look like a dragon?"

Jordan squinted, following the line of his arm, trying to see what her father saw.

"Not really."

He huffed in mock exasperation. "Right there. See? There's the tail, and the wings, and that big puff there is the head. And look, it's blowing smoke."

She could kind of see it now, though to her it looked more like a rabbit on a stick. "I think you're the one blowing smoke, Dad."

He barked out a laugh. "Maybe, honey. Maybe."

He slid his arm underneath her neck and she leaned into him, resting her head on his chest. She listened to his heartbeat, strong and steady. He was her rock, her comfort, her courage. He was the best man she had ever known. She hoped to be just like him someday.

"What about that one?" he asked, pointing with his free arm.

"Looks like a wolf." She didn't know why, but the image filled her with dread. Her father tightened his arm around her.

"Very good," he said. He pointed out another cloud. "And that one?"

Jordan pondered the formation. "Um…teddy bear?"

He laughed again. "No, silly. It's a heart."

"Awfully big heart," Jordan said.

"The bigger the heart, the bigger the love," he said, pressing a kiss to her temple.

They had done this countless times before, lying on their backs in the yard making shapes from the clouds. And yet, it felt different to Jordan this time. Slightly foreign, like they hadn't done this in forever. She burned the memory into her mind, knowing without understanding that this would be the last time.

"Daddy?" she said, turning to her father. He brushed away her tears. "I'm scared."

"You have the biggest heart of anyone I know, Jordan," he said, placing his hand above her heart. "It's where your love lives. And your courage. You need both of those now, more than ever before. You need them to kill the wolf."

"What if I can't?"

"You can."

"I miss you," she said quietly.

"I know, baby." He kissed the top of her head. "I miss you, too. So very much."

Jordan thought it would be lovely to fall asleep in the grass, in the safety of her father's arms.

"You can't fall asleep, Jordan," he said, shaking her gently. "You have to go save your girl."

She sat up, hugging her knees to her chest. She looked back at her father, resting up on his elbows. "What if I can't?" she asked.

"You can, and you will," he said with conviction. "It's who you are."

"I failed once before."

Her father was standing now and pulled her up to face him. The fluffy clouds above them grew darker, blocking out the sun. "You didn't fail. You saved those two kids. The others weren't your fault."

The tears came again, slipping down her cheeks. "They died because of me. *He* died. Because of me."

"No, honey, he didn't." Her father lifted her chin, forcing her to face him. "That boy died because of a madman. Your actions saved the others. If you'd done nothing, they all would have died. And if you do nothing now, so will she."

The words sank into her, infusing new life, new hope. As he always had, her father gave her the strength she needed.

"You don't have to fake-it-till-you-make-it anymore, honey. You're so strong, and I'm so proud of you."

A gentle rain started to fall, mingling with Jordan's tears. It grew darker, her father's face fading with the light.

"Daddy? Don't go. Please," she begged, flinging her arms around his neck. He hugged her tightly.

"I have to, baby. And you have things to do." He pulled back, smiling at her for the last time. "I like her very much, you know. She's good for you. Cute, too." He winked at her.

"I love you, Dad," she said, darkness overtaking them.

She felt him trace his index finger across her forehead. "I love you, too, my darling girl."

All was black, but she felt the rain licking her face, lapping in a familiar rhythm. Jordan opened her eyes. Max whined softly, giving her another swipe with his tongue. The world came rushing back.

She felt so cold, so incredibly weak. Mustering all her strength, she rolled to her side, the pain tearing at her as she moved. Max rolled to his side, too, his mission complete. The snow was red beneath him, the fur of his side bloodstained and matted.

"I'm so sorry, Max," she choked out, pressing her nose to his neck. "You're such a good boy."

Jordan rested for a moment, gathering her strength once more. Propelled by sheer force of will, she threw herself over and up onto her hands and knees, the agony nearly making her black out again. She took deep, shuddering breaths, trying to keep from vomiting. She pushed herself upright until she was leaning back on her knees. She unzipped her jacket, pushing away the material. Her sweatshirt was stained a deep crimson. Gingerly she lifted up her shirt. Blood oozed out of the inch-wide wound. The down-filled coat seemed to have deflected some of the knife's force, otherwise she might be dead already.

Max lay on his side, watching her. She saw a line of blood in the snow and understood at once the magnitude of what it had taken for Max to come to her. She shrugged off her coat and worked it around the dog, using the arms to tie it tightly around Max's injured side. He whined softly but did not move.

"You're going to be fine, Max. I'll be back for you."

He seemed to understand, his gaze never leaving her face. She packed the snow around him tightly, giving his body some limited protection against the wind. She looked in the direction of the cabin and saw a thin, darkened trail. She knew what it meant.

She leaned down to kiss him. "Such a good boy."

Jordan was concerned but grateful that her pain seemed to be lessening. She knew she was falling into shock, but it also meant less pain, which would help.

She was sure she did not have the strength to walk, so she did the only thing she could.

Jordan began to crawl.

CHAPTER TWENTY-NINE

Y ou don't know how I've longed for this moment. For us to
be reunited."

Billy had never felt such elation, such triumph. The pain in his
leg from the mutt's bite was nothing in the face of the endorphins
coursing through him. He'd had only fleeting glimpses of Maddie
until now, mere impressions of cheeks and nose and chin and eyes
from far away that he had pieced together into a portrait. But now,
finally face-to-face, he realized he hadn't done her justice. She was
lovely. Beautiful, really. His heart swelled with pride.

"Look at you. All grown up. My little Maddie."

"My name is not Maddie," she said, her voice low and steely.
"My name is Devon."

"That's right. I forgot," Billy said with a chuckle. "Just how
many names have you had over the years? How many cities? Boston.
Dallas. But no matter how many times you ran, I found you. I found
you at NIU. I found you in Colorado. I found you in Memphis."

He watched her eyes widen, saw the surprise. "Oh, you didn't
know about that one, did you? What was your name then? Theresa
something. I got to Santa Fe not long after you left. Tracked you to
Memphis. But somehow you slipped away again. You were always
slipping away from me. Running away. But the bodies pile up, don't
they?"

Maddie's face drained of color. Billy's heart began to pound, his
adrenaline spiking with each revelation. It felt so good to finally make
his daughter fully understand his skill, his power.

"You know, I really didn't plan to kill that roommate of yours. You were supposed to be in your room, not her. I knew your schedule, and hers. I had waited so long, waited for you to leave Roscoe, for everything to die down, for you to be somewhere else, where no one would connect the dots. But you weren't where you were supposed to be that day. I came for you, and she just wouldn't stop asking questions. Demanding to know who I was, what I wanted. She had no right. She said she would call the cops, and I couldn't let that happen.

"It surprised me, you know, that you figured it out. That you understood it was me. But the police didn't believe you, did they? No, they didn't. You were all the talk at the bar across from the station. That's where I learned about the investigation. They actually thought *you* had killed your roommate!"

Billy laughed at the memory, at the insanity that anyone could believe his dear cowardly daughter capable of his work.

"It was fascinating to see it all play out. So I watched you, and I waited. You were so scared, and so…affected. It intrigued me, I must say, your reaction to her death. I could see your guilt, your shame. How much knowing that it was your fault hurt you. But then you were gone. I hadn't expected that.

"It took me quite some time to find you. Another surprise. You were very good at hiding, Maddie. I hadn't known you had it in you. But finally I found you again. You'd built quite a nice little life for yourself there in Colorado, hadn't you? Tell me something—I've always wanted to know—at what point did you stop looking over your shoulder for me? You must have stopped, or you wouldn't have stayed there so long."

Billy watched the emotions play across Maddie's face, savored the interplay of grief and guilt and memory and despair. She said nothing, but she didn't need to. He understood her perfectly.

"I probably should have just killed you, but I couldn't resist taking out the old woman. You just seemed so attached to her. I debated letting you find her body, but she'd gone to see the sheriff that day, and I didn't want to arouse too much suspicion. Cutting her brake line was simple and effective. But I wanted you to know, to understand. Pain is the only salvation, and the pain of loss was the truest path for you. I watched you find the coin. I saw the understanding wash over you, saw you accept the truth in that one exquisite moment."

Again he saw her surprise and reveled in it. It seemed as if she had always underestimated him, despite all she knew.

"Oh yes, dear one, I was there. I was in the closet, watching you through the cracked door, just waiting for you to find my marker, to understand and to know. But that damn sheriff showed up and spoiled our reunion. And then again, you ran. Always running, Maddie. What kind of life is that? You cannot run from your true destiny. Don't you know that by now? Do you finally understand the Lord's plan for you?"

He studied her, trying to read her thoughts. Her intent. Her surprise, and her pain, had disappeared, replaced by a steely calm. He noticed her eyes darting over the room, to the table and the gun that lay on top. She lunged for it. She was fast, but he was faster.

"Ah, ah, ah," he clucked, his own gun pointed at her forehead. "Is that any way to treat your father?"

He waved the gun at her, indicating for her to come around the table. She didn't budge.

"Do not make me tell you again." He'd said that to her once before, when she was thirteen. She had done as she was told then. She wasn't doing it now. She had changed. He found her resolve surprising, especially now that he had forced her to confront the pain of her failure, of her culpability. The pain of old wounds did not seem to cripple her as he had thought it would, and the threat of force no longer appeared to inspire her. He would have to change tactics. Freshen her pain.

"I would have been here sooner, but this isn't the easiest place to find," he said, rounding the kitchen table slowly. She moved around the far side of the table, as he anticipated she would, trying to keep distance between them. He picked up Salinger's gun as he passed, shoving it into the back of his jeans. "The roads were pretty bad coming up here, made me miss a few turns. I finally found that little store, but then I had to waste hours tearing it apart."

He saw her surprise. It made him laugh. "I figured you were wondering how I found you. Lieutenant Wayne pointed me in the right direction."

He delighted in the fear that flashed across his daughter's face. Not fear for herself, but for a dead man. "He was quite surprised to find me in his home, that's for sure."

He saw tears begin to form. His instincts had been right. These detectives meant something to her. "Don't worry, it didn't last long. He's been reunited with his dearly departed wife."

Billy returned to the cabin's entryway. Maddie was now in the center of the large room, trapped between the couch and the kitchen table.

"For a while there, I almost lost hope. But then I found Wayne's notepad, and it led me to Mel's General Store. I came up empty, but you should be proud of your old man. I didn't give up. I eventually found the notebook where all the local customers' names are logged. And that led me here."

Maddie began shifting again, looking for some means of escape. He was growing tired of her not paying attention to him.

"Sit. Down." He pointed at the sofa. This time, she obeyed. He was getting to her, breaking her down. It pleased him.

"Once I found this place, I took some time to scope it out. The storm made it hard to see, but it also provided me with excellent cover. I almost came in a couple of times, but I knew that damn dog was in here with you. Then I saw the lights come on just as the snow picked up, and I knew. God was giving me my chance. As it has always been. As it ever shall be."

"You know nothing about God," Maddie said evenly, enraging him.

"Don't you dare question the Lord!" he boomed, his voice echoing around the small space. "Twelve years, Maddie! For twelve years, the Lord tested me! But He showed me the way. He never let you get too far. And just when I thought I had lost you, there you were! He led me straight to you, so I could finish my work."

He freed the knife from its sheath, holding it up for her to see.

❖

Devon suppressed a gasp at the sight of the long obsidian blade and the dark red coating that smeared its handle and Billy's gloved hand. The blood glistened in the lamplight, still fresh. It made her gag, for she knew what it meant.

"That's right, honey," Billy said gleefully. "No one's coming to save you."

She felt herself coming apart. This couldn't be happening. All these deaths. Jessica. Mrs. Brindle. Chuck and Sally. And now Henry and…

She couldn't think it. She'd only just found her. She couldn't lose Jordan, not like this. Not when—

"Oh, don't worry, your detective friend is still alive."

The words stunned her. What kind of game was he playing?

"I mean, she's dying, for sure," he said, smirking cruelly. "But I wasn't ready for her to die yet. I want her to see how she failed you first."

Jordan was alive? Jordan was alive. Thank you, God.

The thinnest sliver of hope ignited within her. She pictured her lover lying in the snow, bleeding and alone. She swallowed a sob. How long could she survive? Devon had to get to her.

Hope burned into anger. Anger at the monster before her. Anger at what he had done. Anger burst into bright fury.

She thought of the knife Jordan had given her. It was in their bedroom, in the pocket of her jeans. Her mind raced. She'd never get to it in time, not with Billy holding a gun on her. She noticed his limp for the first time, saw the blood dripping from his torn pants leg. *Max.* She had to force her fear aside. This might be her opening, but she had to distract him somehow. She had to break his focus.

She raised her chin to him with as much defiance as she could muster.

"She didn't fail me. She never could."

Billy blinked at her slowly, realization dawning. "You love her."

"Yes."

Billy cocked his head. "And what does that feel like? To know you've killed someone you love?"

Devon didn't take the bait. She might have once, but not now. Jordan had shown her the truth. This was his doing, not hers. "You tell me. You killed Mom. And your parents."

Billy's lips twitched. "I delivered them."

"Delivered them from what?" She could feel precious seconds ticking by, but she had to keep him talking. She needed to enrage him again if she had any chance of catching him by surprise.

"Not from—to," Billy corrected. "I delivered them to God."

"Why?"

Billy seemed confused by the question. "Because I loved them. Suffering is the only way to salvation."

"But I saw your face that night," Devon said. "You hadn't planned to kill Mom. You lost control."

"I did not," Billy said through gritted teeth, but Devon could see his conflict playing across his features. She was on to something.

"Was it because she stood up to you?" she demanded. "Because she finally saw you for the monster you are?"

Instead of rage, a sickening grin curled his lips. "You'd like to think that, wouldn't you? That she didn't know. But she knew."

Devon felt as though she'd been punched in the gut.

It wasn't true. It couldn't be.

"Oh yes, dear one. She knew. She had to have known. Why do you think she was so afraid of me?"

Devon realized then that Billy was lying. Her mother hadn't known, not for certain, anyway. She never would have let Devon go with Billy on that trip if she had. But even if she had known—and maybe that was why she had stood up to Billy in the end—how would that have made her any different from Devon? Devon had known, had witnessed it, had—God help her—taken part in burying the body. But Devon had been afraid for her mother, for herself, and so she had stayed silent. With Jordan's help, she had forgiven herself for that. And if she could forgive herself, then didn't she owe her mother the same kindness?

"Plus, there was the body." Billy yanked Devon back to the present.

"What body?"

"The body I had stashed in the basement."

Devon felt her face drain of color. She had never been able to figure out that part. At last she understood. Billy lit up with delight.

"Who do you think they found in the ashes?" he asked smugly. "A few weeks before the fire, I stumbled across a woman on my way home from work. Flat tire, out in the middle of nowhere. I felt God telling me to deliver her. So I did."

Billy shifted with nervous excitement. He was getting distracted, lost in his memory and pride. Devon tried to keep her expression neutral.

"There hadn't been anyone on that road for miles. But just as I was loading the body into my trunk, I saw headlights. The car pulled over. A man came up, thinking I had broken down. I hadn't gotten the trunk completely closed, and he saw the body. He turned to run but I chased him down. I cracked him in the back of the head with my flashlight. I guess I broke his skull, because he fell down, dead. Suddenly I had two bodies to deal with. And two cars.

"I hauled his body into my trunk with the woman's. There was a small pond nearby so I sank both their cars into it. Then I drove off. I came to an old abandoned barn a few miles down in the woods. I was going to keep going, but then I saw it."

"Saw what?"

"The eagle," he said simply, as if that explained everything. Devon didn't ask. Billy explained anyway. "It was circling overhead in the tree canopy. Then it swooped into the barn. I knew that's where I needed to bury them. I put her in the ground first, but when I went to drag him out of the trunk, the eagle returned. It landed on my car and just...stared at me. I stared back for a while, and then looked down at the man again. He was roughly my build, same color hair. His face even looked a bit like mine. We could have been brothers.

"God was trying to tell me something. He had stopped me for a reason that night, had brought that man to me. I thought about you. You were getting older, and soon enough you'd be leaving our house, and I wouldn't be able to control you anymore. The time to deliver you and your mother was growing near. And I would need a way out.

"So I brought the man back to the house. I wrapped him in plastic and put him in a trunk in my workroom in the basement. I put a couple gas cans inside, too, and sealed it up tight. A few days later, when you and your mother were at the market, I stashed some more gas cans and plastic bags stuffed with soaked rags in the walls around the house."

Devon remembered coming home one day to find her father patching holes around the house. She hadn't remembered the holes being there before that day. He'd said something about rats. Now she understood.

"It was so the house would burn up completely," she said, astonished.

"Propane in the garage took care of the rest," he said in confirmation. "I just never figured you'd be the one to start the fire."

CHAPTER THIRTY

Billy felt good telling Maddie this story. He wanted her to know, wanted her to understand. Maddie was right. He hadn't planned to kill Marie that night. But when she'd said no to him, he knew it was time. What he'd feared with Maddie had come true with Marie. So he'd killed her. And looking into Maddie's eyes that night, he'd known he would have to kill her, too. And he would have, if it hadn't been for that fire. And the rolling pin she'd slammed against his head.

"I have to admit, I was actually proud of you that night," he said. Maddie looked at him in surprise. "Taking me on like that. I didn't think you had it in you, not after Wisconsin."

He watched her face darken at the mention of it. "You were supposed to follow in my footsteps. But you chickened out. You weren't strong enough. You were such a disappointment."

"If my not being capable of sadistically murdering someone disappointed you," she said hotly, "then I'm glad."

Her righteousness infuriated him. She had no right to act so superior, so saintly. He was God's messenger. She had rejected Him. He edged closer to her.

"You're just like me. It's in your blood. Only you were too much of a coward to see it through."

"No, Billy. I am nothing like you," she spit out. The venom in her voice enraged him.

"You liked burying her."

"No."

"You wanted to go with me again."

"No."

"You would have gone with me again if your mother hadn't interfered."

"No!"

He saw the fire inside her, bright as the sun, and it reminded him of his own. Maybe there was hope for her after all. Maybe this had been God's plan all along.

"It's not too late," Billy said, softening his tone. "You can still join me. I can teach you—"

"I'm not like you," she said, "and I never will be, you sick fuck. I'm no killer! *You* killed those people, not me. I'm not afraid of you anymore. I wasn't strong enough to stand up to you back then, but I am now. You can't hurt me anymore."

The last thread of his control broke in a white-hot rage. He raised the knife high, shouting to the heavens, *"The light of the wicked shall be put out, and the spark of his fire shall not shine!"*

The door crashed open behind him. He turned, eyes flashing. "No!"

❖

Jordan leaned against the doorframe, adrenaline all that was keeping her upright. Time stretched and slowed, giving her an infinitesimal, endless moment to plan her attack. She hadn't had time to strategize. She had just pulled herself up to the doorframe when she heard Billy's shouting. She had understood instantly that she was out of time.

Throwing open the door had sapped the last of her strength. But now, in these milliseconds stretched endless, she drew on her father's courage, on all that she had been and was or ever would be, on her grief and her joy and her infinite love for the astonishing, miraculous woman before her. And it fueled one last, desperate act.

She saw everything at once. The knife in his hand. The gun in the other. Devon's face. The bloody, torn pants leg.

She launched herself at Billy, not caring about the raised knife or the gun. She rammed him in the chest with her shoulder, pumping her legs with all her might, driving him backward. They slammed to the ground, the knife skittering away along the wooden floor. She dug her fingers inside the ripped fabric, into the tears in his flesh. He howled in pain but she was on to her next target, battering his hand over and over on the floor until the gun finally came loose.

She lunged for it, but he slammed his meaty palm into her temple, knocking her off balance. They rolled, wrestling for supremacy. She landed a solid blow to his midsection, but she could feel her strength ebbing.

Not yet. Please, just a few more seconds.

But it was not to be. Billy seized her collar, slamming her head against the floor. Dazed, she could not fend off a devastating fist against her wounded abdomen.

Jordan curled into herself, the agony relentless. She fought to stay conscious.

Billy crawled to the gun. With a final, consuming effort, she grabbed for his bloody leg again but came up with nothing but air. Billy reached out his hand. The sound of a round being chambered stopped him cold.

Jordan followed Billy's gaze to the barrel of the gun clutched firmly in Devon's steady hand.

❖

The fight lasted maybe twenty seconds, but it might as well have been twenty years. It was a slow-motion version of the speed of light.

It had taken Devon at least half that time to shake off the shock of what she was seeing. Time gathered and waned. Her limbs felt leaden and rubbery. She couldn't force her legs to move. She needed to do something, anything. Jordan was fighting for her life, for their lives. Why couldn't she move?

Then she saw Jordan's gun. It had come loose when Jordan had knocked him to the ground. Everything clicked into place. She grabbed the weapon, flicked off the safety, and pulled back the slide, just like Jordan had shown her.

She pointed it at Billy's forehead. His eyes were wide, disbelieving. Every fiber of her being screamed at her to check on

Jordan, but she knew she couldn't take the risk of even the slightest distraction. She could hear Jordan's weak respiration, and it was reassurance enough for now.

"Come on now, let's talk about this," Billy said, hands rising in submission.

"Don't move," Devon ordered. Her finger twitched against the trigger.

"You said it yourself, Maddie. You're no killer." He rose slowly, almost innocently. She wasn't fooled.

"I said. Don't. Move."

"She's going to bleed to death," he said, changing tactics. She saw through him. She shifted her aim to his chest. "Are you going to let her die?"

She heard the shallowness of Jordan's breathing, could almost hear her heartbeat slowing.

Don't look at her. Don't look at her. *Jordan.*

She looked.

It was only for an instant.

Billy lunged.

He was a blur.

Her finger tightened.

He was upon her.

She fired.

Billy's arms closed around her, pulling her into his body.

Devon tried to fire again, but the gun was wedged between them now, singeing her flesh through the fabric of her robe.

Her breath caught and held.

The arms around her began to loosen.

Devon stepped back.

Billy's face contorted in surprise. He looked down, touched the crimson stain blooming over his heart with shaking fingertips. He swayed, staring up at Devon. She stared back at him, this man who had haunted her dreams for so many years, who had brought misery and grief to everything he touched. His mouth moved, the words falling from his lips in a gasping whisper. *"O remember that my life is wind: mine eye shall no more see good."*

He slumped to the floor, sightless eyes gaping up toward heaven.

Her father was dead. She would not mourn him.

A low groan pulled her back to what truly mattered.

❖

"Jordan? Baby?" The words came out on a choking sob. Jordan heard her distantly. She felt Devon next to her, cradling her head. Felt like heaven.

"You're okay?" Jordan's throat felt scratchy and raw.

"I'm fine, my love," Devon whispered. She kissed Jordan's lips, her cheeks, and her lips again. "You saved me."

"You…saved me…first."

Devon shifted beneath her, setting her down gently. She disappeared but was back within moments. Or maybe it was longer. Jordan couldn't tell anymore.

"I need to stop this bleeding." Jordan felt a weight against her stomach, but she no longer felt any pain.

"Where's your phone, love?"

Jordan gazed up at Devon. She hadn't failed her. She hadn't failed.

"Jordan? Baby, I need your phone."

Jordan opened her mouth but nothing came out. She felt Devon search her pockets. She wanted to say something flirty, something ridiculous, but she was having trouble finding words.

"Baby, you have to stay with me." Devon was pleading with her. Why was she pleading? Of course she would stay. Where else would she go?

She took in Devon's face. Her perfect nose. Her delicate chin. Her stunning cheekbones. Her golden hair. Her sparkling blue eyes. No, not sparkling. Shining. With tears.

Don't cry, my love. Don't cry.

She was so, so tired. She had never felt so tired.

"Stay awake, baby. You have to stay awake."

She so desperately wanted to sleep.

Just a little nap, just for a little while.

She heard Devon talking but couldn't make sense of it. She wasn't talking to Jordan.

Jordan heard church bells ringing off in the distance. She didn't remember there being a church nearby. She wondered what kind of church it was. Maybe they would go there sometime.

She felt warm light touching her skin. She searched for its source. Outside the window, shafts of light were beginning to break through the stormy sky. Dawn was breaking. It had finally stopped snowing.

She closed her eyes.

Just for a little while.

CHAPTER THIRTY-ONE

A crisp autumn sky hung high above the trees, the warm cerulean blue a stark contrast to the dirty snow and cold gray stones of Allegheny Cemetery. Devon pulled her coat lapels in a little tighter, fending off the chill.

At least three hundred people had shown up for the funeral. A sea of blue and black. Police officers from miles away had come, marching behind the procession, lining the road leading into the cemetery in a mournful salute to their fallen comrade.

The cemetery didn't usually allow dogs, she'd been told, but they'd made an exception.

Max sat beside her, panting softly, still bandaged from his injuries. Jordan's quick thinking had saved him. Devon still didn't know how Jordan had had the presence of mind to wrap the coat around him. To come for her. To save her, too.

His leash was wrapped snugly in her hand, not that she needed it. Max wasn't going anywhere.

Devon stood at the foot of the grave, gazing at the headstone.

I am so sorry. So sorry.

She knew it was not her fault, but that knowledge did little to assuage her regret. Or her heavy heart.

She felt a hand slide into the crook of her arm.

"Everything okay?" Jordan asked, a sad smile gracing her lips. She wore her dress blues, her jacket draped around her shoulders in deference to her heavily bandaged and tender abdomen.

The knife had damaged her spleen and nicked a kidney. The spleen had been removed and the kidney repaired, but the biggest issue had been the blood loss. The doctors had been amazed that she had survived, let alone crawled to the cabin and taken down Billy. They'd lost her twice in the ambulance on the way to the hospital.

"Yeah," Devon said. She shifted closer, allowing Jordan to lean some of her weight on her.

Devon's grief was nothing compared to Jordan's. Jordan hadn't just lost her partner, but her closest friend. Lieutenant Henry Wayne had been a good man and a fine detective. Without him, she wouldn't have met Jordan. She wouldn't even be here. And for that, he'd lost his life.

"Stop that."

"What?" Devon asked.

"Beating yourself up." She could read Devon too well.

"I didn't say anything," she offered weakly.

"You were thinking it," Jordan said. "This was his fault. Not mine. Not yours. Only his."

Devon knew the *he* in question was not Henry. "I know."

"Do you?" Jordan asked gently. There was a request in Jordan's voice, a plea for Devon to accept the truth.

Devon searched her own heart, looking for the deep-seated shame and condemnation that had followed her for so long. She felt regret, and sadness. At the cabin, Billy had confirmed the terrible truth she had always feared. Except it wasn't the truth. It was all a lie, with Billy at its center. The real truth, the one she had finally begun to understand because of Jordan, was that as much as she might blame herself for all those who had died in relation to her, they had not died *because* of her. They had died because of Billy. And that truth set her free.

The black pit of guilt no longer consumed her. The wolf was finally dead.

"I do," she said with certainty. Jordan kissed her mouth lightly. She turned back to Henry's gravestone, lost in her own thoughts.

Most of the mourners had already left. Captain Buchanan, Special Agent Coleman, and a few others lingered, engaged in hushed conversation.

Jordan sagged, no doubt exhausted by the toll the day was taking on her physically and emotionally.

"We should get you back," Devon said, her concern growing.

"Not yet."

Jordan shouldn't have been out of the hospital, but she had refused to miss Henry's funeral. Devon had promised the doctors she would return Jordan as soon as the funeral was over, but they had remained reluctant. Jordan's mother had settled the matter.

"I don't care if the president of the United States himself orders that she not leave this hospital, my daughter is *not* missing her partner's funeral," Abigail Salinger had insisted. The hospital's chief of staff had actually shrunk back, stunned by the older woman's vehemence. The man had finally relented.

Abigail had been called as Jordan's next of kin. She had gotten on the first plane, arriving just as Jordan was being wheeled out of surgery. The captain had made their introductions, given Abigail a brief summary of events. Devon expected Jordan's mother to be angry with her, to lash out at this stranger at the root of her daughter's life-and-death struggle. Instead, Abigail had studied her for several moments. Then she'd hugged her.

In the days that followed, as Jordan began her slow road to recovery, Devon had barely left her bedside. Neither had Abigail. They'd had a lot of time to talk.

"It was a lovely service," Abigail said, coming up beside Jordan and kissing her softly on the cheek before heading home.

"Henry would have liked it, I think," Jordan said quietly. "He saved my life."

Henry was the reason the police and ambulance were already on their way to the cabin before Devon had dialed 911. At five minutes past five a.m., when Henry had not yet arrived at the station, Detective Lawson had known something was wrong. Henry was never late. He'd called Henry but gotten no answer, so he drove to Henry's house. He had found it unlocked and went inside. He immediately called the state police and raced to the cabin, bringing half the Pittsburgh Bureau of Police and EMS with him. As they were stabilizing Jordan, Devon had demanded that Detective Lawson find Max. He had. He'd ridden with the shepherd in the second ambulance straight to the animal hospital.

Telling Jordan that Henry was dead had been the hardest conversation of Devon's life. She had held Jordan as she wept.

"So, what did the captain say?" Devon asked.

"He said whenever I'm ready to come back, my job will be waiting for me."

"Do you want to go back?"

"I think I do," Jordan said. "Would that be okay with you?"

Devon felt her cheeks flush. It wasn't about her or Jordan anymore. It was about the two of them, together. She cupped Jordan's cheek. "I want whatever you want, my love."

The smile Jordan gave her lit up Devon's heart.

Detective Lawson approached. "You ladies ready to go?"

He had been a godsend. Devon liked the rookie detective, beyond the fact that he had saved Jordan's life. She knew Jordan liked him, too. She said there was a little of Henry in Detective Lawson. Being around him seemed to make Henry's loss a little easier to bear.

Jordan was quiet as they got into the car. She leaned her head on Devon's shoulder. "At least he's with Ella now." She looked out at Henry's grave. "Good-bye, my friend."

Devon kissed Jordan's head as the car pulled away. They had a long road ahead of them, but it was one Devon knew they would walk together.

Madison Montgomery was gone. She was Devon James, now and forever. And she wasn't alone any longer.

About the Author

Robin Summers lives in Pittsburgh, PA, and works in public policy in Washington, DC. Her debut novel, *After the Fall*, is the winner of two 2012 Golden Crown Literary Society Awards, two 2011 Rainbow Awards for LGBT Fiction, and a 2011 Lesbian Fiction Readers Choice Award. Find her on facebook.com/RobinSummersWriting or visit her at robinsummerswriting.com.

Books Available from Bold Strokes Books

The Heat of Angels by Lisa Girolami. Fires burn in more than one place in Los Angeles. (978-1-62639-042-3)

Season of the Wolf by Robin Summers. Two women running from their pasts are thrust together by an unimaginable evil. Can they overcome the horrors that haunt them in time to save each other? (978-1-62639-043-0)

Desperate Measures by P. J. Trebelhorn. Homicide detective Kay Griffith and contractor Brenda Jansen meet amidst turmoil neither of them is aware of until murder suspect Tommy Rayne makes his move to exact revenge on Kay. (978-1-62639-044-7)

The Magic Hunt by L.L. Raand. With her Pack being hunted by human extremists and beset by enemies masquerading as friends, can Sylvan protect them and her mate, or will she succumb to the feral rage that threatens to turn her rogue, destroying them all? A Midnight Hunters novel. (978-1-62639-045-4)

Waiting for the Violins by Justine Saracen. After surviving Dunkirk, a scarred and embittered British nurse returns to Nazi-occupied Brussels to join the Resistance, and finds that nothing is fair in love and war. (978-1-62639-046-1)

Because of Her by KE Payne. When Tabby Morton is forced to move to London, she's convinced her life will never be the same again. But the beautiful and intriguing Eden Palmer is about to show her that this time, change is most definitely for the better. (978-1-62639-049-2)

Wingspan by Karis Walsh. Wildlife biologist Bailey Chase is content to live at the wild bird sanctuary she has created on Washington's Olympic Peninsula until she is lured beyond the safety of isolation by architect Kendall Pearson. (978-1-60282-983-1)

Night Bound by Winter Pennington. Kass struggles to keep her head, her heart, and her relationships in order. She's still having a difficult time accepting being an Alpha female. But her wolf is certain of what she wants and she's intent on securing her power. (978-1-60282-984-8)

Slash and Burn by Valerie Bronwen. The murder of a roundly despised author at a LGBT writer's conference in New Orleans turns Winter Lovelace's relaxing weekend hobnobbing with her peers into a nightmare of suspense—especially when her ex turns up. (978-1-60282-986-2)

The Blush Factor by Gun Brooke. Ice-cold business tycoon Eleanor Ashcroft only cares about the three P's—Power, Profit, and Prosperity—until young Addison Garr makes her doubt both that and the state of her frostbitten heart. (978-1-60282-985-5)

The Quickening: A Sisters of Spirits Novel by Yvonne Heidt. Ghosts, visions, and demons are all in a day's work for Tiffany. But when Kat asks for help on a serial killer case, life takes on another dimension altogether. (978-1-60282-975-6)

Windigo Thrall by Cate Culpepper. Six women trapped in a mountain cabin by a blizzard, stalked by an ancient cannibal demon bent on stealing their sanity—and their lives. (978-1-60282-950-3)

Smoke and Fire by Julie Cannon. Oil and water, passion and desire, a combustible combination. Can two women fight the fire that draws them together and threatens to keep them apart? (978-1-60282-977-0)

Asher's Fault by Elizabeth Wheeler. Fourteen-year-old Asher Price sees the world in black and white, much like the photos he takes, but when his little brother drowns at the same moment Asher experiences his first same-sex kiss, he can no longer hide behind the lens of his camera and eventually discovers he isn't the only one with a secret. (978-1-60282-982-4)

Love and Devotion by Jove Belle. KC Hall trips her way through life, stumbling into an affair with a married bombshell twice her age. Thankfully, her best friend, Emma Reynolds, is there to show her the true meaning of Love and Devotion. (978-1-60282-965-7)

Rush by Carsen Taite. Murder, secrets, and romance combine to create the ultimate rush. (978-1-60282-966-4)

The Shoal of Time by J.M. Redmann. It sounded too easy. Micky Knight is reluctant to take the case because the easy ones often turn into the hard ones, and the hard ones turn into the dangerous ones. In this one, easy turns hard without warning. (978-1-60282-967-1)

In Between by Jane Hoppen. At the age of 14, Sophie Schmidt discovers that she was born an intersexual baby and sets off on a journey to find her place in a world that denies her true existence. (978-1-60282-968-8)

Secret Lies by Amy Dunne. While fleeing from her abuser, Nicola Jackson bumps into Jenny O'Connor, and their unlikely friendship quickly develops into a blossoming romance—but when it comes down to a matter of life or death, are they both willing to face their fears? (978-1-60282-970-1)

Under Her Spell by Maggie Morton. The magic of love brought Terra and Athene together, but now a magical quest stands between them—a quest for Athene's hand in marriage. Will their passion keep them together, or will stronger magic tear them apart? (978-1-60282-973-2)

Homestead by Radclyffe. R. Clayton Sutter figures getting NorthAm Fuel's newest refinery operational on a rolling tract of land in Upstate New York should take a month or two, but then, she hadn't counted on local resistance in the form of vandalism, petitions, and one furious farmer named Tess Rogers. (978-1-60282-956-5)

Battle of Forces: Sera Toujours by Ali Vali. Kendal and Piper return to New Orleans to start the rest of eternity together, but the return of an old enemy makes their peaceful reunion short-lived, especially when they join forces with the new queen of the vampires. (978-1-60282-957-2)

How Sweet It Is by Melissa Brayden. Some things are better than chocolate. Molly O'Brien enjoys her quiet life running the bakeshop in a small town. When the beautiful Jordan Tuscana returns home, Molly can't deny the attraction—or the stirrings of something more. (978-1-60282-958-9)

The Missing Juliet: A Fisher Key Adventure by Sam Cameron. A teenage detective and her friends search for a kidnapped Hollywood star in the Florida Keys. (978-1-60282-959-6)

Amor and More: Love Everafter edited by Radclyffe and Stacia Seaman. Rediscover favorite couples as Bold Strokes Books authors reveal glimpses of life and love beyond the honeymoon in short stories featuring main characters from favorite BSB novels. (978-1-60282-963-3)

First Love by CJ Harte. Finding true love is hard enough, but for Jordan Thompson, daughter of a conservative president, it's challenging, especially when that love is a female rodeo cowgirl. (978-1-60282-949-7)

Pale Wings Protecting by Lesley Davis. Posing as a couple to investigate the abduction of infants, Special Agent Blythe Kent and Detective Daryl Chandler find themselves drawn into a battle over the innocents, with demons on one side and the unlikeliest of protectors on the other. (978-1-60282-964-0)

Mounting Danger by Karis Walsh. Sergeant Rachel Bryce, an outcast on the police force, is put in charge of the department's newly formed mounted division. Can she and polo champion Callan Lanford resist their growing attraction as they struggle to safeguard the disaster-prone unit? (978-1-60282-951-0)

Meeting Chance by Jennifer Lavoie. When man's best friend turns on Aaron Cassidy, the teen keeps his distance until fate puts Chance in his hands. (978-1-60282-952-7)

At Her Feet by Rebekah Weatherspoon. Digital marketing producer Suzanne Kim knows she has found the perfect love in her new mistress Pilar, but before they can make the ultimate commitment, Suzanne's professional life threatens to disrupt their perfectly balanced bliss. (978-1-60282-948-0)

Show of Force by AJ Quinn. A chance meeting between navy pilot Evan Kane and correspondent Tate McKenna takes them on a roller-coaster ride where the stakes are high, but the reward is higher: a chance at love. (978-1-60282-942-8)

Clean Slate by Andrea Bramhall. Can Erin and Morgan work through their individual demons to rediscover their love for each other, or are the unexplainable wounds too deep to heal? (978-1-60282-943-5)

Hold Me Forever by D. Jackson Leigh. An investigation into illegal cloning in the quarter horse racing industry threatens to destroy the growing attraction between Georgia debutante Mae St. John and Louisiana horse trainer Whit Casey. (978-1-60282-944-2)

Trusting Tomorrow by PJ Trebelhorn. Funeral director Logan Swift thinks she's perfectly happy with her solitary life devoted to helping others cope with loss until Brooke Collier moves in next door to care for her elderly grandparents. (978-1-60282-891-9)

Forsaking All Others by Kathleen Knowles. What if what you think you want is the opposite of what makes you happy? (978-1-60282-892-6)

Exit Wounds by VK Powell. When Officer Loane Landry falls in love with ATF informant Abigail Mancuso, she realizes that nothing is as it seems—not the case, not her lover, not even the dead. (978-1-60282-893-3)

Dirty Power by Ashley Bartlett. Cooper's been through hell and back, and she's still broke and on the run. But at least she found the twins. They'll keep her alive. Right? (978-1-60282-896-4)

The Rarest Rose by I. Beacham. After a decade of living in her beloved house, Ele disturbs its past and finds her life being haunted by the presence of a ghost who will show her that true love never dies. (978-1-60282-884-1)

Code of Honor by Radclyffe. The face of terror is hard to recognize—especially when it's homegrown. The next book in the Honor series. (978-1-60282-885-8)

Does She Love You? by Rachel Spangler. When Annabelle and Davis find out they are both in a relationship with the same woman, it leaves them facing life-altering questions about trust, redemption, and the possibility of finding love in the wake of betrayal. (978-1-60282-886-5)

The Road to Her by KE Payne. Sparks fly when actress Holly Croft, star of UK soap Portobello Road, meets her new on-screen love interest, the enigmatic and sexy Elise Manford. (978-1-60282-887-2)

boldstrokesbooks.com

Bold Strokes Books

Quality and Diversity in LGBTQ Literature

victory EDITIONS

Drama

MATINEE BOOKS

SCI-FI

E-BOOKS

MYSTERY

erotica

BSB SOLILOQUY

EROTICA

YOUNG ADULT

BOLD STROKES BOOKS

LIBERTY EDITION

Romance

W·E·B·S·T·O·R·E

PRINT AND EBOOKS